SARAH WEBB

The Loving Kind

MACMILLAN

First published 2010 by Macmillan
an imprint of Pan Macmillan, a division of Macmillan Publishers Limited
Pan Macmillan, 20 New Wharf Road, London N1 9RR
Basingstoke and Oxford
Associated companies throughout the world
www.panmacmillan.com

ISBN 978-0-230-70981-2

Typeset by SetSystems Ltd, Saffron Walden, Essex
Printed in the UK by CPI Mackays, Chatham ME5 8TD

Visit **www.panmacmillan.com** to read more about all our books
and to buy them. You will also find features, author interviews and
news of any author events, and you can sign up for e-newsletters
so that you're always first to hear about our new releases.

This book is dedicated to Ben,
for being the loving kind

'I don't like standard beauty –
there is no beauty without strangeness'

Karl Lagerfeld

Acknowledgements

Firstly I'd like to thank two people in particular – A. and A. – my sources in the plastic surgery industry. Thank you so much for reading the manuscript and for all your helpful comments and suggestions; they were invaluable and I'm so grateful. And thank you to the team of other doctors and surgeons who gave a second (and third and fourth!) opinion on my text. I hasten to add that when it comes to the medical scenes, all mistakes are my own.

I'd like to acknowledge *Plastic Makes Perfect* by Wendy Lewis, a comprehensive insider's guide to cosmetic surgery. And to everyone who has put their tummy tuck or boob job on YouTube, I salute you. You made my research a whole lot more . . . well, um, interesting, to say the least!

Also, to the brave women who talked to me about their breast reductions and other surgical experiences, thank you.

I'd like to point out that Christo's surgical technique is fictional, as is the filler, FreshPearl. I have used artistic licence in both these scenes. But all the other procedures and techniques are as accurate as I could make them in the context of the story. Botox is the registered trade name for the most popular and best known botulinum toxin formula in the world.

On the home front, I must thank my loyal and loving family – Mum, Dad, Kate, Emma, Richard. And my own gang at home – Ben, Sam, Amy and Jago. And, of course, Christina, Sorcha and Miriam for all the babysitting. No writer has a better team behind her.

To my friends Nicky, Tanya and Andrew: after a decade of thanking you all, I can't stop at this stage or someone might think we've fallen out, which we most certainly haven't. Far from it! Your patience and kindness knows no bounds.

To all the newbies in the world: Rua, Skippy (no, my friends are not hippies, these are puppies, my dears, puppies); Isobel, Rose, Sarah, Sam (not puppies this time). It was quite a year for buying baby presents, I can tell you.

To my dear and lovely writer friends, especially Martina Devlin, Clare Dowling, Martina Murphy (Martina O'Reilly), Marita and Mandy Conlon McKenna, Catherine Daly, Vanessa O'Loughlinn and all the Irish Girls. Inspirational, one and all. And to Katie Fforde for making me smile.

To Dee, Jim, Daisy, Seamus, Joseph, Barney and Charlie Boy for making West Cork just that extra bit special.

The amazing gang at Pan Macmillan have done a stellar job on this one, especially Imogen Taylor and Trisha Jackson, my crack editorial team in London, and my Irish boys, David Adamson and Cormac Kinsella. To Robyn Neild for her hilarious 'Lulabelle' on the cover – it made me grin from the first time I saw the early sketches. Robyn is one talented artist and I'm lucky to have her as my cover illustrator.

To my new 'adult' agent, Peta Nightingale – great name, great agent – for her insight and spot-on comments.

And finally to you, the reader. For the supportive and kind emails, for saying such nice things about the books, and for sticking with me during my ten-year writing journey. This is book number nine and I promise there will be a tenth. I do have a rather interesting idea I think you'll all like . . . Better get cracking on it!

Much love,
Sarah XXX

PS Do write to me – sarah@sarahwebb.ie – I love hearing from readers.

Or check out my Facebook page – www.facebook.com/sarahwebb writer or my blog at www.sarahwebb.ie

And if you have young teens or tweens in the house, check out my Amy Green series – see www.askamygreen.com for details.

Chapter 1

Libby

I stood outside the classroom, took a deep breath and smoothed down my shirt. I'd had no idea what to wear today, so I'd played it safe. Black trousers, white shirt, red wedge sandals. The librarian seemed a little taken aback by the bubblegum-pink streaks in my blonde hair, but after the initial wide-eyed stare, she'd given me a warm welcome.

'I'm Maureen Hunter, the librarian here at Monkstown. We're so delighted that you agreed to give these writing workshops. I've read all your books and I'm a huge fan. But I have to say, you look a lot different from your photograph.' She pointed at the poster on the noticeboard behind the desk.

'But that's not me,' I stammered. 'That's Regina O'Reilly. I'm Elizabeth Adams. Please say you were expecting me.'

In fact, Elizabeth Adams was my pen name. I was actually Libby Holliday, but my ex-agent said it didn't have quite the same ring.

Maureen looked confused. 'No, I'm afraid we weren't. I was talking to Regina only two weeks ago and everything seemed fine. I don't understand.'

I sighed. Regina was one of Ireland's most successful novelists; three of her romantic comedies had been made into movies, one into a television show. We shared a publisher and had often done readings together. She was a nice woman, but completely scatty.

1

'Regina was supposed to ring you,' I said. 'She's at a writer's convention in Miami. It was booked a year ago but she'd forgotten all about it. She asked me to fill in for her. I hope it's OK.'

'Are you a writer?' Maureen asked, rather anxiously.

'Oh yes. Yes, I am.' I pulled three books out of my bag and plonked them down on the desk.

She looked relieved. She picked one up. 'Elizabeth Adams. Of course – I've heard of you. I think we even have a few of your books in the library.' She flicked her fingers over the computer keys and stared at the screen. 'Actually, not in this library, but we do have a copy of *Baby, It's You* in Dalkey.' She smiled at me brightly. 'Have you taught workshops before?'

'Yes.' I didn't add 'at my mum's Mother's Union'. I thought it best to leave it vague. This was a well-paid gig and I needed the money. Things with Jeremy, my fiancé, were a mess, and I only had enough in my bank account to see me to the end of the month.

'Excellent. We're short-staffed today and I don't like to leave the desk unattended. If you don't mind introducing yourself to your class, that would be brilliant. And if you need anything, just let me know, won't you? Good luck.' She pointed at the left-hand wall.

I walked over. There were two doors, so I presumed she meant the first. I took a deep breath, wiped my sticky palms on my trousers, swung the door open and strode into the room.

'It's all over in the first few seconds,' Regina had warned me. 'They don't want some nervous loser teaching them. They want someone larger than life, someone successful.'

Channelling 'successful', I walked purposefully towards the desk at the top of the room, dumped my bag and spun round. I smiled at the group, scanning the room from left to right. Men, all men, apart from one woman with short dark hair and boxy shoulders, but maybe she was a man too. It was hard to tell.

Strange. Regina said it was usually all women. I perched on the edge of the desk, pulled out my notes and began to read, the sheets shaking in my hands.

'Welcome, everyone. Thank you for coming out this evening. I know that for most of you this is a passion. For some of you it may be your reason for getting up in the morning. For others, it may be a way of making sense of your life. But you are all in this room for the same reason – because you have a dream. And I'll try to tread softly on those dreams, as Yeats would say.'

There were several nervous coughs. The man nearest to me, young, with a shaved head and a Celtic tattoo on his wrist, pushed his chair back.

'Let's get started,' I continued, trying to ignore the screech of the chair legs on the tiled floor. 'First, I want to talk about inspiration and motivation. So, what are your favourite books? Anyone?'

I looked eagerly around the room.

'Books?' The tattooed man looked confused. 'Here, I'm in the wrong room. Sorry, miss.' He stood up, followed by several others.

Then the door burst open and a very tall man who looked a bit like Jonathan Ross appeared. 'Sorry I'm late. Is this my digital photography group?'

Oh, dear God. My face flushed. 'So sorry.' I shoved my notes back in my bag and scuttled out of the door. I ran towards the exit without looking back.

'Elizabeth,' Maureen called after me. 'Are you all right?'

'Emergency at home,' I said, without turning round. 'So sorry.'

I powered down the road, ducked into someone's drive and pulled out my mobile. In times of disaster there was only one woman to call.

'Celeste, help!'

'What's wrong? You sound terrible. Is it Jeremy again?'

'No! I just ran out of the library.' I explained what had happened. 'I just panicked. I feel such an idiot. What will I do? I can't go back in.'

'You can, and you will. Tell them it was unavoidable. Don't elaborate. And then stun them with your superior knowledge.'

'Stun them?'

'Libby, you're well able to stun. Remember that reading you gave at that literary festival in Cardiff? When you acted out that seduction scene? You had the audience in your lap. Almost literally.' Celeste laughed. 'Remember that old lad with the ruddy face who wouldn't leave you alone during the signing? Kept pawing at your chest.'

I wished I *could* remember that particular night. It wasn't one of my finest hours. 'I was tipsy, Cel. I should never have had that wine at lunch. Or allowed you to come with me. I blame you.'

She gave a laugh. 'You can stun with the best of them, that's all I'm saying. Have a little faith in yourself. You've written six books – that's incredible by any standard. Most people never finish *one*.'

'Five,' I corrected her. '*His Girl Friday* doesn't count. It was never published. Alex hated it.'

'Alex Sharpe is an idiot. I mean, really, what does he know? Some agent!'

'You used to think Alex was cute.'

'That was before he dumped you.'

'He didn't dump me.'

'He didn't take you with him when he set up on his own, Libs. He left you with that tweedy woman at the Franklin Street agency who smells of cats. What's her name again?'

'Polly Eustace.'

'That's right. Polly useless, more like. What's happening with your new one? What's it called again?'

'*Just Like Being in Love.*'

'Has she even sent it out to your editor yet?'

'Yes. And Harriet is now my ex-editor. She rejected it – said it wasn't right for the current market.'

Silence for a moment. 'I'm sorry, babes, you should have said. When did this happen?'

'A few weeks ago. I haven't felt like talking about it, to be honest.'

'Anyway, what does Harriet know? She's a twinkie. What is she? Twenty-one?'

'Twenty-six.' Not only had Harriet rejected it, the seven subsequent editors Polly had tried had also said no. It was all utterly depressing.

A postman walked in through the gates and gave me a funny look. I must have looked a bit suspicious, skulking in the shrubbery. I gave him a smile so he wouldn't think I was a burglar.

'Look, Cel,' I continued, 'this isn't helping. I'm just not cut out for teaching. It's far too stressful. All I really want to do is write.' I gave a deep belly sigh.

Celeste knew better than to give me a motivational lecture. I hadn't been able to write since the day I'd thrown Jeremy out. It wasn't writer's block, exactly, more like writer's anxiety. If I couldn't make my own relationship work, what right did I have to bang on about romance?

'Maybe you're right,' she said gently. 'Where are you? I'll come and collect you. Fancy a sneaky Cosmopolitan? My column's going nowhere. I could do with some inspiration. A cocktail might just do the trick.'

Celeste wrote a weekly column for the *Irish Express*. It was supposed to focus on popular culture and topical news items, treated with a razor-sharp edge, of course – it was Celeste, after all – but sometimes it veered scarily close to what her female friends were currently obsessing about, namely me. Last week's was on the etiquette of reading one's nearest and dearest's emails and text messages. Which is how I'd found out about Jeremy's exploits.

'Why not? It's not as if there's anyone waiting for me at home,' I added glumly.

She laughed. 'Join the club, babes.'

'What about your invisible boyfriend?' I'd never met Celeste's latest, Ross, yet another photographer. He kept odd hours and they tended to meet late, in Celeste's apartment. It was a strange kind of arrangement, but this was Celeste, who specialized in odd relationships.

She gave a hollow laugh. 'Ross is in Croatia. On a sailing holiday with sixteen of his closest friends.' She paused. 'I wasn't invited.'

'I'm sorry, Cel.'

'Don't be. He's an asshole. So, what about those cocktails?'

Chapter 2

Lulabelle

'You have a visitor, Lulabelle – you might want to put some clothes on.'

Lulabelle Ryan was lying on a chaise longue, posing for a photograph. She'd accessorized her half-moon glasses and black satin French knickers with a hardback copy of James Joyce's *Ulysses*, which she was clutching against her ample, naked chest.

She put her hand up to pause the photographer and looked over at Leo, her manager, who had just walked in through the door of her hotel suite. 'Who is it?'

'Your ghostwriter.'

'Send her in. Nothing she hasn't seen before.'

Leo paused. 'Your *new* ghostwriter.'

'What the hell happened to Caroline? I thought we had a connection.'

'Decided the project wasn't for her. She's gone back to writing Regency sagas.'

Lulabelle sighed. 'How unprofessional. Can we sue her?'

'Nope. It was only a trial run, remember? We hadn't drawn up a contract yet. After you sacked your last ghostwriter—'

Lulabelle's back stiffened. 'Don't even go there. She was appalling. All that red hair and pickle breath – yuck. She wanted to turn my book into some sort of ghastly misery-lit sob-fest. As if!'

She flicked back her glossy chestnut hair. 'So who's the new one? She'd better be a damn fine writer. My story deserves the best. You understand, don't you?'

'Of course, Lu. This new writer comes highly recommended. He's won all kinds of awards—'

'Rewind! Did you say *he*?'

'Yes, he. Simon Cadden. He's a crime writer, but he also writes—'

'I specifically asked for a woman – you know that. A man? Ha! That's outrageous. How can a man understand Chloe's complex feelings?'

'I presume he'll make it up,' Leo said dryly. He was in no mood for Lulabelle's histrionics.

'Don't be smart.' She tossed her hair again, dislodging her glasses and then pushing them back up the bridge of her nose. 'I'm not working with a man. Send him away and find me someone else. A woman. Any woman, but she'd better be bloody good. And this time, she'd better not abandon the project at chapter two. Chloe's story deserves to be told. And we're way behind schedule.'

'Tell me about it. The editor from New Haven Books is breathing down my neck.' Lulabelle had already ripped through three ghostwriters – Annie, Pauline and now Caroline. They were fast running out of options.

'You'll sort it all out, won't you, Leo?'

Leo closed his eyes for a couple of seconds, hoping she'd just disappear in a puff of smoke. He opened them again. No such luck. Ireland's reality show darling was still lying on the chaise longue, posing for the author photo to grace the back of 'her' book, glaring at him through those ridiculous glasses. He noticed her copy of *Ulysses* was upside down.

'Lu, the book's—'

'Stop yabbering on and go and find me someone.'

'Fine,' he muttered under his breath, walking towards the door. 'Your wish is my command.'

'What was that?' she asked sharply.

He just kept walking.

Chapter 3

Libby

At noon the following day, I opened the door and gave a little squeak. Alex Sharpe was standing on my doorstep in a slick grey suit and open pink shirt, a wide grin on his face, his dark blond hair, longer than I remember, touching his square jaw. He looked sickeningly good.

'What do you want?' I asked darkly, pulling my dressing gown closed and tying the belt.

'Don't be like that, Libby. You know you're my favourite little romance writer. And I'm sorry about all that business last year.'

'When you dumped me?'

He laughed. 'I didn't dump you, chick. You know that.'

'Get to the point, Alex. I know you're here because Antonia is out, you're a cheap bastard and you want to cadge a cup of coffee.'

Antonia Diggens, aka 'Toni Blade', was a young model turned crime writer who happened to live down the road from me, with her parents. She was perfect for Alex's new agency: just twenty-two, stunning and a horribly talented writer, Antonia had it all. Alex had recently landed Toni a new three-book deal with Griffin House – for half a million euros. Depressing.

He laughed again. 'That's why I like you, Libby. Always so sharp. But this time you're wrong. Toni's on a book tour in Australia. I'm here to see you.' .

'Why?'

'Let me in and I'll tell you.'

'I have no biscuits,' I muttered, standing back. Alex had a fierce sweet tooth.

'Dry coffee is fine.'

He led me into the kitchen. The place was a state – a frying pan lay soaking in the sink, and this morning's half-eaten toast and dirty coffee mug were still on the table – but I made no apology. My head was throbbing from last night's cocktails and Alex was the last person I wanted to see right now.

He made no comment, just sat down at the kitchen table and nodded at the kettle.

'Would you give me a chance?' I snapped.

'What has happened to sweet little Libby?' he asked. 'You used to bring me homemade chocolate brownies when you visited the office. It was adorable.'

He shifted in his seat.

'If you want to scratch your balls, just go right ahead. What is it with you? You're always fiddling with your bloody crotch.'

He looked shocked. 'Are you all right, Libby? It's not like you to be so tetchy.' He cocked his head. 'And what have you done to your hair? You look like a children's telly presenter.'

I ignored both his questions. 'Look, what's this all about? I'm kind of busy right now.'

'Writing?' He looked up at me, his eyebrows slightly raised.

'Yes!'

He crossed his arms. 'Really? I was talking to Polly yesterday, says she hasn't been able to place your latest.'

'How dare you? That's none of your business. Anyway, it's only been a few weeks. There are loads of people interested.'

'A few weeks is a long time in publishing.' He sighed. 'To be honest, it's unlikely to find a home in the current climate. Market's just not there for gentle romantic comedy. Readers are looking for something with a bit more edge.'

I groaned. 'Are you trying to make me suicidal? If that's the aim, I have to tell you, you're doing fabulously well, Alex.'

He gave a short laugh. 'Course not. In fact, I have a business proposition. I cleared it with Polly. In fact, she's not sure there's anything more she can do for you. Says it might be time for you to find another agent.'

A lump formed in my throat, but I was damned if I was going to cry in front of him. 'Well, that's just great. Thanks a lot, Alex. And do thank Polly for breaking the news to me herself. You obviously talk to her more than I do these days.'

'Don't be like that, Libby. It's not all bad news. Do you want to hear my offer or not?'

I shrugged. 'Can't make my day any worse.'

He smiled. 'It's simple. You write a novel for me and I give you a hundred K. Sterling.'

'A hundred thousand?'

He nodded.

I narrowed my eyes. 'OK, where's the catch?'

'You have two months to write it.'

'And?' I stared at Alex.

He blinked quickly, several times. There was something he wasn't telling me.

'And?' I demanded again.

'Have you ever heard of Lulabelle Ryan?'

Chapter

Libby

'I still can't believe you're really doing this.' Celeste stood close beside me at the check-in machine at Dublin airport.

'Like you said, I'm going to reinvent myself. And it's only for two months.'

She smiled. 'A lot can happen in two months.'

'I do hope so!'

She laughed. 'I'll miss you, Libby.'

'I'll ring and email. Every day.' I threw my arms around her. 'Thanks for everything, Cel. You've been amazing. I don't know how to . . .' I noticed something peeping out of the back pocket of her jeans. 'Why are you carrying your passport?'

She pulled away from me, grinning. 'Surprise! I'm coming to London with you.'

'Are you serious?'

'Deadly. I rang my editor yesterday. He said as long as I file my column every Thursday lunchtime as usual and throw the odd feature his way, he doesn't care where I am. To be honest, work's boring me at the moment – I could do with a change of scene. And Ross has been doorstepping me, little creep – wants me to get him some work at the *Express*. As if.'

She broke off and pulled a face. 'Anyway, what do you think? Maybe you'd prefer not to have me hanging around. It's your gig, after all. I'll totally understand if—'

'm over the moon.' I beamed at her, tears of
. 'You know, right at this second, I'm almost glad
gone.'

at's the spirit, Libs. Today – London; tomorrow – the world.'

As I sat on the aeroplane, I thought about what had brought me to this point. Jeremy. Jeremy and his sleazy affair.

It had all come to a head three months ago. Jeremy's BlackBerry had pinged in the pocket of his jacket when he was in the shower. Seizing the opportunity (Jeremy was usually surgically attached to his BlackBerry), I had pulled it out and read the new message. A disgustingly lurid text. I finally snapped. I threw the BlackBerry in my pocket, ran down the stairs, jumped into my car and just drove, not caring where I was going, tears streaming down my cheeks.

I parked in a random housing estate and began to read all Jeremy's recent texts and emails, feeling sicker and sicker. But I just couldn't stop. Some of them were particularly interesting; together they provided a map of Jeremy's year-long affair.

To: jeremysmall42@atlasmail.ie
From: rann@compassdelta.ie
You should see the bruises on my bum, you bad boy.
London was sooooo good. I can't wait to see you
again. Don't forget the you know what. I loved it.
   I'll bring a couple of costumes. You can choose.
   Your sex slave, always, R-A

**I wnt u nw, j. Ht, hrd. Im wt thnkng abt u. Cn u gt awy?
Nw. Nd u nw. R-A**

To: rann@compassdelta.ie
From: jeremysmall42@atlasmail.ie

I'm yours, babe, you know it. I can't get you out of my head. What have you done to me?

What about Paris next week, my treat? Jeremy xxx

To jeremysmall42@atlasmail.ie
From: rann@compassdelta.ie
Paris! Brilliant idea. I'm all yours, literally. Tie me up, tie me down. Beats wet old Brighton any day. I'll bring the new Agent P stuff, darling. You'll love it. I can't wait to get my hands on you, all over you.

And as for your suggestion, let's just say I'll think about it. It would depend on the lady in question. From what you've told me, I don't think Libby would be up for it, do you? Has she toned up, by the way, or is it still like fucking a whale?

Sorry, sorry, I'm being naughty again. It just makes me so cross that she doesn't appreciate you the way I do. How could she not just eat up that delicious lollipop of yours every single day? I just don't know.

Always, R-A.

Im in th aprt. C u in r rm l8r. Hve th chmprs rdy. Wnt 2 lck it off u. Cnt w8 2 c u. R-A

There it was, mapped out in front of me, as clear as day. Jeremy's affair with R-A, otherwise known as our mutual 'friend', Ruth-Ann. I recognized her email address instantly.

Ruth-Ann was an old college friend of Jeremy's. An accountant with a thing for little Italian suits. Small, dark-haired, slim yet curvy; if it wasn't for her fake tan addiction, she'd have a bit of an Anna Friel look about her.

We often had her over for dinner and we always invited her to all our parties. She was good fun and I suppose I felt a bit sorry for her; like Celeste, she never seemed to have straightforward relationships – there was always some sort of complication. Recently she'd broken up with yet another boyfriend (who turned out to be her boss – married or unmarried I had no idea, and didn't think to ask) and started to ring Jeremy to talk about all her disastrous relationship dramas.

Now I knew why his BlackBerry never left his side. The thing that got me most was his disloyalty. I couldn't believe he'd been discussing our sex life with his mistress. It was appalling. We'd been together for nearly six years, lived together for three. Of course some of the passion had waned – that was only natural. But we were supposed to be getting married on New Year's Eve. Didn't that mean anything to him? Clearly not.

Then, as I sat in the car, miserable and fuming, the bloody thing pinged again.

R u thr, j? cn u gt awy?
Fuck off and die, I texted back.

Ping.
Wht? Is tht a jke?

No. It's over. I've met someone else. Someone younger. Sorry, but your droopy ass just doesn't do it for me any more. See you around.

Ping.
U bstrd!!!!!!!!!!!!!!!!!!!

Then the phone rang. I checked the number. It was Ruth-Ann, all right. Then I had a horrible thought. Knowing Ruth-Ann, she was probably jumping into her BMW right now and driving up from Wicklow to give Jeremy an earful. I'd better get home and quick.

I wiped away my tears and checked my face in the mirror, wincing. Red puffy eyes were not a good look. But I didn't care.

When I walked in the door, Jeremy looked up from his car magazine and said, 'Hi. What's for lunch? Have you seen my BlackBerry?'

I'd been gone for over an hour. Had he even noticed?

'Don't you want to know where I was?' I asked.

'I presumed you were out getting the paper.'

'The paper?'

'I thought you might have a review in it or something. You know what you're like about your reviews.'

'Jeremy, I haven't had a book out since last year.'

His BlackBerry rang in my pocket. I handed it to him, not bothering to explain.

'You found it, thanks.' He stared at me, as if he couldn't quite read my expression, then looked down at the screen.

'Aren't you going to answer it?' I asked.

'Nah, probably just work.'

'On a Saturday morning?' I put my hand out. 'I'll talk to them. Tell them you're out.'

'I'd prefer it if you didn't.'

'Really? And why's that?'

We looked at each other for a moment. His eyes were flat, resigned. He looked away, rubbed them with his knuckles. The BlackBerry stopped ringing.

Finally I said, 'I know you're having an affair.'

He gave a wry laugh, but he looked uneasy.

'Where would I find the time?' he said.

'On one of your trips to London.'

'London?' He looked at me uncertainly.

'Or Spain, perhaps? Or what about Brighton? Oh, no, sorry, how silly of me. You never made it to Brighton, did you? You were too busy fucking Ruth-Ann in Paris.'

As soon as I said Ruth-Ann's name his face dropped.

'I'm so sorry,' he said. 'It should never have happened. But you know Ruth-Ann – she's pretty determined. And you have to admit, she's a stunner, really takes care of herself . . .'

As he spoke, I felt exhausted and spaced out, as if this was all happening to someone else. I'd wake up and have my old life back. At the very least, he'd apologize, say it would never happen again, and we'd try to go back to 'normal', whatever normal meant; these days I wasn't all that sure.

Then I tuned back in to what he was saying. 'Sure I care about her, but it doesn't really mean anything; it's just sex.'

'You think that makes it any better?'

'No, but it doesn't have to affect us, Libs. Do you want me to stop seeing her?'

I stared at him. Was he suggesting I turn a blind eye? Was he mad?

'Of course you do,' he said quickly. 'We're due to meet tomorrow night. I'll talk to her then.'

'Tomorrow?' I whispered.

He put his hands in the air. 'Look, do you want me to talk to her now, clear everything up? Just say the word and I'll ring her right this second.'

I sat down on the sofa and stared at the carpet, my mind racing. He hadn't actually said anything about taking me out the following night, but I'd just presumed . . .

I lifted my head. 'Clear everything up? It's not a GP visit, Jeremy. And I don't care what you do. Just get out of the house. This ends now.'

'What are you on about, Libby? I keep telling you, it doesn't mean anything.'

'*GET OUT!*' I screamed. 'Or I won't be responsible for my actions.'

'Jesus, Libby, calm down! What's wrong with you?'

'Tomorrow's our anniversary, you fucking pig. The tenth of

March, our first date. Every year we have dinner on the tenth of March to celebrate.'

'Shit, I'm so sorry, Libby. I completely forgot.'

'You always forget. I bet you don't even know my birthday, do you? Go on, when is it?'

He ran his hands through his wavy blond hair. 'Ah, here, I've never been very good with dates.'

'No, Jeremy, you're far too good with dates – of the female variety. I've had enough. I want you to get the hell out of my life.'

He looked genuinely shocked. 'What about the wedding?'

'A lifetime of wondering where you are every night; waiting by the phone; waiting in bed in my decent underwear just in case you bother your ass coming home before midnight. I've put up with enough shit over the last few years. There's no way I'm marrying you.'

'But it's booked. We'll lose the hotel deposit.'

'God forbid!'

'You can bloody pay it. And you can explain to your mother why her precious wedding production isn't going to happen.'

'Leave my mother out of this.'

'Why? Talk about pain in the ass. Fat ass at that.'

I gasped. 'Jeremy Small. How dare you? She adores you, poor deluded woman. I can't believe you just said that.' I stood up, grabbed a cushion and started battering him over the head.

'Libby!' He wrestled the cushion out of my hands. 'You want to get a grip. Hitting me with soft furnishings is a bit undignified, even for you.'

'I'll give you undignified.' I kicked him in the shins, hard, the toe of my runner impacting with a satisfying crunch.

He rubbed his shin. 'Jesus, stop. That hurt.' He moved away before I could kick him again.

'No, you stop. You said fucking me was like fucking a whale.'

'What?' His face went pale. 'You weren't supposed to read that.'

'And you weren't supposed to say it or to have an affair with Ruth-Ann. But you did. So I'm asking you to get the hell out before I ring Celeste and get her to deal with you.'

'Woo-hoo, Celeste, I'm scared.' He gave me a snide look. 'Don't be so pathetic. And fine, I'll go. But I'll be back. And half of this house is mine – don't forget that. More like three-quarters, in fact. When's the last time you paid the bloody mortgage?'

He walked into the hall. I followed him and watched as he slammed the door behind him without turning round.

'Bastard!' I yelled after him.

Then I crumpled to the floor.

Chapter 5

Libby

An hour later I was still slumped on the hall stairs, staring into space, when someone knocked on the front door.

I ignored them. Whoever it was, I wasn't in the mood for company.

Next thing the letterbox flipped open and a pair of dark blue eyes stared through the slot.

'What are you doing, Libby?' my dad asked. 'Are you all right? You haven't gone and fallen down the stairs, have you, pet?'

'No, Dad, I'm fine. Just thinking. Writer's stuff.' Even though I'd tried to convince him otherwise, Dad still thought writing was a mystical thing, ancient muses whispering in my ear.

'Are you going to let me in?'

'Oh, yes. Sorry.' I checked my face in the hall mirror – not a pretty sight – then licked my index finger and tried to wipe away the mascara stains under my eyes.

Satisfied, I swung the door open.

Dad smiled at me. 'Not stopping. Football on the telly. Your mother asked me to give you this.' He thrust a white paper chemist's bag at me.

I took it from him and pulled out a pot of homemade chicken liver pâté and two packets of tablets.

He said, 'Your mother's worried about you; says you have to keep your iron levels up.'

'But this is folic acid, Dad.'

'She says you need to start taking it months before planning a family.'

'I see.' Normally I'd be furious at her for interfering. But today I didn't have the energy. Instead, tears welled up in my eyes.

'Will I tell her you said thanks?' he suggested.

I nodded. 'Sure.'

'Are you feeling a little off, Libby?'

'Just writing a sad bit in my novel this morning, Dad. You know how it is.'

From the confused look on his face, he clearly didn't. 'Don't upset yourself too much, love.'

After he'd gone, I sat back on the last stair and allowed my tears to roll down my cheeks. My mobile rang and I studied the screen. Celeste. The only person on the planet I could stomach talking to right now.

'Hi, Libs. Your dad rang me. Said you sounded a bit down, wondered if I'd give you a call and cheer you up.'

I smiled through my tears. Dad really was a sweetie. Mum – now that was a different story.

'I don't know what to do,' I began. 'Jeremy's gone . . .' I managed to get some of the story out before my throat constricted so much I couldn't speak.

'I'm on my way,' she said.

Instantly I felt a little better.

Half an hour later, Celeste arrived on the doorstep, a bottle of wine in either hand, held upright like clubs, and a look on her that would kill a T-Rex stone dead.

'Where is he? He'd better not be here or I swear I'll murder him.'

'He's not.'

'Good. Now grab some wine glasses and start talking.'

After I'd told her the whole sorry story, she sat back and blew out her breath.

'I don't know what to say, Libs. This time he's excelled himself. Which is saying a lot for Jeremy. And Ruth-Ann? Didn't she stay with you recently; after one of her many break-ups?'

'At Christmas.' Jesus, I'd forgotten all about that. Ruth-Ann had stayed with us for three days in late December. She'd been on her own and I'd felt sorry for her. I'd gone into the sales on the twenty-seventh with Celeste, leaving Jeremy and Ruth-Ann alone in the house. Ruth-Ann had said she was tired; Jeremy had said he needed to work. Liars!

'The wagon.' She paused and sighed. 'So what now?'

I shrugged helplessly, tears flooding my eyes. Celeste held me as I sobbed, stroking the back of my head.

'It'll be OK,' she murmured. 'That's right, let it all out.'

After a while the tears stopped and I pulled away, tucking damp wisps of hair behind my ears.

Celeste gave me a gentle smile. 'You could start with a great new haircut. And some new clothes. Make him see what he's missing. Moving on quickly will be the best revenge, Libs. He'll hate that.'

She thought for a moment. 'And how about a novel where this cool, amazing heroine wreaks revenge on her scumbag fiancé?'

'Celeste! I couldn't. Jeremy might sue me.'

'Change the names. Vent all your spleen on the page. Better than giving yourself ulcers.'

'I'll think about it.'

I didn't like to tell her I hadn't sat down at my desk in weeks, let alone written anything. My motivation was at rock bottom. Besides, after being rejected by Alex, Harriet and seven other editors, I didn't know if it was actually worth my while writing another book. There wasn't much point if no one was going to publish it.

I hadn't even told Jeremy yet. And I certainly wasn't going to now. I'd have to start looking for other work soon; but I'd been writing full time for so long, I had no idea what I'd actually be qualified to do. Type up students' dissertations? Depressing thought.

'Good,' she said. 'Try not to worry too much, OK? It'll all work out. It's probably for the best.'

My eyes filled up again. I tried to talk and then waved my hand in front of my face. 'Sorry,' I managed. 'I'm a mess.'

Celeste hugged me. 'Ah, Libby-Lu. I'm the one who's sorry. You don't deserve all this.'

'What am I going to do? Who's going to want me now? I feel so stupid. Everyone's going to think I'm crap in bed or something.'

She smiled gently. 'No they won't. Because I'll tell them what a lying, cheating little gnome you were with.'

'*Were*?' I wailed again. 'You think it's over for good?'

She stared at me. 'Libby, this is the third time Jeremy's been unfaithful. That you know of. You can't take him back again. You've been a nervous wreck for the last two years. This has to be the end of it. Please?'

I nodded. I knew Celeste was right. But even after everything he'd done, I still loved him.

The first time it had been a four-month fling with a girl in the office. Jeremy ran the legal department in the Dublin office of a big sports and media agency called Sports Management International. He used to work for Franklin Street, my literary agency, and we'd met at one of their Christmas parties. Jeremy was charming and very funny; that's why I'd fallen for him in the first place.

It was the damn phone calls that had given it away. The house phone would ring, and when I answered it, the line would go dead. Happened for weeks until Jeremy suggested we should change the number. I made him explain and he came clean. I think he was afraid that his recently dumped girlfriend would arrive on the doorstep one day wielding a bread knife. I believed him when he said he was sorry, that it was a stupid mistake, that he'd never do anything to hurt me again; that he loved me. But happen again it did, with another work colleague. I was alerted by an anonymous letter. Probably from the bitter ex-girlfriend. When I confronted him, he apologized, said he'd end it immediately, claimed he was a changed man.

But clearly he'd been lying all along.

The more I thought about it, the more I realized that yes, this time was different. Celeste was right – enough was enough. This time I was going to make a stand, starting with my hair. Bad break-up equals dramatic haircut. You don't mess with tradition. And I'd always rather fancied pink bits.

There was no sign of Jeremy on Sunday, so I spent the day lying on the sofa watching bad television.

At eight o'clock on Monday morning, he arrived with several empty suitcases and began to tip the contents of his drawers and wardrobe into them.

I sat on the bed, still in yesterday's clothes, and watched him, distraught, all my resolutions out of the window.

'Where have you been?' I asked.

'You know where I've been. And that's where you'll find me if there's an emergency.' His voice sounded so harsh, it made me crumble inside.

'You don't have to do this,' I whispered. 'Stay.' I was instantly disgusted with myself.

'Oh, don't start now,' he said without turning round. 'It's too late. And Ruth-Ann's delighted to have me around. She's not surgically attached to her damn laptop like you are. She cooks and everything; makes a change.'

I jumped up and grabbed his arm. 'Say you'll never see her again and we'll forget all about this.'

He peeled my hand off and patted it. 'Libby, you're embarrassing yourself. And what are you wearing?' The look on his face said it all. He was utterly disgusted by me.

I spent the rest of the day sobbing my heart out.

Chapter 6

Libby

'This can't be our room,' I whispered to Celeste as the porter carried our bags into the hall of the plush hotel suite. 'There must be some mistake.'

Celeste frowned at me and said in a low voice, 'Don't you dare say anything in case it is. It's gorgeous, and we might just get away with it. We deserve it after that bloody nightmare of a trip.'

Our flight had been delayed and we'd had to camp in the cramped departure lounge for over two hours with a clump of bored Spanish students who spent the whole time poking each other and squealing. We were supposed to arrive at Heathrow at seven p.m. It was eight before we even boarded.

Celeste ran past the porter and into the large sitting room. She whistled. 'Would you look at that view?'

I stood beside her, my head on her shoulder as she was a good six inches taller than me, and stared out of the huge, green-tinted plate-glass window. The River Thames stretched out in front of us – to the right were the Houses of Parliament and Big Ben. A barge was moored on the river bank, multicoloured lights strung across its deck, and the faint tinkle of cheery piano music drifted through the open window.

Celeste leaned forward and pressed her nose against the thick glass, leaving a greasy make-up smear on its surface. We stood there in silence for a few minutes, drinking in the view.

The porter coughed behind us. 'Will that be all?'

'Yes, thanks.' I handed him five pounds. Probably way too much but I was still awed by the poshness of our room.

'Your champagne is on ice.' He gestured at the shiny black sideboard. 'Handmade chocolates. And if you'd like anything else, just let us know.'

Celeste smiled at him and winked. 'Oh, we will,' she growled.

He practically ran out of the door.

'Celeste! Must you?'

She laughed. 'What? I'm sure he's well used to it. I wasn't serious – he's only a pup. Now, let's pop the bubbly and hit the tiles.'

An hour later Celeste was fast asleep on the sofa, snoring gently, her legs thrown across my lap, an empty champagne glass still clutched in her hand.

The following morning I was woken by a rap on the door. I got up groggily and went to open it. Alex was standing in the hallway, looking like he'd just stepped out of a fashion shoot. Midnight-blue suit, white shirt with three buttons open, showing off several inches of toned chest.

His face was suspiciously smooth and even-coloured.

'Alex, are you wearing make-up?'

'Tinted moisturizer. Do you like it?' He gave me a flirty wink.

I scowled at him and folded my arms across my chest. I wished I was in anything but my baggy cotton pyjamas. 'Are you trying to look camp?'

'No. I just thought Lulabelle might appreciate the extra effort.'

'I doubt if she'll be interested in anyone other than herself.'

'Ouch! Who got out of bed on the wrong side this morning? Off you go and shower. I'll make some calls in your living room, if you don't mind.' He walked past me, looked around and whistled. 'Swish. Hope you appreciate it. Cost me an arm and a leg.'

'Actually, I do mind. Go and make your calls in the lobby. I'd like some privacy while I'm getting dressed.'

'I'll shut the door behind me. You won't hear a thing.' He closed the door of the sitting room in my face.

The man was incorrigible. I stormed into the bathroom, slammed the door and locked it tightly. We had ages yet – the meeting wasn't until ten. It was only five to eight, and I was damned if I was going to waste the incredible red mosaic bath tub and all the posh smelly things. I leaned over the tub, turned on the taps and – splash – covered myself in water. Celeste had obviously had a shower and forgotten to turn the knob back to bath.

'Aagh!' I screamed, jumping backwards. I grabbed a towel and patted my soaked pyjamas.

'Everything OK in there?' Alex asked through the door.

'Fine.' I switched off the water, flicked the knob and started to fill the bath.

'You don't have time for a bath,' Alex said. 'I've ordered your make-up girl for eight sharp.'

I opened the door a crack. 'What?'

'Hair and make-up. We want to make a good impression. There's a lot of money at stake, Libby. A hundred and fifty K, to be precise.'

'I thought you said a hundred?' I narrowed my eyes.

'Fifty is my cut.'

'That's outrageous! You used to take fifteen per cent. Polly takes fifteen per cent – it's standard. That's more like thirty per cent – no agent gets thirty per cent.'

'Thirty-three, actually,' he said mildly. 'But this is a very special deal. A one-off. Look, we're wasting time here. Mush-mush, into the shower. And try not to dress too arty-farty. Lulabelle is a businesswoman.'

I raised my eyebrows at him.

He smiled. 'Among other things.'

Celeste walked out of the bedroom, pressing a hooped gold earring through her ear lobe. 'I wondered what the noise was.'

Alex stared at her in surprise. 'What are *you* doing here?'

'Who were you expecting?' she said. 'Kate Moss?'

'Would have been nice.'

Celeste glared at him. 'And where did you crawl out from? I didn't know they did slimy rocks at the Thames Plaza.'

'I'm here to bring Libby to her meeting.'

'Well, you can just skedaddle, boy-o. We're going to have a civilized breakfast and then I've ordered a taxi for nine. Which should give us oodles of time to get to Soho.'

There was a knock on the door.

'Hair and make-up,' I told Celeste. 'Alex booked it.'

Celeste ran her hand through her still-damp dark chestnut bob. 'Excellent timing. I was about to dry it myself, but this is even better. Sling your hook, Alex. We're busy. And by the way, I think Libby's a damn fool to work with you again. Just for the record. And we'll need that cheque up front, by the way. No cheque, no book. Simple as that.'

Alex smiled. 'You'd make a good agent, Celeste. And you don't need make-up – you look great just as you are. In fact you're looking even better than I remember.'

'Liar,' Celeste said, but I could tell she was trying not to smile.

'Some dames just improve with age,' he said. 'Like crocodile-skin bags.'

Her face dropped. Celeste was touchy about her age.

'Out!' she snapped. 'Right now, before I throw you out.' She swung the door open, right in the face of the rather startled make-up girl.

'And stay out.'

*

30

An hour later we clicked down the white marble floor of the lobby (Alex's leather-soled Italian boots with metal heel-tips making the most noise of all), and climbed into our black London taxi. I walked behind Celeste, admiring her black cigarette pants and pearl-grey top. She'd dressed me in a purple silk jersey-dress. We'd both ignored the fact that it clashed with the pink bits in my hair.

'No one will notice,' she assured me.

'Celeste, you can't come to the meeting with us, I'm sorry,' Alex said as the cab pulled out. 'Libby can meet you for lunch. She's a big girl, she'll be fine on her own.'

Celeste was having none of it. 'If you think I'm letting her out of my sight, you're wrong, lady-boy. God knows what you'd make her sign.'

'Who are you calling lady-boy?'

'That would be the man who's wearing an entire Mac counter on his spotty face.'

'Would the two of you stop it?' I said. 'You're making me nervous. And my hands are shaking as it is.' I showed them.

'Sorry,' Celeste said. 'But he started it.'

'What?' Alex said. 'Celeste, you shouldn't even be in this taxi. In fact – ' he rapped on the plastic partition – 'this lady wants to get out.' The driver grunted and indicated to pull over.

'Pay no attention,' I told the driver. 'Sorry about that. Drive on.'

I looked at Alex. 'She goes, I go. Understand? I need her moral support.'

'Moral?' Alex chuckled.

I'd had enough. 'If I didn't know any better, I'd say the two of you were having it off behind my back and all the bickering is actually the product of a lovers' tiff. In fact, do you fancy each other? Is that why you're both behaving like territorial cats?'

Celeste wrinkled her nose. 'Euew. No! Please, credit me with some taste.'

Alex snorted. 'As if.'

I smiled at both of them smugly. That had shut them up.

'You've been reading too much chick lit,' Celeste muttered. 'All that love nonsense has gone to your head.'

'Hello,' I said. 'I do write romance, remember?'

'I know, but you don't *believe* what you write,' Celeste said. 'Do you?'

I sighed. 'At the moment, no.'

'For God's sake, don't tell Lulabelle that,' Alex said. 'I told her you were Miss Happily Ever After.'

'What else did you tell her?'

'That you've been shortlisted for the Romance Novel of the Year three times.'

'But I've never won it,' I said glumly. 'Always the bridesmaid, never the bride.'

'And that your second book was number one in Ireland for five weeks,' he added.

'But my last book barely scraped into the top twenty.'

Alex tut-tutted. 'Why are you always talking yourself down, Libby?'

'Because people like you keep disappointing her,' Celeste said. 'Look, Alex, Libby's had a pretty shitty year so far. First you dumped her, then her publishers dumped her, now her fiancé has run off with some floozy—'

Alex looked genuinely contrite. 'Libby, I'm so sorry, you never said.'

'As if it would have made any difference to you,' I said. 'You were always forgetting his name, even though you worked with him for two years. You introduced him as my brother once at a book launch.'

Alex said, 'That's not true. 'Course I know his name. It's James.'

'Jeremy,' I corrected.

He nodded. 'That's what I said – Jeremy.'

I stared out of the window, watching some Japanese tourists milling around Trafalgar Square, flapping away the pigeons with their hands and taking cheesy photos of each other with their mobile phones.

'Libby, I've never pretended to be a touchy-feely kind of agent, you know that. But when it comes to deals and contracts, I'm the best.'

'If you're young and pretty, or if you've had a crappy child-hood and want to write a misery memoir, you mean. Otherwise you're not interested, are you, Alex?'

He sucked in his breath. 'That's a bit harsh. What's got into you? Where's the cuddly, sweet Libby I know and love?'

'She's gone.'

He ran his hands through his hair and then wiped them on my raincoat.

I balled my hands tightly. 'Alex!'

'What? Hair gel. They're sticky. Your coat's black.'

'I can't believe you just did that.'

'Look, we're nearly there,' he said. 'We all need to pull together on this. Lulabelle's one of my newest clients and I don't want to piss her off. I have big plans for her. The novel's due out in October and the publishers have already booked ad space in all the magazines. It's one of their big Christmas titles. The cover's almost finished. They dropped the author photo on to the back of it last week and the package looks amazing.'

I gulped. 'Alex, it's nearly June. And I haven't even started writing it yet. How can it possibly be published in October? It can't have been planned with such a crazy schedule. Is there something you're not telling me?'

He dropped his head and started to play with his BlackBerry.

'Alex!'

'OK. Her last ghostwriter walked out. Caroline Saunders. Said she couldn't take the pressure. But she wasn't really suited to the project. Her last book was very gentle. Something about Elizabeth Bennett's daughters. Lulabelle needs someone raunchier, someone who's used to taking risks.'

'Raunchy?' Celeste smiled. 'Libby?'

They both laughed. Charming.

'Hey! I can do raunchy,' I said, slightly miffed. 'There was lots of sex in *Baby, It's You.*'

'Lots of baby-making sex,' Celeste said. 'Libs, it's about infertility – it's hardly the same thing.'

'What's Lulabelle's book about?' I asked Alex, still slightly miffed at them both. 'I need details, Alex. You haven't told me anything useful yet. What's it called, for a start?'

He frowned. 'I could have sworn I emailed you the details. It's called *Stay Beautiful.* It's a rags-to-riches tale about a young girl who wins one of those TV modelling competitions. Against all the odds, crappy childhood, blah blah blah. She has a boyfriend who knocks her about and she kills him.' He stopped for a second. 'Hang on, I think I'm getting it confused with Toni's new book. I don't think there's a murder in *Stay Beautiful,* but I could be wrong. Anyway, Lulabelle has set ideas about the plot. She'll fill you in.'

That didn't sound good. 'Set ideas?' I asked.

'Yep. She wants to have a lot of input into the story. Wants you to email her the book as you go along so she can OK each chapter.'

'That sounds appalling,' I said, pushing the back of my skull against the headrest. 'No wonder her last ghostwriter walked out. I'm not having some page-three girl editing my work. Tell her to write the bloody thing herself if she's that much of a control freak. What do you think, Cel?'

Celeste looked at Alex, her eyes narrowing. 'Will Libby's name be on the cover?'

'No,' he said. 'Just Lulabelle's. And she's never done any glamour modelling as far as I know, so less of the attitude, Libby.'

'Will the publishers know who's behind it?' Celeste asked.

'Yes. But no one else. And if the trade or the press ask, we'll give them a pen name.'

Celeste shrugged. 'You do need the money, Libs. Think of it as an experience. For a hundred grand, I'd do it. What do I know? I'm just a lowly journalist.'

I gave a laugh. 'The highest-paid columnist in Ireland.'

Alex looked impressed. 'Really?'

'Yep,' I said. 'One of the youngest, too. She's always on the radio talking about her columns. Telly as well. She's quite the media star.'

Alex looked at her with interest. 'I had no idea.'

'Now you do.' Celeste's eyes met his, challenging him to say something.

But instead he looked out of the window.

After a moment he said, 'We're here.'

The taxi pulled up outside an anonymous-looking wooden door nestled between a jewellery shop and an upmarket hairdresser's.

'What's it to be, Libby?' he asked. 'Are you in or out?'

Chapter 7

Libby

'Private members' club?' Celeste sniggered. 'Sounds a bit rude. How's your private member, Alex?'

'Shush!' he warned her. 'Somebody's coming. You're Libby's PA, remember? But keep your mouth firmly shut. Understand?'

Celeste just rolled her eyes theatrically, making me laugh.

We were perched on a leather banquette in the bar at the Soho Regent Private Members' Club, a very swish affair – brown velvet drapes surrounded the bar counter and all the windows, teamed with low oak tables with brushed steel inlay and matching benches and stools. My feet didn't touch the ground, so I was swinging my legs nervously, feeling like Alice in Wonderland after she'd just fallen down the rabbit hole.

A tall, well-built man in jeans, black linen jacket and white T-shirt walked through the doorway. He oozed alpha-male confidence. And make-up would have been wasted on *his* tanned skin and dark stubble.

Celeste drew in her breath and kicked me under the table.

'I think we're about to be summoned by He-Man,' she whispered. 'Wow. Take me now.'

I giggled again. He was quite something, all right.

'Celeste,' Alex warned. He jumped to his feet. 'Leo, good to see you.' He wrapped both his hands around the man's.

Leo looked at Alex carefully. 'You look different, Alex.'

'I've been away.' Alex withdrew his hands and stepped back a little. 'And this gorgeous specimen here—' he spread his arms theatrically – 'ta-da! – is the number-one bestselling Irish author Elizabeth Adams. And her PA, Celeste O'Connor.'

I cringed. Did he have to be such a drama queen?

'Everyone calls me Libby,' I told him.

'Leo Knight. Delighted to meet you both.' He shook our hands, his palm cool and firm, and then cocked his head and looked at me curiously. 'You're not what I expected.'

My heart sank. He'd obviously expected someone far more glamorous.

'Sorry,' I mumbled, too embarrassed to look at him.

'I thought you'd be older,' he said. 'You've written so many books. I've been reading *Baby, It's You* and it's quite an eye-opener. Thrillers would be more my thing.'

Celeste batted her eyelashes at him. 'I can see that.'

'Is Lulabelle ready to see us?' Alex said, glaring at Celeste and regaining control.

Leo pulled his eyes off Celeste and nodded. 'She's upstairs doing a photo shoot for *VIP* magazine. "My New Life as a Bestselling Novelist".'

'Bestselling?' I gulped. 'Isn't that a bit presumptuous?'

Alex threw me a look and then gave a laugh. 'As you can see, Libby has a great sense of humour,' he told Leo. 'Of course it's going to be a bestseller, Libby. The publishers have spent thousands on marketing already. The booksellers have been wined and dined, slots have been booked in all the major Christmas catalogues, the supermarkets adore the cover.' He patted my hand. 'All we need now is the book.' My heart started to race and I could barely breathe. I grabbed Celeste's hand, and silently pleaded with her to help me.

She murmured, 'Can you excuse us for just one second?' and pulled me up by the arm. She held on to me as I staggered out of the room and collapsed on the marble stairs outside. She pressed my forehead gently against the cool marble wall.

'Breathe,' she told me. 'In, out. In, out. That's it. You're going to be fine, Libs. Just take it easy. I think you're having a mini panic attack.'

'But it's . . .' I paused to puff '. . . too . . . much . . . They're expecting . . .' I took more shallow breaths '. . . a bestseller.'

'Don't try to talk,' Celeste said. 'Just concentrate on breathing.'

When my breathing returned to normal, I said, 'Celeste, I'm freaking out here. They have such high expectations. What if I write the book and everyone hates it?'

Celeste sucked on her teeth. 'To be honest, Libs, from what Alex was saying, the actual contents don't matter all that much. It's the "package" Joe public will be buying. If the book's actually good, that will be a bonus.'

I stiffened. 'But *I* care, Celeste. I know my name won't be on the cover, but they'll still be my words inside. I can't sell out like that. My work still means something to me.'

Celeste shrugged. 'Then write the best book you can. A book you can be proud of. You can do it. You wrote *Baby, It's You* in three months, and it's always been your most popular. How many translations?'

'Seven.'

'See!'

'Marian Keyes's books are in forty languages. I'll never get to forty! And I hate to think how many translations Maeve Binchy has.'

'Stop comparing yourself with other people, Libby. It's not helpful. There are hundreds of people out there – hell, millions – who'd love to have one book published. This is a great opportunity to get back on your feet. It could be the start of a whole new writing career. And besides, you've always hated the publicity side of things. With this book, that's Lulabelle's job. At the very least it will stop you thinking about Jeremy for a while –

you'll be so busy, you won't have a choice. Ready to meet Lulabelle?' she asked gently.

My stomach churned. 'I can't. I feel sick.'

'Yes you can. I'll be right beside you every step of the way.'

Lulabelle Ryan was even more extraordinary in the flesh. If you could call it 'flesh'. I'd never seen skin quite like it – luminous and silky – and her round cheeks were as smooth as a baby's. Her make-up was immaculate: fluttering Bambi eyelashes, perfectly blended smoky eyeshadow making her startling green irises pop, pouty rosebud lips. I wanted to reach out and poke her, see if she was real, but I stopped myself.

Celeste was equally mesmerized. I caught her checking out the area behind Lulabelle's ears for plastic surgery scars.

And as for Lulabelle's infamous cleavage, it was gravity-defying. She was wearing a white Grecian dress which clung in all the right places, with a gold belt clenching in her impossibly tiny waist. Her chest and limbs were lightly tanned, her conker-coloured hair a silky sheet.

Standing beside her, I felt like I'd been put together from her leftovers.

Leo had a word with the magazine team, who promptly left the room.

He then walked back towards us and stopped just beside Lulabelle.

'This, of course, is Lulabelle Ryan,' he said. 'Lulabelle, you know Alex. And this is Elizabeth Adams and her PA, Celeste O'Connor.'

Lulabelle's green eyes swept us all in regally. She was holding court and she knew it. Her gaze lingered on me. Her lips were smiling but the smile hadn't hit her eyes.

'So delighted to meet you, Elizabeth,' she said. 'I've heard a lot about your work from Leo and Alex. They both tell me you write wonderfully. I'm not much of a reader myself, but I do so admire people who can type quickly.'

'Call me Libby, everyone does. And there's a lot more to writing than that,' I said.

Alex glared at me. 'What Libby means—'

'You also have to have a vivid imagination,' I continued, ignoring him. 'And, to be honest, a lot of it is just hard slog until you have the first draft finished. Then you start the rewriting. That's the most difficult bit. For me, anyway. I'm a bit of a per-fectionist and—'

'Quite.' Lulabelle cut me off. She seemed a bit put out that I'd dared interrupt her. 'But for this project, it's my story that will be driving the plot. I'll be doing the work for you.'

'Lulabelle knows exactly what she'd like to happen in the book,' Leo explained. 'She just needs help getting her ideas down on paper.'

'So you have the plot all planned out?' I asked her.

'In my head, yes.'

I thought about this for a second, then said, 'What happens if your main character takes on a life of her own and won't do what you want her to do?'

Lulabelle gave a short laugh. 'She'll just have to toe the line. She's only a character. She's not real.'

'If she's not real to you, she won't be real to your readers,' I said. 'You have to believe in her one hundred per cent, Lulabelle. You have to know everything about her – what she eats for breakfast, what she thinks of Green issues, what—'

'I do know her!' Lulabelle said strongly. 'But she still has to do what I want.'

I wasn't budging. 'I can't write this book for you unless you give me some leeway to change the plot as the story develops.'

'Alex,' Lulabelle said, still staring at me, 'You said she'd be compliant. This woman is not compliant.'

'Excuse me, I'm right here in front of you,' I said, waving my hand in Lulabelle's face.

'*Libby!*' Alex hissed. 'I'm sorry, I don't know what's got into her, Lulabelle. She's so excited about this project. I think it's stress.'

'It's not stress,' I said. 'And would you all stop talking about me as if I'm not in the room.'

Celeste stepped forward. 'Look, Lulabelle, Libby's a writer, not a robot. And when it comes to novels, she knows what she's doing. I understand you have two months to get this book finished, otherwise the whole project goes down the toilet. No book, no moolah for anyone, your good self included. Why don't you and Libby put some writing guidelines in place, so you're both happy? Leave the business side of things to Leo and Alex. You concentrate on the book.'

Lulabelle looked at Leo. He gave her a nod.

'Fine,' Lulabelle said. 'The business side is simple. My profile is excellent in Ireland, and I'm starting to break through over here in the UK. I'm currently filming a reality show for Channel 7 which will help raise my profile in both countries and be my calling card for the States. The book's a vital element of the Lulabelle brand. I want to be big worldwide.'

Leo caught my eye, a smile playing on his lips. He dropped his eyes to Lulabelle's pneumatic chest then raised his eyebrows. I stifled a giggle. He was ultra cute. Funny too. And miraculously he seemed to be on my side.

'Europe, America,' Lulabelle continued. 'A girl's gotta make a living.'

'Absolutely,' Alex agreed enthusiastically. I could practically see the ch-ching of dollar signs reflected in his eyeballs.

Celeste harrumphed under her breath. She'd obviously seen them too.

'That's all well and good,' I said. 'But when it comes to the book—'

Lulabelle was staring at me. I stopped mid-sentence. She didn't look too pleased.

'Sorry,' I murmured. 'Do continue.'

Her eyes bored into mine. 'Elizabeth, are you going to be my ghostwriter or are we all just wasting our time here?'

I gulped. 'Libby.'

'What?'

'OK, I'll do the book, but I'd prefer it if you called me Libby. Only my mother calls me Elizabeth.'

I could hear Alex mutter something under his breath.

Lulabelle looked at me. 'I prefer Elizabeth. Sounds far more literary, don't you think?'

'You're quite right, Lulabelle,' Alex said.

'So Elizabeth it is,' she said, ignoring him. She was obviously well used to sycophants. 'I think we're done here. Leo, can you see them out? And arrange a meeting with *Elizabeth* for tomorrow morning in my suite. Six a.m. sharp. We'll work on the book for two hours before my appointment.'

Leo guided us all towards the door.

'Lulabelle, there are a few things—' Alex began.

She put her hand up to stop him. 'Talk to Leo. I'm frightfully busy today.'

'Nice to meet you, Libby,' Leo said, falling into step beside me as we walked back down the marble stairs. He lowered his voice. 'You'll be fine. Under all that camouflage, she's a pussy cat; wait till you get to know her better.'

I stared at him, speechless. Was he joking?

He smiled at me. 'Don't look so incredulous. It's good to have you on board. See you bright and early.'

I gave a laugh. 'There'll be nothing bright about me at six in the morning, I can assure you.'

Chapter 8

Libby

Celeste yawned deeply, making her jawbone crack.

'Ouch!' she said, rubbing it. 'I'm falling apart.' She pulled out a black compact from her bag, flicked it open and began to study her under-eye area, poking and prodding the skin with her fingertips.

'More bloody lines,' she muttered.

'It's ten to six in the morning,' I said. 'Of course there are lines. Your skin hasn't had time to stretch out yet.'

She placed her fingers on her temples and drew the skin back.

I laughed. 'You look like that catwoman. You know, the American millionaire's wife who's had all that plastic surgery.'

'Not quite the look I'm aiming for. But did you see Lulabelle's skin yesterday? It's so perfect. Not a spot or line in sight.'

'But she's had loads of work done. She's one of the few people who actually admits to it.'

'Do you think she'd give me the name of her plastic surgeon?'

'Celeste! Are you serious?'

She shrugged. 'Maybe. I'm twenty-nine, Libs. Twenty-bloody-nine. In a few years I'll be completely washed-up. No man's going to look at me when there are women like Lulabelle out there giving the rest of us prune-skinned folk a bad name.'

'What are you talking about? You look fantastic for ... for anyone.'

'For someone my age. Go on, you know you were going to say it. God, I wish I was your age again.'

'In case it's slipped your attention, there are only two years between us, and I'm also single. And I have pink bits in my hair, and enough emotional scars to put me off men for life.'

'Even a man like Leo? Do you think he and Lulabelle are a couple?'

'No! He's her manager.'

'Loads of celebs marry their managers. Look at Celine Dion. And Madonna got it on with one of her dancers.'

'And look how that turned out.'

The taxi pulled up outside Number 12, a huge Georgian-style hotel with bay trees in brass pots on either side of the entrance, and a doorman in top hat and tails.

I started to feel dizzy again.

'Celeste, I can't do this.'

'You can and you will.'

She pushed me out of the taxi with such force I fell on to the pavement.

'Celeste!' I stood up and brushed my trousers down. Celeste was taking her role as my pretend PA a little too seriously. She'd even laid my clothes out this morning.

I looked up at the hotel. Five-star-plus. Way out of my league. According to Alex, Lulabelle had been living here for two weeks, holding ongoing meetings with her publishers and Channel 7, and giving various media interviews in the build-up to publication date.

I knew this because last night, Alex had taken Celeste and me to dinner in a swish Italian restaurant in Knightsbridge – the kind with starched napkins and a special waiter to brush the tablecloth between courses.

Alex had filled us in on Lulabelle's schedule.

'You'll need to be at her hotel every morning this week,' he'd said, flicking through the diary on his BlackBerry. 'Then we fly on

Saturday morning to San Francisco, where Lulabelle's filming her first *Plastic Fantastic* show.'

'Rewind,' Celeste said, putting her palm up. 'Did you say San Francisco? And *we*?'

He looked at her. 'Obviously, when I say *we*, I don't mean you, Celeste. I mean myself and Libby. First class.' He smirked at her.

'We'll see about that.' Celeste folded her arms across her chest. The lacy strap of her bra fell off her shoulder and I reached over to hook it back up.

When we were getting dressed for dinner, Celeste had padded her C-cups with socks, put her hands on her hips, and pretended to be Lulabelle, pouting her lips and fluttering her eyelashes.

'Hello, boys,' she'd purred. 'Go on, take a look. I know you wanna.' She'd grabbed the bottom of the bra cups and squeezed, and a pair of socks had shot out, hitting me in the face. We'd fallen around the place laughing.

'What's *Plastic Fantastic*?' I asked Alex. 'Explain.'

He stared at me. 'Surely I told you?'

'No, Alex, you didn't.'

'Really?' He looked genuinely puzzled. 'I remember telling someone. In detail. Must have been another writer.'

'So I wasn't your first choice to ghost Lulabelle's book?'

'No.' He shrugged. 'But that's irrelevant now.'

Charming. 'Gee, Alex,' I said. 'You sure know how to make a girl feel wanted.'

'Don't get all huffy on me. Do you want to hear about *Plastic Fantastic* or not?'

'Suppose,' I said grumpily.

He picked up his BlackBerry again and navigated through the pages, his practised forefinger barely touching the mouse ball. Then he stopped.

'OK, found it. *Plastic Fantastic* is a reality show – a travelogue-cum-medical documentary. *Wish You Were Here . . . ?* meets *Nip/ Tuck*.'

'*Nip/Tuck*?' Celeste said with interest. She used to be in lust with one of the doctors – the dark-haired one with the funny-looking sideburns. 'Let me guess, Lulabelle's having plastic surgery all over the world and it's going to be filmed live.'

'Almost.'

'Euew,' I said. I couldn't even watch *Grey's Anatomy* without feeling squeamish. There was no way I was watching a real live operation. All that blood and gore. No thank you.

Alex ignored me. 'It will concentrate on the three most popular cosmetic procedures for women: number one – breasts, number two – Botox, number three – liposuction.'

'For women?' I asked. 'What about men? Are they different?'

'Yep. Apparently permanent hair removal is numero uno, followed by male breast reduction.'

'Who's paying for all this expensive surgery exactly?' Celeste demanded. 'Channel 7 is hardly loaded.'

Channel 7 was a new digital channel that mostly showed reruns of American sitcoms and reality shows.

'The surgeons are donating their services for free,' Alex said.

Celeste didn't look impressed. 'What kind of doctors do that? It all sounds a bit fishy to me.'

'The kind that like being in the limelight,' he said. 'The kind that just might be after a reality show of their very own.'

Celeste gave a dry laugh. 'Now I've heard it all. Celebrity chefs, celebrity gardeners, and now celebrity plastic surgeons.'

'And to finish answering your question about the cost,' Alex said, 'according to Leo, Lulabelle's putting up some of the production money herself. As you say, Channel 7 don't have much budget to play with and she's determined to make the show a success.'

'Here.' Alex passed me his BlackBerry. A balding man, greying at the temples, smiled out from the small screen. He had a large, slim nose with a bulbous tip, thin lips and hooded eyes. 'That's

Tony Sisk. Otherwise known as Mr Botox. He's going to work on Lulabelle's armpits.'

I snorted. 'Her armpits? Come on, you're not serious. What's wrong with her armpits?'

He smiled. 'The whole world's going to know soon, so I might as well tell you. Mr Sisk specializes in Botox and fillers. He's developed a special procedure for dealing with underarm sweat. It's vital for stars who wear red-carpet dresses on a weekly basis. Next up is Paris and Christophe de La Tour who will give Lulabelle breast implants.'

'New ones, you mean?' Celeste asked. 'I presume they'll whip out the old ones first?'

I wriggled uncomfortably in my seat.

Alex made a face at her and then continued. 'Finally we'll meet Raul Avelon, who's from Buenos Aires originally but has a clinic in Antigua. Raul will work on Lulabelle's body – liposculpture they're calling it here.'

'That's just a fancy word for liposuction,' Celeste said. 'Which she doesn't need – she's far too skinny for her build as it is.'

He shrugged and looked down at his BlackBerry again. 'And he's going to throw in a belly-button elongation on the side.'

'Isn't it dangerous to have so much plastic surgery in such a short time?' I asked.

Alex looked nonplussed. 'I guess it's a risk she's prepared to take. If it's successful, *Plastic Fantastic* will make her a household name. This is only a pilot, remember; if it takes off, Lulabelle's happy to do a whole series featuring different operations.'

'If she lives through all that invasive surgery,' Celeste said. 'People die on operating tables all the time.'

'Says who?' Alex said.

'Don't you read newspapers, Alex, or are you too busy preening yourself for that?'

'Keep out of this, Celeste. And I don't want to hear any more scaremongering from you, understand? Lulabelle knows what she's doing. And all you need to know, Libby, is that you're flying to San Francisco on Saturday, and to Paris the following weekend. You'll work around Lulabelle's surgical schedule and email the chapters back to the editor as soon as you're both happy with them.' He rapped the table with his finger. 'Be very clear, there's no time to mess around. What you send to the editor must be the final text. No edits or rewrites, get it? And they need at least ninety thousand words. I know it's a tall order, but I have every confidence in you.'

I sat back in my chair and said nothing. There was so much to take in. A few days ago I'd been back in Dublin, trying to make sense of Jeremy's betrayal. Now I didn't have a second to think about it – my brain was awash with Botox and boob jobs.

'Can I interview Lulabelle about the show?' Celeste asked.

'Absolutely not,' Alex snapped. 'Leo's in charge of the *Plastic Fantastic* media partners, and I doubt if the *Irish Express* is on his list.'

'He's lucky I'm even interested,' Celeste said indignantly. 'Lulabelle is hardly *Irish Times* material.'

Celeste was right. 'Alex, if Celeste travelled with us she could write an in-depth piece about Lulabelle's transformation,' I suggested. 'You could syndicate it worldwide a few months before the show airs to create a buzz. Top Irish model interviewed by one of her own. Has a certain ring to it.'

'Enough,' Alex said. 'I'll mention it to Leo, OK?'

He studied the menu.

'Celeste,' he said, without lifting his head, 'kindly don't order the white truffle on anything unless you intend to pay for it yourself. It's an extra forty quid.' He put the menu down. 'And let's get this straight – you're not coming to San Francisco. Or New York, or Paris, or Antigua. Especially not Antigua. And that's final. As soon as Libby signs her contract, which I just happen to have with me – ' he patted the inside pocket of his jacket – 'you're on the next flight back to Dublin. Alone.'

'Wrong.' Celeste reached over and snaked her hand towards his pocket. He pushed it away.

'This is an amazing opportunity for Libby and you're very close to screwing it up for her. Lulabelle wasn't impressed with your superior, know-it-all attitude. She doesn't like to be interrupted and she didn't take kindly to your intervention. We have a finely tuned working relationship, Lulabelle and I, something I don't want to put in jeopardy. That's why I'm sending you home on the next plane.'

Celeste just smiled. 'Don't be pathetic, Alex. You're not sending me anywhere. And if you have such a finely tuned working relationship, why did she dismiss you so quickly yesterday and tell you to talk to Leo?'

'Are you ready to order, Libby?' he said, picking up the menu again and ignoring Celeste's dig. 'I'm having a steak.' He caught our waiter's eye, and he walked over.

'Madame?' the waiter said.

'I think I'll have the lobster,' Celeste told him with a wide smile. 'With white truffle please.'

'Celeste!' Alex exploded.

'Don't worry, Alex, dinner's on me. Unlike some, I'm not a scabby little runt whose clients have no respect for him.'

Alex stood up, almost knocking the table over. 'That's it. I'm going outside to make a call. When I get back you'd better not be here, Celeste. I'm warning you.'

'You go right ahead,' she said. 'But Libby's not signing anything unless I'm here. Isn't that right, Libs?'

They both stared at me. Although I did feel slightly sorry for Alex, I knew where my loyalty lay.

'That's right,' I said. 'Make your call, and then Celeste and I will have a look at the contract while we're waiting for our food.'

'Fine,' he said through tight lips, and stormed out. Heads turned to watch him go.

'Everything all right, madame?' the waiter asked me.

I nodded and smiled. 'Yes, thank you.'

'Poor man has terrible wind,' Celeste told him. 'Suffers dreadfully.'

The waiter was too professional to react. 'Very good, madame. Can I get you anything else to drink?'

'A bottle of your best champagne, please. We're celebrating.'

Chapter 9

Libby

Alex had decided not to accompany us to Lulabelle's hotel the following morning. He said he didn't want to get in the way of our creative flow, but I suspected he was still smarting. After dinner and after several careful readings, not to mention seven amended clauses and two deletions, I signed his contract, binding me to the *Stay Beautiful* project.

Celeste was invaluable. Without her eagle eyes, I would have given away all digital rights to the book, for no extra payment. As Celeste rightly pointed out, the whole digital market was only in its infancy, and if mobile-phone books took off the way they had in Japan, it could be a huge money-spinner.

'The bloody man's supposed to be your agent,' she'd said later that evening back at the hotel, swiping at her make-up with a cotton-wool ball dripping with cleanser and throwing it in the bin. 'He's not acting in your best interests, Libs. Or else he's clueless about contracts, and I very much doubt that. He may be a lot of things, but stupid he's not.'

'That's the nicest thing I've ever heard you say about him.' I frowned. 'Do you think I should get another agent to look at the contract for me?'

'Nah, we've caught everything. I've been reading your contracts for years, remember? And I do have a law degree. Not that I've ever used the damn thing.'

'I know. I trust you. But I just want to make sure everything's above board. Lulabelle just makes me so nervous, you know?'

'I understand, babes. But we just have to find what makes her tick, what gets under her skin. Everyone has a weakness.'

'Really? What's yours?'

'Men. I specialize in bastards – you know that.'

I winced. Unfortunately it was true. But who was I to judge? I was no slouch in the bad choice department myself.

'What's mine then?' I asked her.

She smiled at me gently. 'You need to work it out for yourself.'

As we walked into Number 12, its air of calm, quiet elegance began to have a soothing effect on my nerves. By the time we'd reached Lulabelle's suite, up eleven floors in the lift and down a long corridor scented by fresh lilies, I felt rather drowsy and ready for a nap.

'Ready?' Celeste asked.

I nodded.

She gave a single rap on the door.

Leo appeared. 'Come on in. Good to see you both.'

His dark hair was still wet from the shower, and as we followed behind him I breathed in his fresh clean smell.

Celeste sucked in her cheeks and mouthed 'Hot' at me and I laughed. I turned my palms up and clenched my fingers, as if I was about to squeeze his bum.

'Elizabeth!'

I looked up. Lulabelle was standing in front of us. And from the scowl on her face, she'd seen me. Blood rushed to my cheeks.

'Lulabelle,' Celeste said confidently. 'You look stunning this morning. Tell me about this underarm Botox business. I'm intrigued. I'm a real sweaty Betty and it sounds like a great idea.'

I held my breath. This could go either way.

Lulabelle stared at Celeste for several long seconds before saying anything. Finally her lips twitched into a smile.

'Sweaty Betty? I haven't heard that one since school. And yes, underarm Botox is very useful. But painful.'

'How many injections do you need?' Celeste asked. 'Does it stop the sweat completely?'

'Let's have some coffee,' Lulabelle said. 'Then I'll tell you all about it.'

'I'll leave you girls to it. I'll be in the study if you need me, Lulabelle.' Leo excused himself and left the room. I resisted the urge to check out his rather fine bum once more. I was in enough trouble with Lulabelle already.

As we followed her into the sitting room, I wondered why she seemed so different this morning – almost human.

A black-haired man in his early thirties was sitting at the round table by the window, munching on toast and reading the newspaper. He was wearing navy boxer shorts and nothing else, his tanned legs stretched out in front of him, his hairless chest perfectly toned. He looked strangely familiar.

As we walked in, he put down the paper and smiled.

'Hi, girls.' He winked at me and Celeste. 'I've just had the most wonderful shag. Lulabelle's a gem.' He smiled at her. 'I'm off to the gym, sweets.'

He stood up, and I couldn't help my eyes darting to his crotch. I pulled them away and he looked at me knowingly, one eyebrow arched.

'Will I see you later, Lulu?' he asked. 'Dinner?'

'Oh, yes,' she said, sounding quite flustered. 'Lovely. What time?'

'I'll meet you in the bar downstairs at eight.'

As soon as he'd left, it came to me.

'He's on the telly,' I whispered in Celeste's ear. 'The new Galaxy ads.'

'Yes! George Fox. I knew he looked familiar. He can lick chocolate off me any day. Hubba-hubba.'

Lulabelle seemed oblivious to our interest in her boyfriend, her mind clearly elsewhere. She flopped down on to the sofa and sighed.

'Are you all right, Lulabelle?' I asked.

She straightened her back. 'Of course I'm all right,' she snapped. 'Why wouldn't I be all right? Now, let's get to work.' She sat down behind the leather-topped desk and pulled a plastic folder out of her Kelly bag.

'Where are we?' she said.

'You were going to tell me about underarm Botox,' Celeste said.

'No, no.' Lulabelle scowled at her. 'I mean the book. Where are we with the book? Elizabeth?'

'We're not really anywhere,' I said nervously.

Lulabelle cocked her head. 'Did that Alex creature not send you the notes?'

'No.'

I could hear Celeste laugh under her breath at Lulabelle's description.

'Oh, for God's sake.' Lulabelle pulled some A4 sheets out of the folder and passed them to me. 'It's the opening chapter. Alex said you'd rewrite it in your own style. But I want the story to remain the same. Understand?' She nodded at the chair opposite her. 'Read!'

I sat down and did as I was told, while Lulabelle tapped a hotel pen against the top of the desk impatiently.

'If you don't need me, I'll just slip out and have a word with Leo, if that's OK,' Celeste murmured.

Lulabelle ignored her. Celeste took this as a yes.

Before I had the chance to consider what Celeste was up to, Lulabelle said, 'Well? What do you think?'

I put down the sheets. I'd read enough. I had to say something.

If I didn't, this whole project would be a nightmare. I took a deep breath.

'The opening's flat,' I said.

Lulabelle's eyes narrowed. 'What do you mean, flat?'

'Dull. The opening is crucial. It needs to sparkle, to grab the reader's attention from the very start. To be frank, this is boring.'

'Are you saying Chloe is boring?'

'No. But we don't need to know every single detail of her life from the time she was born. The main focus of the book is Chloe's rise to fame, isn't it? And how she wins a modelling competition, against all the odds.'

'That's right.'

'So we don't really need all this backstory. We can knit that in as we go along, where it's relevant, using flashbacks. But I think we should start again. Our target market is, what – women in their late teens, twenties and thirties, right? And they'll be looking for a fun, entertaining and thought-provoking read.' I paused. 'Is all this rather turgid family history any of those things?'

Lulabelle twisted her mouth, then said, 'No, I suppose not.'

'So we change the opening. Here's what I suggest – we start at the most important moment in Chloe's life.' I put my hands out in front of me. 'Picture this. It's the final of the competition, she's about to step on the stage, sorry, catwalk. She has two choices. She can go forward and embrace her destiny, or she can run away. Then she hears a voice from her past . . .'

'She hears her father's voice,' Lulabelle said. 'And it says, "You'll never amount to anything, Chloe Lane."'

'Excellent! And then we cut back to the point when she decides to take control of her destiny.'

Lulabelle nodded. 'When she runs away to London at seventeen.'

'Brilliant. Spot on, Lulabelle.' I quickly jotted this down in my notebook. 'Now we're sucking diesel.' I gave her a grin.

She looked at me with interest. 'This isn't how the last woman did it. She didn't get as animated about Chloe's story.'

'Every writer is different. Some writers act out each scene before they write down a thing. But back to Chloe. Before I start writing the opening and the first scene, I need to know everything about her. What happens when she goes to London? Wait, wait – before you tell me that, first person or third person?'

'Sorry?'

'Is Chloe telling this story herself – I did this, I did that – or do you want it to be "Chloe did this", "Chloe did that"?'

'Which is more popular?'

'I tend to write in the first person – I think it makes it more personal. Or close third, where the reader sees the action through the eyes of one main character. In this case, Chloe's. But the writer still says "Chloe did this, Chloe did that." It's still nice and personal, but it might give you a bit of distance from the story. But it's your book – it's up to you.'

'I don't want readers to think it's Lulabelle's thinly disguised biography. Stick with the one that shows it through Chloe's eyes.'

'Close third. Good.' I looked down at my notes. 'So, London. What happens when Chloe gets to London?'

'She stays with her best friend, Liam.'

'Liam? Is he the love interest?'

'No, he's her best friend. The only man who never tries to sleep with her and who doesn't judge her on her looks. And then she goes to work in a bar, where she meets—'

'Hang on a second, a bar? What kind of bar?'

'A traditional English bar. Lots of wood and ale and stuff.'

'Not going to work for this market. Especially if we're going down the rags-to-riches route.' I rapped my pen against my teeth. 'I'll need to spice it up a bit. Can I make it a pole-dancing club?'

'No!' Lulabelle wrinkled her nose. 'Chloe's not that kind of girl. She'd be Charlotte in *Sex and the City*, not Samantha.'

'OK. How about a burlesque club? More tasteful. Nice and theatrical. Lots of red velvet and tassels.'

'That sounds a bit more like Chloe. She's very theatrical, but shy. Keeps herself to herself.'

'She sounds like an interesting character. But I'll need to get a better feel for her before I start writing. Have you done any character sketches?'

Lulabelle looked at me blankly.

'Notes on the different characters and what they're like. Physical details, likes, dislikes, that kind of thing.'

'No, it's all in my head.'

'We'll need to back up a bit here. We'll list the main characters, then I'll ask you questions about them and you can answer as best you can. OK?'

Lulabelle didn't look pleased. In fact, she was practically glaring at me. 'Look, can't you just write? This seems like an awful lot of time-wasting. The last woman didn't do all this. She just got on with it.'

It was on the tip of my tongue to say, 'But she didn't last very long, did she?' but I stopped myself. I had to keep Lulabelle on side.

'It'll make the book better in the long run, I promise. So we have Chloe and Liam, they're the main characters, right?'

'Yes.'

'But we still don't have a love interest. Are you sure Chloe and Liam don't get it together in the end?'

'No. I keep telling you, they're just friends.'

'We need a love interest.'

'Chloe meets someone when she's working in the bar. He's in a band. I thought we could call him Fly Peters.'

I smiled. 'Love the name. Go on.'

'He doesn't treat her very well. There's drink and drugs involved. Wild parties. He overdoses and she saves him. But he still leaves her. Then, after the modelling competition, she decides to forget about relationships and concentrate on her career.'

'But she's beautiful – she must have men crawling all over her. What about male models? And photographers?'

Lulabelle scowled. 'Not the right kind of men. Chloe's holding out for true love. It's what she deserves.'

'I understand. But we can't disappoint the reader like that. Can't we give her true love?'

'Maybe in the sequel. This is only the first part of her story. It doesn't end when she wins the modelling competition.'

'I see.' I sat back in my chair. Alex hadn't said anything about a sequel. Maybe he had someone else in mind.

Lulabelle noticed my discomfort. 'I've signed a one-book deal. If I'm happy with the way New Haven have marketed my book, and it gets to number one, I'll sign another contract. Otherwise I'll find another home for Chloe's story.'

I tried not to laugh manically.

'What?' She stared at me. 'Why are you smiling like that? Tell me!'

'Lulabelle, I admire your confidence.'

'What do you mean?'

'Most authors are grateful to have a publisher at all.'

'Lulabelle is more than just an author – Lulabelle's the whole package. And this book is only a small part of that brand.' She glanced at her watch. I looked too. Cartier. On closer inspection the edges looked tarnished.

She put her hand over the face and I looked away.

'We're wasting time,' she said. 'Ask your questions about Chloe.'

'OK – full name,' I said immediately.

'Chloe Jasmine Lane.'

'Age.'

'At the start of the book or at the end?'

'At the modelling competition.'

'Twenty-two.'

'What does she look like?'

I kept asking questions until I was satisfied I knew a little bit more about what made Chloe tick.

'Final question,' I said. 'What are her flaws and what motivates her?'

'Flaws? She doesn't have any.'

'Uh-uh.' I shook my head. 'Everyone has flaws. It's what makes us human.'

'Chloe is perfect.'

'Perfect isn't real, Lulabelle. Flaws make a character more likeable. Go on, she must have some weakness.'

'No.' She shook her head firmly.

'OK, we can work on the flaws later. But finally, motivation – what motivates her?'

'She wants to make something of herself, prove her father wrong.'

'Excellent.' I looked down at my notebook. 'Lulabelle, I think we're getting somewhere.'

We went through the same process for Liam and Fly, and then worked on plot notes.

A little later Leo walked in. 'It's eight o'clock, Lulabelle. You have an appointment.'

'But Elizabeth hasn't written a thing.' She grabbed my notebook and flicked back several pages. 'It's all just scribbles.'

'But we've made a good start,' I said. 'We have a strong idea for the opening and we know what's going to happen in the early chapters. We're doing really well, Lulabelle, believe me. Sometimes it takes me months to get to this stage. You have the makings of a great book here.'

She sniffed. 'After all my hard work, I should think so. I will expect you to do some actual writing tomorrow, Elizabeth. That's what I'm paying you for. Not sitting on your fat bottom and scribbling in a notebook.'

I opened my mouth to protest at the 'fat bottom' slur, but Leo put his hand on my arm and smiled down at me.

'Libby's a professional, Lulabelle. She knows what she's doing. I'm sure the notes are a vital part of the process.'

'They are.' I nodded gratefully. 'I'm going back to my hotel right now to write the first chapter.'

'Email it to me as soon as you're through,' Lulabelle said. 'I want to read it before anyone else. And don't let that muppet Alex get his hands on it, understand?'

I chuckled. 'Clear as crystal.'

I worked like a maniac all day, stopping only for a quick sandwich and coffee at two. Celeste had disappeared while I was working with Lulabelle. I'd asked Leo where she'd gone, but he had no idea, and she wasn't answering her mobile, so I got stuck in, lost in Chloe's world.

I wrote the opening scene, where Lulabelle, aka Chloe, faces her destiny. I was under no illusion that this novel was a thinly veiled autobiography.

I wrote the next chapter, setting it in 'Laces', the tasteful yet edgy burlesque bar I created from my rather vague memories of the film *Moulin Rouge*, all red velvet and tassels.

It was fun conjuring up its number-one bartender, Liam – tanned skin, bulging muscles, gruff manner, heart of gold. As I thought about Liam, Leo's face floated in front of my eyes. Leo was Liam, it was obvious. I set about making Liam the romantic hero of my dreams. If it wasn't for Lulabelle, this job wouldn't be half bad.

At seven that evening, Celeste finally arrived back. I looked over from the sofa where I'd been crashed out watching TV on the hotel's huge plasma screen.

'Where've you been, Cel? I was worried about you.'

'The library. Wanted to get some work done and I didn't want to disturb your writing.' She sat down beside me, kicked off her heels and threw her long legs out in front of her. 'I fired off a column on the enduring attraction of Alpha males. And get this, Leo said I can interview Lulabelle about the show and all the procedures. My editor's delighted. Wants to run the pieces as a series in the weekend mag. Says every time they have Lulabelle on the cover the circulation soars. In fact, Leo thought it was a great idea. I really don't see why Alex has such a problem with my work.'

I smiled at her. 'I keep telling you – he fancies you.'

'Yeah, right. His idea of the perfect woman is someone with Lulabelle's body and the brain of a chipmunk.'

I laughed. 'What's he been up to today, anyway? He's been suspiciously absent.'

She shrugged. 'He's hardly on my speed-dial, babes. I don't know and I don't care. So how did you get on with Lulabelle? Any progress?'

'Actually, we had a pretty productive morning. And I think she's in love with Leo, but she won't admit it.'

'Really? I would have thought he'd have better taste. But I did try to warn you about divas and their managers. So where are we off to tonight?'

'If you don't mind, I'm going to press on with *Stay Beautiful*. I'll lose a day on Saturday when we're travelling.'

Celeste frowned. 'So I guess clubbing is off?'

'Sorry, Cel. But there's always Alex.'

She groaned. 'I'm not that desperate.'

Chapter 10

Lulabelle

Lulabelle leaned in close and stared at her face in the mirror. She squinted her left eye up and studied the crow's feet and then did the same with her right eye. Just as well Simone was coming tomorrow – the Botox definitely needed a top-up. Lulabelle knew from experience that television cameras picked up every little imperfection, and although she'd never let it show, she was very worried about *Plastic Fantastic* and how she'd look on screen. It was make-or-break time for brand Lulabelle, and the pressure was on.

She pressed the apples of her cheeks. The filler was holding up well; Simone had a delicate yet firm hand, the sign of a true artist. Badly injected filler could look horrific, but this was perfect, plumping out her cheeks like down-filled pillows, making her look young and fresh.

It was a word Simone used a lot – 'fresh'. 'I'll just freshen you up a little.' Never 'I'll knock years off you', which was what everyone really wanted to hear. Lulabelle hated injecting her body with toxins, but it was a means to an end. She had to make the most of her few assets, and if that meant giving her skin, boobs and body a little extra help, so be it. She wanted the whole world to know her name, talk about her, listen to her. Anything less would be failure.

Her mobile was sitting on the bathroom counter, silent and

accusing. She checked her watch. Five to nine. Where the hell was George? Leo had been waiting in the bar since ten past eight and he still hadn't shown.

She stared in the mirror again. The arch of her brows had dropped a little, and the vertical lines above the bridge of her nose were starting to look more defined. Simone would have to do something about that. Lulabelle wanted perfect. Nothing less would do.

There was a knock on her bedroom door. She smiled, relieved. Thank God. George. She ran over and swung it open.

'I'm sorry, Lu,' Leo said. 'No sign of him. I'll take you out for dinner. Shame to waste that beautiful dress.'

'What's wrong with me? Why would he do that?' Lulabelle burst into tears.

Leo pulled her to his chest and stroked the top of her hair. Even in heels she was tiny, like a doll. 'Because he's an asshole who doesn't deserve you. Let me take you out, please?'

She pulled away and shook her head. 'I'm going to bed.'

Lulabelle shut the door in Leo's face, threw off her gold Chanel dress and sat on the edge of the bed, naked apart from her lacy thong. She picked up the remote control and flicked on the news.

'And at the world premiere of *Lying Eyes*, Bond girl Sabrina Garnet paraded up the red carpet with none other than the Galaxy man himself, George Fox. London's hottest new couple appeared to—'

She switched it off and threw the remote control at the screen. Then she grabbed her mobile. Before she could change her mind, she keyed in the familiar number.

'Hey, Lu, I wondered how long it would take you,' came the slurred voice. 'Sorry about running off on you like that, but the guys in the band—'

'Oh, shut up, Karl, and get over here. I'm in Number 12. Princess Grace Suite.'

She clicked off her phone, went straight to the minibar, and placed several small bottles of spirits in a row on the floor. Then she sat down on the carpet and started to throw each of them systematically down her throat. The whisky inflamed her chest, making her cough, splutter and almost vomit, but she held the burning liquid down, feeling the familiar alcoholic warmth hit her stomach and spread though her veins.

Chapter 11

Libby

I'd just got to sleep when my mobile rang. I slapped my hand around the large bedside table until I reached it. Celeste and I were sharing the bed and I didn't want to wake her.

'Hello?' I said groggily.

'Libby, can you talk?'

It was Jeremy.

'*What do you want?*' I hissed.

'Need to talk to you.'

'No!'

'Please, Libby? S'important.'

'Have you been drinking?'

He laughed. 'Only a bit. I was at a barbecue at the O'Reilly's. Wrecked my neck head-banging to Guns N' Roses. Come on, Libby.'

Against my better judgement I whispered, 'Hang on,' and crept out of bed and into the sitting room. I sat down on the sofa and looked at my watch. 'Jeremy, it's almost one in the morning.'

'Sorry. Didn't realize it was so late. Your mum said you were in London for the week. When are you back?'

'None of your business. And why were you talking to Mum?'

'Don't be like that. She rang, said she was worried about the wedding. Hoped we could work everything out. And she wanted to show me some material she'd found for the cravats.'

'She's deranged. She knows the wedding's off. And I don't want you talking to her, understand?' I paused. 'What do you really want, Jeremy? You hardly rang for a chat. Not at this hour.'

'I'm in the house. Where are your car keys?'

'What? Why?'

'I'm getting some work done on the Audi. It's going to the garage tomorrow. Saw your car's outside and thought I could use it in the morning. You hardly need it if you're in London.'

The cheek of him. Daisy, my convertible Golf, was my pride and joy, bought with the *Baby, It's You* royalties and named after the main character.

'Stay away from Daisy and don't bother looking for the keys, I have them with me. And get Ruth-Ann to drive you around, you're her problem now. Or here's a novel idea, Jeremy – use the bloody train. Goodbye. And don't ring me again.'

I heard a noise in the background, then a giggle, and then Jeremy whispered, 'Stop.'

'Is *she* there with you?' I demanded. 'In our house?'

'I have every right to stay here, Libby. It's my house too, remember? It's no biggie. The O'Reillys are only down the road and you're away, so we thought we could have a few drinks and—'

I cut him off, then threw my mobile on the floor. I closed my eyes, pressed my head into the back of the sofa and gave a huge sob.

After a few minutes I felt someone sit down beside me. Celeste. She put her arm round my shoulders.

'Jeremy?' she asked.

I nodded, tears splattering my bare arm. 'Wanted to borrow Daisy.'

'He rang at one in the morning for that?'

I nodded again. 'He was at a barbecue at the O'Reilly's and he's staying at the house. With *her*.'

She gasped. 'What? I thought Cliona O'Reilly was a friend of yours?'

'So did I.'

Celeste held my hand and stroked it. 'Do I have to say it?'

'You're right – he's a pig. But it still hurts.'

'I know, babes, but it'll get easier, I promise. Now, let's get back to bed.'

But I couldn't sleep. I lay there until five, Jeremy and Ruth-Ann's faces floating in front of my eyes, mocking me. Ruth-Ann wearing black lacy underwear, Jeremy naked apart from a pair of Guns N' Roses Y-fronts.

The sad thing was, he actually owned a pair. I bought them for him in New York as a joke. He'd booked the holiday as a birthday surprise, proposed to me on Ellis Island. And now I was going back to America, to watch Lulabelle's armpit procedure. How pathetic was that?

'Libs, it's almost six. You're going to be late.' I could hear Celeste's voice from above.

I squeezed my eyes shut even harder.

'No,' I moaned. 'I've only just got to sleep.'

'Lulabelle's going to have a freak attack if you don't show.'

'I can't. I need some rest.'

She sat down on the side of the bed. 'I've ordered some strong coffee. That should help. You jump into the shower, I'll ring Leo and tell him you're stuck in traffic.'

'At six in the morning?'

'It's London – there's always traffic. Now – shower, pronto. Otherwise I'll throw this glass of water over you.'

I opened my eyes. She was holding a glass over my head. 'You wouldn't dare.'

Cold drops hit my face. I jumped up, hitting my head against the glass and splattering water all over myself.

'Celeste! I'm soaked.'

She just smiled. 'You'll be even wetter in the shower.'

I was almost an hour late. Lulabelle wasn't amused.

'I have an appointment at eight, Elizabeth. We have less than an hour and I still haven't received yesterday's pages. You were supposed to email them to me, remember?' She strummed her fingers on the desk. 'I'm not impressed.'

'I'm sorry, I was up all night writing and I plain forgot. The good news is I've done five thousand words already.'

'Really?' Lulabelle looked at me through her reading glasses. I watched her forehead wrinkle a little and she touched her fingers against it.

'What are you staring at?' she asked rather rudely.

'Nothing,' I lied.

'It's my wrinkles, isn't it?'

'Everyone has a few lines, Lulabelle. It's nothing to worry about.'

'If you're photographed as much as I am, it most certainly is.' She pressed the fingers of both hands into her skin and began to feel her way around her face, inch by inch. She jotted down a few notes on the hotel stationery. I saw a few 'x2's and 'x3's and wondered what she was doing. She seemed very distracted.

'Would you like me to leave?' I asked.

'No, no. Where were we?'

'I was just saying that Chloe's story is coming along well. I've finished the opening and the first chapter. Today I need some more information about Fly and his relationship with Chloe.'

She nodded. 'Good. And I'll read over what you've done after my appointment. Do you mind waiting?'

'Not at all. I'll make some notes while you're having your . . . um . . . appointment.'

'Botox,' she said evenly. 'You may as well get used to my

routine. I have my hair cut every two weeks, a weekly manicure and pedicure, spray-tan when I need it, depending on photo shoots – some magazines don't like my colour to be too deep – and regular Botox and fillers. Different areas, of course – my doctor works around my face. I had the fillers done last month, so it's Botox time today. Forehead area.'

'That's a lot of injections.' I tried not to wince, but I couldn't help it. I hated needles.

'Yes. And don't look at me like that. I'm not some sort of freak – it's quite normal for a model. It's just maintenance. My body and my face are my living – I have to take care of them. Just like your hands and your brain are your living.'

'Sorry?'

'Writing. I presume you have to take great care of your hands. But clearly your appearance is of little importance.'

Charming! And did she say take care of my hands? That was a joke. I stared down at my nails, which needed a good manicure. And the pink bits in my hair would have to come out – beside Lulabelle's chestnut mane they looked ridiculous. She had the hair of a thoroughbred horse. I had the hair of a seaside donkey. Maybe I should start wearing make-up, even at seven in the morning. Smarten up my image. Use some fake tan. Maybe if I looked bit more like Lulabelle and Ruth-Ann, glossy and groomed, Jeremy wouldn't have strayed. To my utter mortification, tears sprung to my eyes. I wiped them away with the back of my hands.

'Sorry,' I murmured. I jumped up, ran out of the room and locked myself in the guest bathroom off the hall. I sat down on the closed loo seat and put my head in my hands. I was such a mess. Lulabelle wanted perfection, and I was imperfection personified.

Several minutes later I heard a gentle knock on the door.

'Libby?'

It sounded like Leo. I opened the door a crack.

It was Leo – how embarrassing.

'Lulabelle's worried about you. She said you ran off crying.'

'If she's so worried, why isn't she checking on me herself?' I dabbed at my damp eyes with some balled-up loo paper.

I heard him chuckle. 'Good question. Let's just say she doesn't like to get involved.'

'So you have to do all the dirty emotional stuff for her? Do you have to break up with her boyfriends for her too?'

He laughed again, this time wryly. 'No, that isn't really a problem with Lulabelle.' He lowered his voice. 'They don't tend to stick around long enough.'

'What about Galaxy man? He seemed pretty keen.'

'George? Stood her up last night. She was devastated. Didn't show it, of course, but she's ordered extra Botox syringes today. That means she's in a stinker.'

I smiled a little.

'That's better. She didn't make you cry, did she?'

'No, nothing like that. I didn't get much sleep last night – things on my mind. I'm a bit fragile this morning.'

'Celeste told me about your fiancé. I'm really sorry.'

'Thanks.' I wondered what else she'd told him. 'But I think it's best if I just go. If it's all right with Lulabelle, I'll work from the hotel today.'

'Are you sure? Celeste will be here soon. She's coming over to watch Lulabelle's Botox session, to get some material for her *Plastic Fantastic* articles. And I'd like to take you both out tonight. Celeste is one funny lady, and I could do with a good laugh.'

'I'll be busy writing tonight. Besides, I'm a bit of a wet weekend at the moment. I don't want to cry over your dinner.'

'I think you deserve a night out.' He smiled. 'Come with us. Please?'

I must have been hypnotized by his melty eyes, because I nodded a yes.

'*Elizabeth!*' Lulabelle yelled.

'I can't face her, Leo,' I said. 'Please don't make me go back out there.'

'Be brave,' he whispered.

He took my hand, his palm smooth and warm. Then he touched my cheek with his other hand, running his fingers over my flesh and making my breath quicken.

'Think about tonight. I'd really like you to come.'

Was it my imagination, or was he putting extra emphasis on the last word? My stomach flipped. *Stop it, Libby*, I told myself. *Of course it's your imagination*. Then he lifted my hand to his lips and kissed it. My knees buckled, and to my embarrassment I nearly fell over.

'You have such beautiful eyes. That ex of yours is one stupid man.'

With that he walked away, leaving me floundering in the hall, my heart pounding, staring after him in shock. Until a few weeks ago I was a happily engaged woman; now I was a ghostwriter and a Greek god was flirting with me.

Extraordinary.

The next thing I knew, Lulabelle was standing in front of me, her hands on her hips.

'You're very flushed, Elizabeth. Don't tell me you're ill. If you are, you'll have to wear a surgical mask. I can't afford to be sick.'

I shook my head, still unable to speak. What had just happened there? Was Leo really interested in me or had Lulabelle sent him out to cheer me up? I wouldn't put it past her – she was a machine.

'I'm sorry about your fiancé,' she said, her eyes meeting mine, softer. Leo must have said something to her. 'Break-ups are hard.'

'Can I base Fly on him?'

'Only if your fiancé is an unworthy, selfish prick.'

I laughed. 'That he is.'

'Then feel free.' She paused for a second. 'Elizabeth, tell me this – do you base a lot of characters on real people?'

'Yes. Especially people I don't like. I make them the baddies and give them horrible lives.' I smiled at her. 'Most writers do. But don't tell anyone.'

She smiled back. 'It's our little secret.' Lulabelle sat down behind her desk, and I asked her to describe Fly. I scribbled down notes as she talked.

'He's tall, dark-haired and mysterious,' she said. 'At least, he likes to think he is. Actually he had a very privileged background – public school, the works. Dropped out of college when the band started taking off.'

'Band's name?' I asked, looking up from my notebook.

'Gosh, something a man with arrested development would think is cool. You suggest a name.'

'What kind of band are they?'

'Indie guitar band. They'd like to think they're the Red Hot Chili Peppers, but they're so not.'

I laughed. 'How about Scar Tissue?'

She smiled, showing her teeth. Even her dentalwork was flawless. 'Perfect.'

We continued, creating detailed notes on what Fly looked like (scar on his eyebrow which he liked to tell people he got in a fight, not falling off a polo pony at eleven), his likes and dislikes, and how he talked – practised West London smeared thickly over his original Home Counties accent.

'Vanity and self-obsession,' Lulabelle said when I asked what made him tick.

'And hormones?' I suggested. 'Is he Testosterone Central?'

'Definitely. He doesn't care who he hurts to get what he wants. Chloe has no idea what he's really like.'

'Ouch,' I said. 'And why would she be with someone like Fly in the first place?'

'She's lonely and she doesn't know any better. As far as she's concerned, all men are like that. She comes from a very dysfunctional background. Plus, he can be very charming when he wants to be.'

'But Liam sounds decent.'

'He's one of life's good guys, all right.'

'But she's still not going to fall in love with Liam and live happily ever after?'

'No! Elizabeth, I keep telling you, there's no Cinderella ending to this book. After everything that's happened, you're still a romantic?'

'I suppose.' I shrugged. 'What's the alternative?'

I looked back over my notes. 'I think I have enough now to write chapter three. Fly's going to spot Chloe in Laces; he's there with his band after a gig. He takes a shine to her and she finds him waiting for her once the club's closed. He walks her home. Do they have sex or does she make him wait?'

'She makes him wait,' Lulabelle said firmly. 'But she does a private striptease for him in her apartment.'

'Fab! You're really getting the hang of this, Lulabelle.'

'There's a lot of waiting around involved in modelling. Deadly boring for anyone with half a brain. So when I'm getting my make-up or hair done, or sitting around waiting for the photographers to set up a shot, I think about Chloe's story. That's why I want to be so involved with the writing process. It's all in my head, but I don't have the time or the experience to put it down on paper. Alex told me most celebrities take a back seat and let their ghostwriters drive the plot. But I wouldn't be happy to work like that. I may not have a college education like you, but I know how to grab people's attention.'

'I don't doubt it. And you certainly know your characters.'

Leo poked his head round the door. 'Celeste's here. Will I show her in or ask her to wait?'

'She's early,' Lulabelle said. 'Ask her to wait. We'll be two minutes.'

I smiled to myself. Celeste would be more than happy to wait, especially if it meant having Leo all to herself. Then I remembered he'd been flirting with me and I felt divided.

'Show me what you've done so far,' Lulabelle said once Leo had left.

I handed over the fifteen double-spaced pages. She read the first few lines of the prologue out loud.

'Chloe! Chloe! You're up next,' the stage manager shouted.

Chloe stared out from the wings at the floodlit catwalk. Her heart was thumping in her ears, even louder than the hammer of the drum and bass music. This was it, the final of So You Want to Be a Supermodel, UK.

It was everything she'd ever dreamed of and more. She was one of only three finalists. The other girls were extraordinary: Londoner Vita Petrov, six foot tall, with sculptural cheekbones, and the legs of a racehorse; Sophie Blow, a peaches and cream Cornwall girl with strawberry blonde hair and the wiry body of a surfer. What chance did Chloe have with her curves? Yes, her navy blue eyes were striking, and at five foot eleven, she had all the height of a catwalk model, but she didn't have Vita's Amazonian body or Sophie's complexion.

'Chloe,' the stage manager called again. 'Everyone's waiting.'

'I can't,' she whispered, terrified. 'I shouldn't even be here.' Her father's words rang in her ears. 'You'll never amount to anything, Chloe Lane. Never.' Chloe tried to block them out, but she couldn't.

'It's now or never, Chloe,' the stage manager said. 'We can't stall any longer. What's it to be?'

Lulabelle looked up.

'Well?' I asked her, horribly nervous.

She shrugged, putting the sheets back down on the table. 'It's much better than the last two writers' attempts. It brings the reader into the story quickly and makes them want to continue. You're not bad, Elizabeth.'

Not bad? Did that mean good? I wasn't sure whether to be pleased or offended.

'I'll read the rest later,' she said. 'Keep writing. No changes will be necessary.'

'Thank you.'

She looked at me as if trying to decide whether I was being smart or not.

Leo walked in again. 'Simone's here, Libby. Would you like to work in the study while you wait? She won't be long.'

I nodded and smiled at him. 'Thanks.'

He opened a panelled door. Celeste and a slim, blonde woman with smooth skin and movie-star teeth were sitting on a green buttoned velvet sofa, chatting.

'And does it hurt?' I heard Celeste ask as we walked towards them.

'A little,' the woman admitted. 'Depends on your pain threshold. I can use a topical cream first to dull the area. But it wears off pretty quickly.'

Celeste looked up. 'Hi, Libs. Simone's just telling me about this filler stuff.' She ran her fingers down the creases between her nose and her cheeks. 'To plump out these babies. What do you call them, Simone?'

'Nasolabial folds,' Simone said in a plummy voice. 'It's a very common procedure. One of the most popular, in fact. After the glabella and crow's feet. And the horizontal foreheads, of course. I use Botox for all of those.'

'Glabella?' Celeste frowned. 'In English, please?'

Simone laughed. From the lack of lines, she'd clearly been self-medicating.

'The vertical creases between your eyebrows.' She touched the middle of Celeste's brow area. 'Here. I would do this area with Botox.' She made the word extra long – 'beau-taux'.

'Simone used to be a dentist,' Celeste told me.

'I still do some cosmetic dental work,' Simone said. 'For special clients. I liked dentistry, but I have two children now, and this work is far more family-friendly.'

'And lucrative?' Celeste asked.

Simone smiled. 'That too. But I like making women feel good about themselves.'

'And men?'

'Most of my clients are women.'

'Simone's very discreet,' Celeste told me. 'She won't tell me any of her clients' names, but I intend to find out.'

Simone laughed again. 'Celeste!'

'I won't write about them, if that's what you're worried about,' Celeste promised her.

'You have to excuse Celeste,' I said. 'She's terminally nosy. Probably why she makes such a good journalist. She's a columnist with the *Irish Express*,' I added proudly. 'She's won awards and everything.'

'I'm impressed,' Simone said.

Celeste deserved Simone's awe. She'd worked her butt off in college, winning a scholarship, which was just as well as her mum, a widow, was struggling to find the fees. After graduating top of her Law class, Celeste had taken a summer job in a local newspaper and had loved it so much, she'd completely changed career track, signing up for an MA in Journalism, and working part-time at the paper to pay for it. A year later she was snapped up by the *Irish Express*, where she'd been rising through the ranks ever since.

'Ladies,' Leo interrupted. 'I hate to break up the party, but you're keeping Lulabelle waiting.'

'Can't have that,' Simone murmured. She took a doctor's coat from the back of a chair and put it on.

Celeste winked at me, jumped up and followed Simone and Leo into the sitting room. She left it open a crack. I waited a few seconds, then crept towards the door.

Leo said, 'I'll leave you to it. Lulabelle, I have a meeting with

Channel 7 – I'll be back before three.' He walked out of the other door, directly into the hall.

I moved even closer to the crack. Lulabelle was sitting in the office chair, which was tilted right back, her skull pressed firmly against the white leather headrest.

'Today we're going to focus on your forehead and eyebrows, Lulabelle.' Simone took some small glass vials with metal tops out of her bag and placed them in a neat row on the desk. 'Botox this time, fillers next month. And how are the nipples? Any side effects?'

'No, none at all,' Lulabelle said. 'They were a bit tender for a few days, but nothing too dramatic. The swimsuit shoot went really well. The photographer was most impressed with the wet T-shirt shots.'

'I'd say he was.' Simone stood in front of Lulabelle. 'I'd say your nipples look lovely and perky. Now, are you comfortable?'

Lulabelle nodded.

'Just lie back,' Simone said. 'And if you have any questions, Celeste, just ask away.' She swabbed Lulabelle's forehead with a surgical wipe. Even from the doorway I could smell the sharp, acidic smell of the alcohol. Then she pressed small, fine needles on to the tops of two syringes. She stuck one of the needle tips into a vial and filled it with a clear liquid, flicked the end of the syringe with the tip of a nail and pressed down the small plunger, making a bead of liquid squirt out of the top.

'What's in the syringes?' Celeste asked.

'Botox,' Simone said. 'Or Botulinum toxin. It works on the muscles to make them relax. It was originally used for stroke patients and for people with conditions like cerebral palsy. It can even help writer's cramp, if you're interested. Now, I'm going to work on Lulabelle's glabellas, or 11s, Celeste, and her forehead. I'll do five small injections in a V-shape – three in the middle, on the bridge of her nose, one on each side of her eyebrows about a centimetre up. I'll also do the forehead lines, to avoid what we call "Spock Sign" – abnormal arching of the eyebrows. Ready, Lulabelle?'

'Yes.'

'As you know, you'll feel a slight prick and then a slight burning sensation.' Simone picked up a syringe with her right hand.

'Can you frown for me, Lulabelle?'

Lulabelle tried but there was minimal skin movement.

'Good.'

With her other hand, Simone firmly pinched the skin from the bridge of Lulabelle's nose between her thumb and forefinger. Then she broke the skin with the needle and pressed gently on the plunger for a couple of seconds.

I watched as she repeated the procedure all over Lulabelle's forehead. Tiny dots of blood marked each puncture hole, and Simone pressed on each gently with a surgical wipe.

'Why are there little lumps under the skin?' Celeste asked.

'I call them mosquito bites. The Botox takes a little while to be absorbed. They'll be gone in a few minutes.'

Simone stood back for a second, studying her work.

'Wonderful. I'll move on to the brows now. I'll inject her temples to lift the eyebrows and give Lulabelle a nice, fresh, alert look. And finally I'll work on the horizontal forehead lines.'

After a few more minutes, Simone said, 'All finished, Lulabelle.' She handed her a small mirror and Lulabelle checked out the work.

'Any more questions, Celeste?' Simone asked.

'Are they addictive? Botox and fillers, I mean.'

'Substance-wise, no. But most people who have a treatment do come back for more. Like Lulabelle, they like to look after themselves.'

'Lulabelle, what do you think?' Celeste asked. 'Are they addictive?'

'Safe as daytime telly,' she said, but judging by her slightly tetchy tone, Celeste had obviously struck a nerve.

'Thanks, Simone, you've been really helpful,' Celeste said. 'I'm only just starting my research, but I think it's going to be a fascinating piece. This morning's been a real eye-opener.'

Literally, for Lulabelle, I thought, moving away from the door. I couldn't wait to see the effect of Lulabelle's eyebrow-lift. I sat down on the sofa, feeling slightly queasy.

Chapter 12

Libby

'What are you wearing tonight?' Celeste asked me.

I looked up from my magazine. 'It's only dinner – I haven't really thought about it.'

'Libby! It's dinner with a gorgeous and, as far as we know, single man. An endangered species.'

'Cel, he only invited me to get you along. I could wear a nurse's uniform and he wouldn't notice.'

She raised her eyebrows. 'If you're talking an Ann Summers' nurse's outfit, he most certainly would.'

'Your mind is in the gutter.'

'But it's reaching for the stars.' She smiled. 'Come on, Libs, you should be sipping champagne in the bath, not reading *Grazia*. Where's your sense of occasion? It's our big night out in London – don't put a dampener on the whole thing.'

I stood up. 'If it makes you happy, I'll have a bath.'

'And you'll let me style you?'

'If you must. But the magazine comes with me.' I hugged it against my chest.

As I lay back in the lavender-scented bubbles, I continued to read the interview with Lulabelle. It was very surreal – she was talking about our book.

The Loving Kind

Tell the readers about your new book, Lulabelle.
It's a rags-to-riches story about a beautiful girl called Chloe.

Where do you find the time to write?
I manage to squeeze it in. If you want something badly enough, you have to make sacrifices. Writing is important to me; it's part of who I am.

And do you have any words of advice for would-be writers?
Yes – be honest on the page. Sit down at your computer and open a vein.

I smiled to myself. She'd robbed that quote from an American writer called Red Smith. I'd found it while making notes for my ill-fated creative writing class in the library. But I was impressed she'd looked it up, let alone remembered it.

I closed the magazine shut and slipped further down into the bath until the warm water caressed the back of my neck.

Thump-thump! I sat up, sloshing water over the side of the bath. It sounded like someone was breaking down the door to our suite.

'I'm not decent,' I heard Celeste shout. 'Give me a second.' And then, 'Oh! Not you again. What do you want this time?'

'Nice dress. Are you sure it's short enough?'

Alex.

'It's not supposed to be a dress. It's a T-shirt. If you must call at the door unannounced, deal with it. And I asked you a question.'

I could imagine her standing in front of him, eyes sparking, hands on hips, Alex staring at her long legs.

'I'm joining you for dinner. I have a taxi waiting downstairs. Where's Libby?'

'In the bath,' I yelled. 'Go away!'

'I'll wait for you both in the living room,' he said. 'Hurry up.'

'Go and wait in your own bloody room,' I shouted.

I sighed. So much for my bath.

I got out, wrapped a towel tightly round my body and padded out of the bathroom. The air felt cool against my skin. I ran into the bedroom, where Celeste was sitting at the dressing table, layering her eyelashes with mascara.

'I hate Alex,' I said grumpily, sitting down on the bed. 'Why does he always have to ruin everything? You know what he's like – he'll bang on about work, and I was hoping to have a night away from all that.'

Celeste shrugged. 'Leo obviously invited him. It'll still be a lovely evening. You leave Alex to me, babe. Concentrate on Leo.'

'But I thought you liked him.'

'I do.' She swivelled round and smiled at me. 'But your needs are greater than mine.'

When we walked into Balthazar, Leo was already sitting on a red velvet banquette. He lifted his head from the menu and waved us over.

He whistled and grinned. 'Nice dress, Libby.'

I felt my cheeks flame. I'd told Celeste the midnight-blue sequinned number was a tunic, not a dress, but oh no, she'd known better. I'd kill her later. At least I'd had the good sense to cover my bare legs with black footless tights and swap the stilettos she'd picked out for Marni-style wedges.

I slid in beside him and Celeste took the chair opposite.

'What do you think?' Leo asked us, gesturing at the long, dimly lit room. I took in the signed photographs of famous actors, the tasselled brocade curtains, the smartly dressed waiting staff bustling between the packed tables.

'Very luvvy,' I said. 'I like it.'

'Good. And they serve proper food, too. Listen to this.' He picked up the menu. 'Lasagne, steak and chips, salmon.' He looked around. 'Now, where's our waiter? Let's get some drinks in.'

Only then did he notice Alex loitering behind us.

'Alex, what a surprise. I'll get an extra place set. It shouldn't be a problem.'

I glared at Alex and opened my mouth to say something, but Celeste got in first.

She narrowed her eyes. 'We presumed Leo had invited you.'

'Actually, I was talking to Lulabelle earlier,' Alex said easily. 'She happened to mention Leo had booked a table here. I was at a loose end this evening, I didn't think anyone would mind.'

'I was hoping to have these two beauties to myself,' Leo told him, his voice slightly sharp. 'But this is even better. I'm treating Libby and Celeste to dinner and I'm sure you'd like to pick up the wine, Alex. Celeste, would you do the honours?'

He handed her the wine menu.

I looked at Celeste and she gave me a wink. Leo was obviously no fool. And he didn't appreciate Alex muscling in.

Celeste held the menu up in front of her face and leaned towards me. 'I am cave man, hear me roar,' she whispered. 'This should be fun.'

I grinned.

Celeste chose the second most expensive wine on the menu, a Sancerre. I expected nothing less. By the time our main courses arrived (steak for Alex and Celeste, lasagne for me and Leo), we'd already polished off two bottles and ordered another, much to Alex's chagrin. He suggested a Pinot Grigio instead of the Sancerre, but Celeste was having none of it.

As soon as Leo excused himself to have a cigarette outside, Celeste said, 'Stop being so tight about the wine, Alex. And Libby,' she added, 'why don't you go outside and keep Leo company? Our desserts won't be here for a while. I'll make sure Alex doesn't do a runner with his credit card.'

I nodded. 'OK, I could do with some fresh air. And I still can't believe you gate-crashed our dinner, Alex.'

'Get over it, the pair of you,' he said tetchily, pulling out his BlackBerry and fiddling with it.

'What do you think you're doing?' Celeste demanded. 'That's incredibly rude.'

Alex smiled rather nastily. 'Entertain me, then. Go on.'

God, they were exhausting.

I wove my way through the tables and walked outside. I was standing beside Leo for several seconds before he noticed me.

'Sorry,' he said. 'I was miles away. I didn't know you smoked.'

'I don't. Felt like some air. Left Alex and Celeste bickering inside.'

'The lady protests too much, methinks,' he murmured.

'Sorry?'

'Shakespeare. *Hamlet.* Celeste's crazy about Alex but hates herself for it.'

I grinned. 'That's what I think too. But she's not exactly Alex's type. His last girlfriend was a model.'

'Celeste's worth a hundred models.' He pulled heartily on his cigarette and blew the smoke out in a grey-blue plume. I couldn't drag my eyes away from his strong, firm lips. 'Believe me. There's only so much inane chatter and self-obsession a man can take. Give me a smart, funny girl any day.'

'You're just saying that.' The wine was making me bold. 'If a stunning, five-foot-ten beauty sashayed past you right now, there's no way you'd be talking to the midget with the pink streaks in her hair.'

He laughed. 'Libby! You're not a midget. You're just right. Look.' He put his arm around my shoulder, and, sure enough, my shoulder rested just under his armpit, a perfect fit. Disappointingly, he took his arm away.

'And Lulabelle would pay thousands for your peachy skin.' He smiled. 'Scratch that; does pay thousands.'

'Even with chicken-pox marks?' I pointed at my forehead.

He lifted his short fringe and pointed. 'We're twins.' There were two faded circular dips in the skin just below his hairline.

'You could get Simone to do something about those,' I said. 'With her magic needles.'

He winced. 'No thanks. I hate needles. And I think it's a mistake to mess with nature unless you have to.'

'Do you think Lulabelle has to?'

He shrugged. 'It's her job to stay beautiful. I know you don't approve of Lulabelle and what she does to her body, but—'

'I never said that!'

'It's pretty obvious.'

'Does *she* think that?'

'Yes. But don't let it bother you. She's used to people being judgemental.'

'Hey, that's not fair. I think she has every right to do what she wants with her body. But I just wonder if she's doing all the Botox and plastic surgery to fill some sort of emptiness or need. She told me what her father said, that she'd never amount to anything. Maybe she's doing all the surgery to prove him wrong. Maybe she wants to be perfect for *him*. She seems to think she's ugly, which is a complete joke.'

Silence. After a long drag of his cigarette, Leo said, 'He's dead.'

'Who?'

'Her father. Died when she was fifteen. Hit her pretty hard.'

I was mortified. 'I'm so sorry, I had no idea. I shouldn't have said anything.'

'It's OK. But did she really talk about him?'

I shook my head. 'No. But she told me about Chloe's father. Most first novels are thinly disguised autobiographies. I've been reading up about Lulabelle, and it all checks out. OK, Lulabelle was runner-up for Miss Ireland, which isn't in *Stay Beautiful*, but, like Chloe, she ran away to London and worked in a bar, and she kick-started her modelling career by winning a reality show.

Picture Perfect in Lulabelle's case. That was a great show, by the way. I only caught bits of it, but the shots of Lulabelle in the rainforest were amazing. Plus she dated that singer, Marcus Valentine. Chloe's story is Lulabelle's story. So I just presumed the bit about her father . . . I'm sorry, I'm being terribly indiscreet. You're Lulabelle's manager and, for all I know, her boyfriend, too . . .' Oops, now I'd done it.

'Boyfriend?' He just laughed heartily. 'That's a good one. If only you knew, Libby.' He shook his head, still smiling to himself.

He took a packet of Marlboro Red out of his jacket pocket.

'This book is very important to her,' he continued, after lighting up and sucking deeply on a fresh cigarette, making the paper crackle. 'And, to be frank, I'm surprised she's allowed you to make any changes to the storyline. She wouldn't let the last two writers touch a thing – that's why they walked out. But I think she recognizes an artist when she sees one.'

An artist? I was flattered. I looked down at the pavement, smiling to myself.

'She loves what you've done with Chloe's story so far,' he continued. 'And it looks like we might even get the damn thing to bed within the deadline. You're quite something, Libby.'

'Thanks. So what about you? How did you end up managing Lulabelle?'

'You know that book you're writing? I'm Liam.'

I gave a laugh. 'I'd kind of guessed. So you're originally from Dublin, but you came over to London to find work and ended up managing a bar.'

'Correct. Not a burlesque club, although Laces does sound like fun.' He grinned. I must have looked surprised because he added, 'I'm reading your chapters along with Lulabelle. Anyway, to cut a long story short, I knew Lulabelle in Dublin, and she looked me up in London. We became, well, friends, I suppose. Hey, don't look so incredulous.'

I smiled. 'Sorry. Go on.'

'When she won *Picture Perfect*, this talent agent contacted her, a slimy Essex wide-boy called Robbie, used to come into a room leading with his crotch – you know the type. Nowadays the shows sign the winner up immediately with a proper modelling company, but it wasn't the case back then. You just got a short contract, some clothes and jewellery if you were lucky. Anyway, Robbie found her a few jobs, some photo shoots for men's magazines, some high-end car show gigs, nothing too sleazy; but it wasn't what Lulabelle wanted to do. They dated for a while, which only complicated matters.'

He paused, pulled on his cigarette again. 'Anyway, she arrived on my doorstep one night in tears. They'd got into an argument about the direction her career was taking, and he'd hit her across the face; almost broke her nose.'

I winced. 'Poor Lulabelle,' I murmured.

Leo nodded. 'Stupid prick. I had words with him, made him tear up her contract. Then I became her manager. It was a steep learning curve, but the modelling world isn't all that different from any other business – a lot of it's about perception and luck, being in the right place at the right time. There are hundreds of good models out there, but my job is to make people remember Lulabelle: casting agents for catalogues, magazine editors, all the people that matter. Lulabelle doesn't have the build for catwalk modelling.'

'That's why she's made Chloe a catwalk model in the book,' I said.

'Maybe. But long term, television is her natural home. That's where the *Plastic Fantastic* show comes in – it will showcase her talent. Plastic surgery is her USP. We're pitching her as the thinking woman's expert. Someone who knows everything there is to know about surgery; someone other women can relate to.'

I gave a wry laugh. I couldn't help myself. 'Relate to? You're kidding.'

'Libby, do you have any idea how many people use Botox?

And Botox is only the tip of the iceberg. As the demand for plastic surgery increases, the prices go down. Basic business rule. Supply and demand.'

I sighed. 'How depressing. Soon the world is going to be full of perfect-looking women. I'll be a freak of nature.'

He cupped my chin in his hand. 'You'll look beautiful, just like you do now.' He moved his own head towards mine, tilting it softly. My God, was he going to kiss me?

'You two look cosy,' Celeste said.

Leo quickly dropped his hand.

'Libs,' she continued, oblivious. 'Your hot chocolate fudge thingy is going cold.'

I glared at her and the penny dropped.

'Oh, sorry,' she said. 'Am I interrupting something?'

'No!' I said, my voice sounding all high and mouse-like. I was still reeling from Leo's touch.

Leo ground his cigarette out with the toe of his shoe. 'Lead on, Macduff,' he said.

'You do like your Shakespeare,' I said.

He nodded. 'Among other things,' he murmured, his eyes meeting mine.

My heart skipped a beat.

The evening ended rather abruptly. Leo's mobile rang just after midnight.

'It's Lulabelle.' He stood up. 'I'll take it outside.'

When he returned, I couldn't read the expression on his face. Was it exasperation or annoyance?

'Sorry about this, folks – trouble at the ranch.' He looked at me. 'I'll see you in the morning, Libby.'

'What was all that about?' Celeste said after he'd left.

'Booty call?' Alex suggested.

'Alex, you're disgusting,' she said.

'What? Woman like that – ' he whistled – 'must have needs.'

Celeste slapped him across the face with her napkin.

'What?' He swatted the napkin away. 'I'm just saying.'

'Keep your sordid little thoughts to yourself. Libby and I are leaving. And don't follow us. You're not invited.'

'That was a bit mean,' I said as we sped away in the back of a black London taxi, jiggling up and down on the highly sprung seats. Our driver had obviously taken Celeste's 'Thames Plaza Hotel and step on it' to heart.

'He deserved it.' She rolled her shoulders. 'God, I'm wrecked. I can't deal with early starts. There are some advantages to working for the *Express*.'

'Neither can Alex, in case you haven't noticed.'

Celeste stared out of the window for a while and then said, 'I really don't get men. One minute you think you're starting to understand them, then – boom – they hit you with their stupid Neanderthal opinions and you're back to square one again.'

'I'm afraid you've lost me, Celeste.'

'Alex. While you were outside with the delicious Leo, Alex told me something. Actually he told me a lot.'

'What?'

'First, tell me what happened with Leo.'

'That's blackmail.'

'Too right. Spill.'

I stared down at my hands. 'I think he was building up to kissing me, but then we were rudely interrupted by some woman wittering on about my dessert going cold.'

Celeste hit her forehead with her hand. 'Doh! Sorry, Libs. Was he really moving in for the kill?'

'I think so. Hard to tell, really. He's a bit of a closed book. And I can't make out his relationship with Lulabelle. Surely you don't ring your manager at midnight and ask for his help? I wouldn't dream of ringing Alex outside working hours.'

'Maybe that's your problem. You should be more demanding.'

'Speaking of Alex, tell me what he said. Please, Celeste?'

'OK, OK. But don't let on I've told you. We were talking about Lulabelle. Just after you went outside I asked him if her name was real.'

'And?'

'What parents in their right mind would call a child Lulabelle?' I smiled. 'So what's her real name then?'

'He swore me to secrecy.'

'Cel, Alex is the most indiscreet man on the planet. You know that. He won't expect you to keep your promise.'

She smiled. 'It's Lucy. Plain old Lucy Ryan. Doesn't have quite the same ring, does it? And then I asked him had he ever used his full name, Alexander. He said his dad used to call him that all right, but he was Alex to everyone else. Then I asked him "What do you mean, used to?" And he told me his dad was dead. He said it so baldly I was a bit taken aback, so I asked him, "What about your mum?", and this is where it gets interesting. Alex is Irish.'

'No! He has such a strong London accent. I don't believe you.'

'It's true,' Celeste insisted. 'He's from Bray, to be exact.'

Celeste began to recount the whole conversation verbatim.

'"Don't look so shocked," he told me. "My mum's Irish, moved to Dublin when she got married."'

'Where does she live now?'

'Nowhere. She died. When I was fifteen.'

'That must have been hard for you.'

'Don't pretend you give a shit, Celeste.'

'Jesus, Alex, give me some credit. Dad died when I was eight. Heart attack. I don't really remember him. Mum had to raise me on her own and it was no picnic. She worked two jobs most of her life, cleaning houses during the day, waitressing at night, nearly wiped her out, but she's pretty much retired now, thank God. And at least she's still around. Losing your mum at fifteen – that's gotta be tough.'

'Yeah. I lived with my gran for a while, then she died, so my aunt took me in. Then my uncle lost his job and he was offered work up north. I didn't want to leave London, so I stayed down here with my cousin. Big mistake. Ended up failing my O-levels and getting expelled for dealing in school.'

'Dealing?'

'Don't look at me like that, Celeste. It was only hash. He bullied me into it, said he'd kick me out. He was in some sort of trouble with his own dealer; I never got the full story. After I got expelled, he was banged up for aggravated burglary and I couldn't pay the rent on the flat. A friend's dad took pity on me and gave me a part-time job at his bookshop. Bit of cleaning, unpacking boxes, covering the booksellers' breaks, that kind of thing.

'Anyway, within three months he offered me a proper job as a bookseller, said I could sell tea to China.'

'Wasn't wrong. After two years I applied for a job as a publisher's sales rep – much better dosh – worked my way up to sales director. Then Franklin Street headhunted me, and then I set up on my own. Easy-peasy, lemon . . . Anyway, why am I telling you all this, Celeste? Must be all the overpriced wine. Did you have to order the bloody Sancerre?'

'Ta-da! So there you have it,' Celeste said. 'The potted life-history of one Alex Sharpe.'

I whistled. 'I had no idea. What a shitty childhood. No wonder he's such a mess. He needs the lurve of a good woman.' I looked at Celeste and wiggled my eyebrows suggestively.

She snorted. 'Would you listen to yourself? Yes, he's had a rough time of it. But what he needs most of the time is a good kick up the ass. When it comes to relationships, he's a lost cause.'

'But he had that lovely girlfriend, Hannah. She put up with him for years, so he must have some redeeming boyfriend fea-tures.' Hannah was Alex's assistant at Franklin Street, from Belfast originally. I'd really liked her – she had a warm smile and dark blonde hair which she wore in Heidi plaits. She always knew how to make me feel better when my books were slated in the papers. She'd given Alex an ultimatum – get married or break up.

Celeste said, 'That was a long time ago. He's been a complete slut ever since.'

'Only 'cause Hannah got engaged three months after they'd split up.'

'It was his own fault. If he was that mad about her, he should have married her while he could. And I don't know why you're such a big Alex fan all of a sudden. He dumped you too, remember? Anyway, enough about Alex. Let's talk Leo. Did he have anything interesting to say for himself?'

'We spent most of the time discussing Lulabelle,' I admitted.

'Why doesn't that surprise me? You're obsessed, Libs.'

'I am not!'

'What were you reading earlier, then, in the bath?'

I ignored her.

She smiled knowingly. 'Admit it – you're caught in her Botoxed web.'

'Rubbish. I can't stand the woman.'

I turned away from her in a huff and gazed out of the window, the bright lights of late-night London flashing by.

Chapter 13

Libby

'You're making that up, Libs,' Celeste said, looking up from her notebook in which she was scribbling down notes for her latest column (I spotted the word 'sex' ringed several times). 'They don't do suites on planes.'

'You'll see,' I said confidently, my head still stuck in *OK!* magazine. This time Lulabelle was talking about her favourite holiday destination. The Caribbean. No wonder she was having *Plastic Fantastic* surgery in Antigua.

Celeste and I were sitting in the wi-fi area of the transatlantic departures lounge, waiting for our flight to San Francisco. Alex was pacing the floor beside us, BlackBerry pinned to his ear. Leo was using his laptop two seats away.

'I should be working,' I said a little anxiously. 'You're making me feel guilty.' I stuffed the magazine into my carry-on bag. I was already behind schedule. Unless I got my words in today, I'd be even more behind. But I didn't feel like writing. At home, I had procrastination down to a fine art. I'd been known to vacuum my laptop keyboard, clean out the microwave, polish the bathroom taps, Facebook for hours, invite Jehovah's Witnesses in for a chat – anything other than actually write.

'Forget that,' Celeste said. 'We'll be boarding soon. How many men have you slept with?'

'*What?*'

'It's for my column. I'm writing about the difference in sexual standards between men and women. At least I think that's what it's about. It doesn't really matter. Once my editor sees the word "sex" in the first line, he'll be happy. So, go on – how many? Ballpark figure.'

'I don't need to give you a ball-park figure,' I said in a low voice. 'Unlike some people I know, I can count them all on one hand.'

'Five?' she said.

'No! Two.' I thought for a second. Number one: Hughie, when I was nineteen, sweet guy from my English class. The whole thing was a bit of a let-down. Number two: Ronan, Biology student, not that you'd know it. All I remember were his gritty sheets. And finally Jeremy. Who knew exactly what he was doing. I thought I'd died and gone to heaven.

'Actually, three,' I said. 'But do we have to have this conversation here?' I nodded at Leo.

'It's on the low side, Libs,' she said, oblivious. 'But you were a late starter and Jeremy hasn't been good for your batting average.'

'OK, that's enough.' I stood up. 'I'm off to find Lulabelle. Book research.'

'Can I come?'

'No, go and quiz Alex.'

'Good idea. And then I can ask the air hostesses.'

'Please don't, Celeste – you'll get us all thrown off the flight.'

I walked over to Leo. 'Where's Lulabelle?' I asked.

He stopped typing, looked up at me and grinned. 'Three, eh?'

I blushed and put my hands over my cheeks. 'Celeste and her stupid columns.'

'I hope she doesn't ask me. I don't think my total would impress her.'

I smiled. 'She's all talk. She'll just make the whole thing up. Is Lulabelle around?'

'She's in the spa in the first class lounge. If you tell them it's urgent, I'm sure they'll let you in. Say you're her manager. Here, take this.'

He handed me a business card. Gold script on heavy cream card. Very tasteful. *Knight Management*, it read. *Representing Lulabelle Ryan* – and his mobile number.

'Thanks.' I smiled at him.

He smiled back, his eyes lingering on mine. Zing! There it was again. Blush city.

I had no trouble getting into the first class lounge and finding the spa's reception desk. A blonde girl in a white beautician's dress pottered off to find Lulabelle for me.

She came back a few minutes later. 'I'm sorry, Ms Ryan is having her skin hydrated for the flight. She says she'll speak to you on the plane.'

The girl sat down behind the desk and studied the appointments book intently.

I'd been dismissed.

'I told you she had a suite.'

Celeste and I were sitting in our seats, waiting for take-off.

'You were right, but I can't believe they let her board first. Before that man in the wheelchair, or any of the families with babies. And did you see the state of her? She looked like the Queen Mother in that headscarf. And what was that gunk on her face?'

I laughed. 'Layers and layers of extremely expensive face cream. But I did like her sunglasses.'

The entire queue had stared as Lulabelle stalked past on Leo's arm, her head held high. She was wearing a white cashmere tracksuit, and Leo was carrying her oversized Gucci handbag as well as his own laptop case. We could hear the whispers all around us.

'Who's that?'

'Must be someone famous.'

'Posh Spice? Na, the boobs are too big.'

Even with the fake look of resignation on her face, I could tell Lulabelle was lapping it up.

I'd traded my first-class ticket for two economy tickets, much to Alex's disgust. He'd wanted to make Celeste pay her own way, or to get the *Irish Express* to cover her expenses. Problem was, Celeste's editor said the paper's feature department was so skint that she'd only get paid after the pieces ran in the paper, not before. And as Celeste's credit card was maxed out from several recent shopping splurges, travelling economy was the only option. I was actually a bit disappointed – I'd always wanted to travel at the front of the plane. But having Celeste along more than made up for it.

As soon as we were in the air and the lights had pinged off, Celeste and I clambered into the side aisle.

'Leo said to ask one of the air hostesses for Miss Smith,' Celeste said.

'Smith?' I gave a laugh. 'Isn't that a bit of a cliché? I would have called myself the Crown Princess of Muldovia or something.'

Celeste patted my shoulder. 'She's clearly doesn't have your imagination, doll.'

I asked a blonde hostess for 'Miss Smith', trying not to giggle. She smiled. 'Follow me,' and led us through business class and first class, towards the very front of the plane. She stopped and pointed at a small door to her right.

'Miss Smith's suite.'

A moment after Celeste knocked, Leo swung the door open, nearly taking it off its hinges. He beamed at us.

'Come on in, girls.' He stood back.

'Suite' was a bit of a misnomer. It looked like the interior of a tiny caravan, with four average-sized aeroplane windows, a neat desk, a built-in sofa, and, instead of seats, a queen-sized bed slotted under the windows, complete with fresh white bedding. Lulabelle was lying on the bed, her head propped up on several full-sized pillows. She wafted her hand at us and then closed her eyes, the lids glistening with heavy cream. Her feet were elevated on yet more pillows, and she was sipping a deep red drink through a straw.

Leo gestured towards the built-in sofa. 'Sit down. Can I get you a drink from the minibar? Or a snack? We have sushi, caviar, fruit or olives.' He smiled. 'And I've just ordered chips.'

'Leo,' Lulabelle said without opening her eyes. 'The grease will stink the place out.'

'Sorry, Lu, I need my carbs.'

She sighed. 'And I need my rest. I have a gruelling operation ahead of me, remember?'

Leo winked at us and smiled. 'I know, Lulabelle, and you're being very brave.'

Lulabelle's eyes snapped open. 'I'm not an idiot, Leo. Make fun of me and you're out of here, understand? I'm sure they can give you one of those pull-out seats. And what do you want, Libby? Is it really all that urgent?' She glared at me.

'I was hoping to do some work on the flight,' I said meekly. 'I've started the second section now, where Chloe meets Fly. I'm confused. I know we've talked about it a little, but what does she see in him? Why is she so taken in?'

Lulabelle sighed. 'It's simple. She's young; she doesn't have all that much experience with men. He's nice to her at first, makes her feel special. Plus he's gorgeous, of course, and the whole rock thing gives him a bit of an edge.'

'And she's attracted by his fame, I presume,' I said. 'Does she see it as a way of getting into the papers?'

Lulabelle sat up sharply. 'No! Not at all. And I'll thank you not to put that into the book.'

'But maybe that's Chloe's weakness – she needs to be the centre of attention, craves notoriety. We were talking about giving her flaws, remember? To make her really come alive on the page. So our readers will believe in her, understand her, maybe even relate to her. Make her perfect and you'll lose them.'

'You clearly haven't been listening to me. Chloe is *not* flawed, Elizabeth. And you're wrong. Chloe's attracted by Fly's personality, not his fame.'

Lulabelle put her hand up in the air like a traffic cop. Even her fingertips were slick with cream. 'Enough, I must sleep. The paparazzi will be waiting for me at San Francisco airport and I don't want to look like a dog's dinner. Out!'

'Lu,' Leo said, 'surely the girls can stay? They haven't even finished their drinks yet.'

'Absolutely not. I won't have anyone watching me sleep. It's creepy.'

As we walked out of the suite, Leo closed the door behind him. 'Sorry, she's a bit of a control freak,' he said in a low voice. 'And I think you touched a nerve there, Libby; she loved being photographed on Marcus's arm. Gave her a real kick.'

I nodded. 'Thought so. I suppose we'd better squeeze back into our teeny tiny seats now. Thanks for the brief taste of the high life.'

He chuckled. 'You're welcome.'

The flight was uneventful. I scribbled away in my notebook for as long as I could before eventually dozing off. When I woke up, we were about to land. We peered to our left, across the aisle to the nearest window, eager for our first glimpse of the Golden Gate Bridge. The aquamarine of the bay filled the window as we swooped, and the aeroplane turned in the sky.

Celeste gripped my hand and squeezed. 'Sun, babes,' she squealed. 'God I've missed it. We're going to have a ball.'

'We're both supposed to be working, remember?'

'Work, smirk. We're in the big, beautiful U-S-of-A, babes. Embrace it.'

I smiled. I hoped Celeste was right.

Chapter 14

Libby

'Alex! Tell me you're joking.' I was hopping mad. He'd really done it this time.

Alex shrugged. 'I didn't think you'd mind. It's not as if you'll be spending much time in your room.'

'The place is a flea pit. The beds have orange nylon sheets. And there's no desk. Where exactly do you want me to write? In the bar?'

He smiled. 'I'm sure they have plenty of tables.'

'Don't be so flippant. And don't you dare smile at me like that, you patronizing git. If I don't deliver on time, you don't get paid, remember? Maybe I should get Lulabelle on the case. You'd listen to her, all right.'

He ran his hand through his hair. 'Don't go bothering Lulabelle. I guess you can move if you must.'

'Where are you staying?' Celeste asked. 'If it's good enough for you and Lulabelle, it's good enough for Elizabeth Adams.'

'Whoa there,' Alex said. 'I don't mean the Stanza.'

Celeste folded her arms across her chest. 'And why not?'

'It's bloody expensive, that's why not. There's a perfectly good Holiday Inn—'

'Don't even think about it,' I said. 'We're staying at the Stanza and that's that.'

'Fine. But you're sharing a room, and she's paying for half of it.' He pointed at Celeste.

'A quarter,' Celeste said. 'And that's my final offer.'

He muttered something under his breath. It sounded suspiciously like 'Bloody women'.

The moment we stepped into the huge, dimly lit lobby of the Stanza, we clutched each other in disbelief.

'Score!' Celeste hissed.

To our right, two cute guys were perched on the edge of a sofa, playing an intense-looking game of chess; to our left was a long black desk; behind it stood an identikit row of cute male receptionists in dark suits. The wall behind the desk was covered in shimmering grey silk.

'Look,' Celeste pointed at the floor. As we watched, the tiles changed colour, from dark red to priest's purple. 'I could get used to this.'

Our room was equally dramatic – a huge bed with a white leather headboard buttoned like an old-fashioned sofa; floor-to-ceiling windows with slick remote-control blinds; cream marble en suite with walk-in shower.

Celeste jumped on the bed and sank into the duvet, scissoring her arms and legs as if she was making a snow angel.

'I've died and gone to heaven.' She closed her eyes and gave a swoony sigh. 'I'm going to sleep well tonight.'

I looked at my watch. 'It is night. Three in the morning, London time. No wonder I feel like the living dead.' But Celeste was already snoring gently.

There was a knock on the bedroom door. My heart skipped. Leo?

I swung open the door.

'Oh, it's you, Alex.'

'Don't look so disappointed. Can I come in?'

'No, Celeste's asleep. And I'm about to join her.'

He brushed past me. 'I'll only stay a second.' He whistled. 'Nice room. Almost as big as mine.'

He stared down at Celeste, who had flipped over, her stomach now pressed against the mattress, head turned towards the wall.

'She looks quite sweet when she's asleep. A lot less intimidating.'

'Celeste isn't intimidating.'

He gave me a look, then sat down on one of the clear Perspex chairs and wriggled around for a moment before moving to the sofa.

'She's loyal,' he continued. 'I'll give her that much. Rang and gave me a right earful when I started up on my own and didn't take you with me. Shrieked so much she nearly deafened me.'

I smiled. 'Good for her. You haven't said anything to her, have you?'

'About what?'

'Don't be so obtuse, Alex. You know quite well what I'm talking about. About you dumping me and all the business after that.'

'No. Why would I? That's between me and you.' He looked at me, his eyebrows lifted. 'And I didn't dump you – it's not as simple as that. I've always been on your side, Libby. Have a bit of confidence in me.'

Now he was starting to annoy me. 'What do you want, Alex? I'm tired.'

'I'll come straight to the point. Lulabelle wants you to update her website, freshen up the content. Nothing major, just details of her *Plastic Fantastic* procedures, her recovery, a bit about the noble history of plastic surgery . . .'

I stared at him. 'You're joking? How many pages?'

'Ten, maybe twelve.'

'Stop right there. You know how much pressure I'm under. And you're asking me to take on more work? Are you insane?'

He shrugged. 'Enid Blyton used to write ten thousand words a day.'

'Jeez, Alex – about enchanted trees and ginger beer. And she didn't have to deal with Lulabelle.'

'There's a couple of grand in it. And most of the pages will have big photographs.'

'The answer's still no.'

'I'll do it,' said a voice. Celeste sat up.

'You're awake.' Alex coloured and stared down at his hands.

'I've already written one article,' she continued. 'I can bang out some web content, no problem.'

Alex blew out his breath. 'OK. I'll draw up a contract just to keep everything professional. You'll have it first thing in the morning.'

'Is that it?' Celeste stared at him. 'You're giving me the job?'

'I don't have much choice. This Lulabelle project is turning into a circus. My other clients are starting to complain. Toni's sent some rather sharp emails about missing her launch. The sooner I get back to London the better.'

'I thought Antonia was a sweet girl?' Celeste said, clearly enjoying his discomfort.

'I thought she was,' he said. 'Success has gone to her head. She's completely stressed out at the moment, convinced her new book's going to be slated by the press. She may be right. Her publishers are already calling her the new Martina Cole, but personally I think that's a bit premature. She needs time to develop. And sometimes reviewers can turn on writers who've been paid big advances.'

'For a seven-figure advance, I'd put up with a lot of bad press,' Celeste said. 'Anyway, let's forget about work, who's coming to the bar? It's famous for its cocktails.'

'Count me out,' I said. 'Sorry, Cel, I'm wiped.'

'I suppose that leaves you, Alex.' She looked at him as if he was something the cat dragged in.

He nodded once and they left together, wordlessly.

I tried to sleep, but tossed and turned for ages. I pulled out my book, but it was no use, I was too tired to concentrate. Eventually I drifted off, my mind conjuring up vivid dreams involving blood-splattered surgeons and crazed, Joker-smiling musicians with wings.

'Celeste?' I opened my eyes and rolled over.

'Hi, babes – wondered when you'd stir.' She was sitting on the sofa, flicking through a magazine. 'We need to get cracking. Doctor Sisk awaits. Day one of *Plastic Fantastic*, remember? Now I'm officially working on her website, I get to watch all the procedures and operations. I've said I need you along as my artistic advisor. We're meeting everyone in the lobby in ten minutes, so chop-chop.'

'Cel! I have my own work to do. *Stay Beautiful* won't write itself.'

'Can't you hook your plot and characters into some sort of computer programme?'

I scowled at her. 'I'm deeply insulted.'

'You know I'm joking. You have to come, Libs. Plus you'll get to check out the cameraman. Dion. I met him at breakfast. Bom-chicka-wah-wah.'

I groaned. 'Stop being so chirpy.'

'Come on, Libs, it'll be fun.'

'Watching someone inject Lulabelle's pits? You're one twisted sister, Celeste O'Connor.'

Chapter 15

Lulabelle

Lulabelle looked around the surgeon's consulting room. Bertram, her director, was sitting beside her. Did he have to wear those rectangular architect's glasses? So pretentious.

She swung round. Giselle Cuttey, the pet Channel 7 presenter – all 1950s chignon, red lips and va-va-voom dress – was standing behind them with the cameraman, and she'd spotted Elizabeth and Celeste loitering against the wall.

She glared at Elizabeth – silly woman was supposed to be back at the hotel writing, but Lulabelle didn't like to make a scene. Because sitting behind a huge green leather-topped mahogany desk, holding court, was Mr Tony E. Sisk, one of the most celebrated aesthetic surgeons in the world.

So far Lulabelle wasn't impressed. The man was no beauty. Mid-fifties. Hooded dark brown eyes, long angular face, thin lips, pasty, wrinkled skin. He'd practically invented Botox – why didn't he use it?

'Are you sure I can't tempt you into something a little more dramatic, Lulabelle?' he was saying, oblivious to her questioning stare. 'I've just perfected the most beautiful anatomic breast implant – looks like a giant teardrop. Looks awesome.'

'Lulabelle is having her breasts done in Paris,' Bertram said firmly. 'Christophe de La Tour.'

Tony nodded. 'Sure, I understand. The man is a breast genius.'

'As you pioneered the use of Botox and fillers, we'd like to concentrate on that area of your expertise,' Bertram continued.

'No problem. I'd be happy to work on such a beautiful young woman. Most of my clients are considerably older and less . . .' He stopped.

'Fresh?' Celeste suggested from the back of the room.

'You got it,' he said with a wide smile. 'And who are you, honey?'

'Celeste O'Connor. Journalist. I'm also writing Lulabelle's website content, tracking these procedures for her fans.'

'Really? I do hope you'll be complimentary about me.' He puffed out his chest. 'Say, perhaps you'd like to fire a few questions at me while my nurse prepares Ms Ryan in a few minutes?'

'That would be great, thanks.'

Lulabelle scowled at Celeste, but the bloody woman had the cheek to smile back at her. Who the hell did she think she was? Lulabelle was the star here, not Celeste, not Giselle bloody Cuttey. She still couldn't believe Alex had given Celeste the website job. But apparently Elizabeth was too busy with the book. If she was so fecking busy, what was she doing here?

Lulabelle bristled. These women hadn't a clue. They wouldn't survive a day in Lulabelle's shoes. They had no idea how exhausting it was staying thin and beautiful – the styling and grooming, the constant demands for signed photographs, the ladies' lunches, the charity balls, not to mention the constant stream of interviews, especially now the book was nearing publication. The questions the reporters dreamed up made her want to scream. *What's in your handbag? What's your favourite ice cream? If you could be any animal in the world, what animal would you be? What's your favourite holiday destination?* Were people really interested in such inane trivia? She felt prickly all over just thinking about this afternoon's phone interview with *Lush* magazine.

God, she wished she'd been able to sleep last night – she was in no humour for any of this.

'And I'm the presenter,' she heard Giselle pipe up from the back of the room. 'Giselle Cuttey.' Giselle strutted forward and held out her hand. 'So honoured to meet you, Mr Sisk,' she gushed. 'You're much younger than I thought you'd be. And may I say, much more attractive.'

Lulabelle's jaw dropped. Liar! What a nerve.

Tony Sisk visibly preened. He smiled around the room. 'Isn't she a sweetheart?'

This was getting out of hand.

'I'm the main presenter of *Plastic Fantastic*,' Lulabelle said firmly. 'And let's get cracking. Giselle, you won't be needed today. These are not invasive procedures – I'll be well able to talk while Tony is working on me. Why don't you pop back to the hotel and deal with the paperwork? I'm sure there's mountains of it.'

'But that's not fair,' Giselle said. 'I'm part of the production team. Tell her, Bertram,' she whined.

'We do need to get the Alcatraz filming permit sorted out, Giselle,' he said. 'You can do a piece to camera tomorrow, I promise.'

'But Bertram—'

'We've made our decision, Giselle,' Lulabelle said smugly.

'Fine! At least my tits are real.' With that Giselle stormed out of the room.

'Get your own show,' Lulabelle shouted after her. 'Bloody parasite.'

'Sorry about that, Tony,' Bertram said, walking forward and putting a hand on Lulabelle's shoulder. 'It's our first day of filming. Emotions are high.'

Tony smiled. 'No need to apologize. Now, maybe Lulabelle would like a Valium before her procedures.'

Lulabelle scowled at him. 'I don't need a Valium.' She paused for a split second. 'But I will take an Anxicalm if there's one going.'

Tony smiled at her. 'Of course, sweetie. We aim to please.'

Chapter 16

Libby

Mr Sisk looked at Celeste. 'You had some questions. About my art?' He rested his fingers on her wrist.

Cel and I were alone with Mr Sisk in his consulting room. Lulabelle was being prepped and Bertram and Dion, the cameraman, were setting up their equipment in the operating theatre. It was unnerving. He had a spooky smile. And the thick pan-stick he'd applied for the camera made him look even stranger.

'You collect art?' Celeste said, taking her wrist away. She pulled her notebook out of her bag and set her Dictaphone on the table.

'Sure. But I was talking about my work. To be a great aesthetic surgeon, you must also be a great artist. As well as sculpting faces, I also sculpt clay.'

He pointed at a terracotta figure on a plinth. She – and judging by her Lulabelle-sized breasts, it was certainly a she – was sitting in a rather unladylike position, legs akimbo, lady-bits displayed to the world.

'I call this my psycho-erotic sculpture,' he continued. 'Like an iceberg, the surface of the sculpture is only part of the work; the rest is hidden deep inside.' He clasped his hand to his chest.

I bit my lip, trying not to laugh.

'It's, um, really something,' Celeste managed.

'I'm a very creative being,' he continued. 'People say, "Tony, you're in aesthetic surgery for the money," and I admit, yeah, the money is a nice perk, but it's not my *raison d'être*. I love making my clients feel wonderful about themselves. I give them the ultimate gift – confidence. I'm like a psychiatrist. I cure people's imperfections, and, by doing that, cure their minds. Is that machine working?' He pointed at the Dictaphone.

Celeste checked it. 'Oops, sorry.' She turned it on. 'Can you repeat the part about surgeons being like psychiatrists? Fascinating.'

He did, embellishing even more, while I stared at the paintings on his walls. I'm no art expert, but even I recognized some of the names. I squinted at the signature on one picture, a scribbled drawing of a sausage dog.

'You like that?' Tony asked me. 'One of my many Picasso charcoals. I have two of his paintings at home.'

Celeste whistled. 'I think I'm in the wrong job.'

He laughed. 'Of course, as well as running my practice, I also write.'

'Novels?' I asked brightly. 'Don't tell me, you're the Dan Brown of medical thrillers?'

He gave me a rather condescending smile. 'I'm an academic. Thrillers would be kinda beneath me, don't you think? No, I write textbooks. Of aesthetic surgery. Bestsellers in their field.' He moved a pen around his desk. 'Now, do you have any other questions, hon?' he asked Celeste. 'I'm sure Bertram is ready by now, and Lulabelle doesn't seem like a lady who likes to be kept waiting.'

Celeste looked in her notebook. 'Who is the most beautiful woman in the world?'

'Ah, good question. Our idea of beauty has changed over the years. Nowadays Marilyn Monroe would be considered on the chubby side. Beauty is very subjective. For me it also comes from within. For example, I think my wife Cindy's very beautiful, both inside and out. But perhaps not everyone would agree.'

He took a silver-framed picture off his desk and passed it to me. A blonde woman with cheerleader looks smiled back. From the lack of lines and crows-feet she seemed about thirty-five, but it was hard to tell.

'Oh she's definitely beautiful,' I said. I passed the photograph to Celeste.

'Has she had any work done?' Celeste asked, studying her features.

I gulped.

'Cindy is a natural beauty,' he said firmly, taking the frame out of Celeste's hands and putting it back on the desk.

'And what about yourself?' she asked, her eyes flicking over his face. 'Anything done?'

'Nope,' he snapped. 'Now, where's Lulabelle? Time is money.'

'Nearly finished, Mr Sisk,' Celeste said. 'Do you have any famous clients? Pop stars or actors?'

'Honey, I'm a physician. I've taken the Hippocratic oath. I couldn't possibly divulge such sensitive information. Let's just say some of my clients are regular red carpet material.'

'One final question.' Celeste looked down at her notebook. She pointed at one of her questions and angled it at me, eyebrows arched.

Have you ever performed sexual reassignment surgery – i.e. a sex change?

I shook my head vigorously and pointed at the one beneath it.

'Are attractive people happier than unattractive people?' she asked him.

He considered this. 'It's all about perception. In order to be happy, a person must be content with their looks. If they consider themselves unattractive, that's certainly a problem. But in my experience, some of the most beautiful people in San Francisco are also the most miserable.' He shook himself. 'That last bit's off the record.'

'Of course,' Celeste said, switching off her Dictaphone. 'Thank you, Mr Sisk. It's been most enlightening.'

*

'That's disgusting. I think I'm going to faint,' Dion said. He did look rather pale, like Robert Patterson in *Twilight*, complete with tawny quiff.

'Shush,' Bertram warned him. 'It's just a needle.'

Dion made a face. 'A bloody big needle.'

I looked closer. He was right. Mr Sisk was moving the needle about under Lulabelle's skin, pressing firmly down on the syringe with one hand and manipulating the injected filler with the other.

Bertram was currently holding the sound boom and, if his protracted sighs were anything to go by, I think he felt it rather beneath him.

'Reality TV credit-crunch style,' he'd told us earlier when Celeste asked him if it was usual for everyone in the crew to double-job.

'I didn't expect it to be like this,' Celeste whispered to me. 'It's not exactly a glam procedure, is it?'

Dion winced as Mr Sisk squirted some more filler into place. 'Poor Lulabelle. That has to hurt.'

'Concentrate, Dion,' Bertram snapped. 'And not another word. The boom will pick you up and I want to get this done in one take. Lulabelle's cheeks are a national treasure.'

'Thank you, Bertram,' Lulabelle said, her voice sounding a little woozy. She winced and pressed her head against the white leather headrest of the reclining chair. Her hair was pulled back off her forehead with a thick towelling band; her face was fully made-up.

Mr Sisk hadn't looked impressed when he'd first seen it, but he'd made no comment, instructing his nurse to clean the area around the large marker dots (the injection sites) with sterile wipes, making the room stink of raw alcohol.

'Are you nearly finished with the filler, Mr Sisk?' Lulabelle asked. Not surprisingly, after all the prodding and poking, her voice sounded a little pinched.

'Yep. But you wanna do something about those marionette lines while you're here?'

Lulabelle's fingers jumped to either sound of her mouth and she pressed her skin with her fingertips.

'At the moment they're very faint,' Mr Sisk added. 'But in time . . .'

'Deal with them,' Lulabelle said firmly.

Mr Sisk filled Lulabelle's marionette lines – not that I could spot so much as a crease, and, believe me, I looked – and then injected Botox under her arms, leaving her armpits looking red-raw and pitted, like the skin of a freshly plucked chicken. Afterwards, Lulabelle was escorted off to get dressed (she'd refused the offer of rest, saying she'd rest in the hotel), leaving Bertram and Dion to pack away their equipment.

'Face down, boobs and blubber to go,' Bertram said and then yawned. 'God, that was exhausting. I'm going back to the hotel to get some kip. See you lot in the bar later, yeah?'

I went down the corridor to use the loo. When I opened the door, Lulabelle was standing in front of the fiercely lit mirror, her face pressed against the glass.

'How are you feeling?' I asked.

'Like a pincushion,' she admitted. 'I don't care what they say, women are much better at giving injections. Give me Simone any day. Can you see any marionette lines?' She pointed at the edges of her mouth.

I peered and then shook my head.

She sighed. 'I suppose it's important to blast them before they get hold of my mouth and make me look grumpy.'

I nodded. Maybe she was right. She rarely smiled as it was.

'When did you start with the Botox and fillers?' I asked her. 'Have you been doing it long?'

She looked at me for a moment. She obviously decided I was genuinely interested because she shrugged and said, 'A few years.

Modelling's a tough business. You have to do everything you can to stay on top. Especially if you start with my disadvantages.'

'Disadvantages?'

'Wrinkles. Sagging tits. Bingo wings.' She held up one arm and prodded the flesh underneath. 'My arms have no tone.'

I smiled. 'You don't have bingo wings. But if you're worried about tone, I'm sure a few sessions in the gym or a few press-ups would help.'

'I can't go to the gym.'

'Why not?'

'Exercise loosens up the tiny attachments that fix the muscles to the skin. It makes your skin sag. It's a scientific fact.'

'Who told you that?'

'I read it somewhere. And have you seen the state of your average gym bunny? Gaunt faces are not pretty.'

'But surely you do some exercise? How do you stay so thin?'

She looked at me as if I was crazy. 'I don't eat much. Salads mostly. Diet Coke. And popcorn. And Leo makes me do boring yoga stretches every morning.'

'That's it? The secret of your tiny waist? Not eating? How depressing. Don't you miss food? Ice cream with lashings of chocolate sauce? A big old steak? Pizza washed down with some nice red wine?'

Her face flickered but she said nothing.

'What happens when you're out for dinner?' I continued, intrigued.

'Salads happen. With no dressing. Look, this conversation stays strictly between us. I do not want my nutritional deficiencies splashed all over the *Irish Express*, understand? One word to Celeste and you're fired.'

'Celeste's not like that—'

She put her hand up to stop me. 'Yeah, right! I've learned not to trust anyone in the media business, especially not journalists.'

'You have to trust people sometimes, Lulabelle. Not everyone's out to get you. In fact, some of us are actually on your side.'

From the way her lips were curling, she was deeply amused.

'Oh, Elizabeth, I'm not that naive. You're here because I'm paying you. Far too much, in fact. And there's something about Celeste I don't trust. Her eyes – they're too narrow-set, and her lips are a little thin—'

Now she'd crossed the line.

'Listen, you trumped-up twiglet, you're not paying me, your publishers are. And stop being such a bitch about Celeste – she's doing you a favour. There's no way you'd have found someone else to do your website at such short notice. Oh, and Lulabelle, just so you know, this evening I intend to stuff myself with pizza and cocktails. Every night I'm here, in fact. *Stuff* myself!'

Lulabelle looked horrified. 'You can't speak to me like that. I won't have it.'

'I just did. Deal with it.'

She gasped, and then flounced out of the door.

'I'm sorry, Alex. How many times do I have to say it? I don't know what came over me. Lulabelle was making personal remarks about Celeste and I just lost it.'

Lulabelle had rung him in a state and, after talking to Leo, Alex had called a crisis meeting in the Starbucks beside the hotel. I'd just told him my version of what had happened.

He ran his hands through his hair. 'She's not happy. I hope you haven't banjaxed this for all of us, Libby.' He shook his head.

'Hello?' Celeste said, glaring at him. 'You're supposed to be Libby's agent too. How about a bit of support, Mr Big Shot.'

His BlackBerry jumped in his hands. He looked at the screen. 'Leo again.'

He answered it. 'Yes. She's right here.'

'He wants to talk to you,' he hissed. 'Be humble.' He thrust his BlackBerry towards me.

'This isn't *Charlotte's Web*, Alex. And I'm not Wilbur the pig.'

'I have no idea what you're talking about.'

'*Charlotte's Web*? Humble pig? The children's book?'

His face looked blank.

'It was made into a movie,' I added. Still nothing

'Ah, of course, how silly of me,' I said. 'You're the literary agent who doesn't actually read.'

'Just answer the bloody thing.' Alex pressed his BlackBerry to my ear.

'OK, OK, no need to get aggressive. Hello?' I could feel my stomach tighten, preparing for Leo to bawl me out of it.

'Libby. Are you OK?' Leo sounded surprisingly calm.

'Um, yes, thanks.' I tried to sound breezy. 'And you?'

'Look, Lulabelle's really sorry about what happened in the loo.'

'I am not!' I heard Lulabelle's shriek in the background. 'She was out of order. Tell her I demand an apology.'

'Lulabelle's not used to people being so direct,' he continued, ignoring Lulabelle's interruption. There was another noise in the background, but it was muffled and I couldn't make out what Lulabelle was saying. There was a bang and then silence.

'I hope that was a door and not a gun,' I said.

'Libby!' Alex snapped, making me miss what Leo said next.

'. . . grateful for everything you and Celeste are doing for her,' I managed to pick up. 'And she wants to work on *Stay Beautiful* this evening. After having a talk.'

A talk? Dear Lord, he made it sound like being sent to the headmaster's office.

'Will you be there?' I gulped.

'Yes.' He lowered his voice. 'Celeste can come with you if it helps. We'll see you in Lulabelle's suite at eight. OK?'

I nodded silently, feeling sick with nerves already, and it wasn't even three yet.

'Libby? Are you still there?'

'Sorry, yes. See you at eight.'

'What did he say?' Alex asked as soon as I handed back his BlackBerry.

'Everything's fine. Lulabelle wants to work on the novel this evening.'

'She hasn't fired you?'

'Don't look so surprised. Leo said she doesn't want to lose me; she's very happy with my work and thinks I'm a gifted writer.'

Alex frowned. 'Are you sure? You don't have to apologize?'

'No. In fact, *she* apologized to *me*.'

He shook his head. 'I really don't understand women.'

'No kidding,' Celeste murmured.

'Don't you start,' he said.

'Surrounded by strong, super-intelligent women, Alex.' Celeste grinned. 'How does it feel, baby boy?' She ran her hand up his leg.

He swatted it away. 'Celeste!'

I rubbed his head with both my hands, ruining his carefully teased hairstyle.

He jumped away from me. 'Libby! What's got into the pair of you?'

'You be careful, Alex Sharpe, or you'll see what we're really made of.' Celeste gave a fruity laugh and tried to grab his black leather man-bag from his lap.

He swatted her off and hugged it tightly to his chest.

'You two make Lulabelle look sane.'

Chapter 17

Lulabelle

Leo put his hands up to protect himself. 'Jesus, Lulabelle, stop slapping me!'

'I'll hit you if I want to, you disloyal snake. I can't believe you made me sound so feeble. That woman will have no respect for me now. You should have made her grovel.'

'Why? So she'd hate you? Do you want this book finished or not, Lu?'

Lulabelle scowled and then moaned, touching her cheek. 'I need some more painkillers. What's the strongest thing we've got?'

'Difene? And Mr Sisk said you can take another Anxicalm if you need to.'

'No. If I have to deal with Elizabeth later, I want all my wits about me. I already feel a bit peculiar.'

'You're pumped full of chemicals, Lu. And when was the last time you ate?'

'Don't you start. Elizabeth kept going on about pizza and how she was going to stuff herself every night.'

A smile crept across Leo's mouth.

'What?' Lulabelle demanded.

He just shook his head. 'What am I going to do with you? Look, I'm meeting Bertram and Dion for an early dinner. Why don't you join us? When was the last time you had a bit of fun?'

Lulabelle opened her mouth to say something, but Leo interrupted.

'Shagging male models doesn't count. It always ends in tears.'

'Shut up, Leo! This trip isn't about having fun. It's about building brand Lulabelle, remember? And I've just been injected to shit, in case you've forgotten. Even moving my arms stings.'

'In that case, you shouldn't be working tonight. Call it off, Lu. Libby won't mind.'

That sounded so tempting – all she wanted to do was lie on her bed, remote control in her hand. But she was damned if she was going to let Elizabeth go off gallivanting while she felt so rotten. Not after her disrespectful behaviour earlier. Who did she think she was, speaking to her like that?

'Absolutely not. We're behind as it is.'

'Maybe tomorrow night, then. You've got to loosen up a bit. Cut loose. Libby and Celeste are nice women – I think you'd enjoy hanging out with them. We're off to Paris in a few days and I still can't believe you've never been. You must be excited.'

'Thrilled,' Lulabelle said flatly.

'Jesus, Lu, snap out of it. The old Lu would have been so psyched about the trip. She'd have dragged me round the Louvre, up and down the Eiffel Tower, had me climbing the cloisters at Notre Dame, all in the first morning. What's happened to you?'

'I've grown up.'

There was a short rap on the door.

'Must be Elizabeth. I need a few minutes, Leo. Stall her. And please have a word with her about her manners.'

'There's nothing wrong with her manners. Get over yourself. Go and plaster on your slap if it makes you happy. But I've had just about enough of doing your dirty work. I've a good mind to leave you.'

'You wouldn't do that.'

He raised his eyebrows and gave her an icy look. 'Try me.'

'Don't look at me like that.' She gave a loud sob, then began to cry, then winced and tried to stop. 'Ow, ow! Crying makes my face hurt. Don't leave me, Leo. Please?' She threw her arms around his waist. 'You're all I've got. I'm sorry if I've been a bit difficult lately. It's all the stress. I don't mean to be—'

'Quit the drama, Lu – I'm not going anywhere. And you have to stop acting like such a diva.'

There was another knock at the door, this time a little louder. He peeled her arms off his body and walked towards it. Lulabelle ran into her bedroom and shut the door behind her. She blinked back the tears. She felt wretched.

She walked into the en suite and a shiny, blotched face with swollen cheeks stared back at her from the mirror. Even with the painkillers her armpits were still throbbing uncomfortably.

She turned her head from side to side. She was pleased with the extra filler in her cheeks – once the swelling died down it would make her look like a cat. She made her face frown. Was it her imagination or was Simone's Botox already wearing off? And there was something about her eyes . . .

Lulabelle squinted. She couldn't have any more Botox for a while or her eyebrows would arch into the middle of her forehead. But she certainly needed something. Her eyes didn't look quite right. They weren't perfectly symmetrical. Maybe an eyelid lift would help, she thought. And there was something funny about the tip of her nose . . .

'Lulabelle, are you nearly ready? Libby's waiting in the study.'

'I'll be right out.' Lulabelle grabbed her make-up and her foundation brush and went into auto-pilot, dabbing the heavy beige liquid all over her deeply flawed face.

Chapter 18

Libby

'Are you sure you're up to working this evening?' I asked Lulabelle, who had just wafted into the room in a mist of perfume and hairspray and settled herself behind the desk.

She gave her head a little shake, flicking her hair behind her shoulders. 'Let's get straight into it,' she said, paying no attention to my question. She opened her notebook. 'Section two. Chloe meets Fly for the first time.'

She noticed Celeste sitting on the small sofa at the back of the room. 'To what do we owe the pleasure, Celeste? Planning to take shorthand?'

Celeste laughed. 'Not likely. You should see my Pitman's. It's shocking.'

'Why are you here, then?' Lulabelle sounded tetchy.

'To stop you eating the head off Libby. She was only trying to talk to you as a normal human being earlier, Lulabelle. She didn't mean to offend you.'

'I don't want to discuss it.' Lulabelle pointed at the door. 'Kindly leave. You can see yourself out. Leo's busy.'

Celeste folded her arms across her chest. 'Actually, it was Leo who suggested I come here in the first place.'

'I find that hard to believe.'

'Ask him, then.'

'I certainly will. *Leo!*' she bellowed.

He walked in to the room. 'You called, m'lady.' He gave a little bow.

'Stop acting the fool,' Lulabelle said. 'Did you ask Celeste to accompany Elizabeth this afternoon? Yes or no?'

'Yes.'

'Why exactly?'

'I had to see her,' he said simply, giving me a sly wink. 'She sets my heart alight.'

Lulabelle's face was a picture – shock mingled with repulsion.

Celeste started to laugh and I joined in. Within seconds the two of us were falling around the place, holding our stomachs. Leo grinned, clearly delighted we found him so entertaining.

'What's so funny?' Lulabelle demanded. 'Is it true? Why are you all laughing?'

'He's joking,' Celeste said, wiping tears away from the edges of her eyes. 'He's actually in love with Alex. You should have seen them in the bar last night. All over each other. It was disgusting.'

I hooted with laughter again.

'Stop being so childish.' Lulabelle banged both hands on the table. 'All of you. This is ridiculous. I asked you a perfectly logical question, Leo. I don't know what's got into you.'

'Sorry,' he said, trying to reign in his belly laughs. 'You're right. You want the truth, Lu? I warn you, it's not half as amusing.'

She glared at him. 'Go on.'

'Libby was terrified you'd scream at her. Celeste's here to back her up.'

'Scream at her?' Lulabelle looked surprised. 'Why would I scream at her?'

'For daring to talk to you like a real person,' Celeste said. 'Now, are you going to work on your book or not? At this rate you'll never get it finished in time.'

'As soon as you leave we'll get right to it,' Lulabelle snapped.

'Writing fiction is very different to writing a column, Celeste. Elizabeth and I need to get in touch with our creative muses.'

Celeste grinned. 'I think you'll find Libby's is called Mr Bank Manager.'

'You're both right,' I said, feeling a little sorry for Lulabelle, who, like Dad, clearly had quaint ideas about the writing process. 'We do need to get cracking on Chloe's story. But we also need to concentrate, Celeste. And you would be a bit of a distraction. So if you don't mind . . .' I gestured at the door.

Celeste sniffed, clearly put out. 'I was only trying to help. Me and Leo will find something to do, I'm sure. Maybe we could consummate our burning passion for each other.'

Leo laughed. 'Why don't we do that over a coffee?'

'Deal.'

'So where were we?' Lulabelle asked as soon as they'd left the room.

'Are we OK, Lulabelle?' I asked nervously, eager to clear the air.

She nodded without raising her head and went straight into business mode. 'Fly's about to introduce Chloe to the dark underbelly of the music world.'

I grinned. 'I like writing dark underbellies.'

The edges of Lulabelle's mouth flickered. She was thawing.

'Why does Chloe have to save Fly from his overdose?' Lulabelle demanded an hour later. 'Why can't he die?' We were plotting the Chloe and Fly section, and I knew I had to tread carefully.

'I'd like to make her triumph in this situation, save him,' I explained. 'I think it would really develop her character and make the readers root for her even more. Chloe's had enough trauma in her life without a man dying on her, don't you think? Especially one she loves.'

'She doesn't love him, she hates him.'

'She may think she hates him, but from the way she's acting, she's actually still in love with him. She hates the way he treats her, hates his lifestyle, hates his so-called friends; but she can't shake him from her heart quite yet. She still hasn't learned how to spot a man who is truly good. That will come later.'

'Do they exist?'

'To our readers, yes. In real life, I don't know, to be honest. Mine started out OK, but turned into a toad.'

'What did he do?'

'Old story. Affair with a mutual friend.'

'Ouch, that's gotta hurt.'

'Yep, but I'm doing OK. Getting back to work is helping. And being away from home. And my mother. She's furious at me for calling off the wedding. She's determined to have a grandchild before she's sixty, and I'm an only child.' I grimaced.

'I'd like a baby some day,' Lulabelle said. 'I'm very maternal.'

I was so gobsmacked, all I could say was, 'Oh.' It was just as well Celeste wasn't in the room. She wouldn't have been able to contain herself.

'What?' She looked at me, wide-eyed. 'You don't think I'm maternal?'

'You're just so busy. Babies take a lot of time.'

'I'd have a nanny, obviously.'

'Obviously.' Oops, did I say that out loud? 'And maybe the father would help out?' I suggested, fascinated.

'I wouldn't bother with all that,' she said, waving her hand in the air. 'I've already done some research into sperm donation, and Amsterdam looks like the best place for high-quality sperm.'

I didn't know quite what to say to that.

'As soon as I've made my first million,' she continued, 'I'm prepared to take some time out to do the baby thing.'

'Million?' I spluttered. 'Really?'

'Lulabelle will be a global brand in less than three years if all goes to plan. The novel is only a small part of the jigsaw.'

'If we're ever going to finish that jigsaw, we'd better start fitting all those little pieces together, namely your plot. Now, can we agree that Chloe saves Fly?'

'All right. As long as you give him permanent liver damage and a nasty facial tic.'

'A facial tic? From an overdose?'

'It's my final offer.'

'OK, maybe I can give him a mini stroke.' I thought of something. 'And once he recovers, Chloe takes him back and he leaves her again. It's the final nail in the coffin for her self-esteem, and she hits absolute rock bottom. She locks herself away and won't speak to anyone for weeks, even Liam. She spends the whole day and night lying on the sofa, sleeping and watching rubbish on the telly. That's when she spots the ads for the model competition.'

I paused, tapping my pen against my top teeth. 'But hang on, if she's at her lowest ebb, what on earth would make her pick herself up and answer that ad?' I looked at Lulabelle expectantly.

'Her father's voice in her head,' she murmured. She sat up. 'And the fact that Fly then took up with her best friend. A double betrayal.'

Then I remembered what had happened to Lulabelle. Her ex, the smarmy singer Marcus Valentine, and his new girlfriend had had a baby pretty swiftly after he'd dumped Lulabelle. The press had asked Lulabelle about the pregnancy and she'd said, 'No comment. But they'd better not ask me to be godmother.' It was a bloody good storyline.

'And then the friend announces she's pregnant with Fly's baby?' I suggested cautiously.

'Yes, yes! Which makes Chloe even more determined to win. To show them all. Every damn one of them. The ugly girl wins a modelling competition. Ha!'

'But Chloe's not ugly.'

'Fly says she is. Her father says she is.'

'And what about Liam?'

'He's biased.'

'And does Chloe think she's ugly?'

'Chloe *knows* she's ugly. That's why it's all such a triumph.'

I stared at her, confused. 'Why would Chloe win a modelling competition if she's ugly?'

'Because people are stupid. They don't see what she sees. Yes, she's pretty, yes, she has a passable body, but it's all an illusion.'

I caught Lulabelle's eye. 'I don't think she's ugly,' I said gently. 'The Chloe in my head is beautiful.'

She looked away and snapped her notebook shut. 'We're done for today. Kindly leave.'

'But Lulabelle—'

She stood up and stalked out of the room, leaving me staring after her. I gathered up my things, wondering if I'd gone too far, yet again.

Leo walked into the room. 'Everything all right?'

I nodded. 'I think so. But I think I touched a nerve. Does Lulabelle really think she's ugly?'

He blew out his breath. 'It's complicated. We both know Chloe's story isn't exactly fiction, and I only agreed to this whole novel thing in the first place because I thought it might be good for Lu to put her past behind her, focus on how far she's come.' He ran his hand over his face. 'Look, if things come up that you can't deal with, or that seem to upset her, come and get me immediately, OK?'

'What kind of things?'

He shrugged. 'She's had a tough life. There are things in her past that are best left alone. One day I'll tell you everything, I promise. But not when she's in the room next door. She has quite a past. Tread softly.'

'I will.' Now I really was intrigued. Celeste had dug around a little, unearthed some of Lulabelle's old Miss Ireland qualifier shots – all back-combed hair and frosted pink lips – plus a string of dodgy ex-boyfriends, but from what Leo had just said, there was a lot more juicy stuff that Celeste hadn't discovered. I couldn't wait to find out.

Chapter 19

Libby

'*Look!*' I hissed, pointing at the arched doorway. Celeste followed my gaze. Within seconds the animated chatter in the Redwood Bar had died to a graveyard hush, the tinkle of jazz piano the only sound.

Framed in the arch was Lulabelle, utterly still apart from her eyes, which scanned the darkened room. I remembered the curve-hugging Grecian dress from the day I'd first met her. She'd teamed it with vertiginous gold heels, her hair had been teased into a chocolate fountain, and her eyelids dripped with burnished gold. She looked extraordinary.

'Hubba-hubba,' Bertram said in a low, husky voice. 'I'd so give her one.'

'Hey,' Leo said. 'That's my—' He broke off. 'That's Lulabelle you're talking about.'

Bertram just grinned at him. 'Mate, if you're not interested, then I most certainly am.'

'Be my guest,' Leo said dryly. 'But treat her with respect or you'll have me to deal with.'

'That's so sweet,' Celeste whispered in my ear. 'Wish I had someone to stick up for me like that.'

'You do,' I said with a sloppy grin. We were several cocktails down at this stage. 'Me.'

She gave me a kiss on the cheek. 'Thanks, babe.'

'Girl-on-girl action!' Bertram whooped. 'Loving it.'

'Down, boy,' Celeste said.

We'd been in the bar for several hours now, and everyone was in flying form. Bertram's cool façade had melted away with every drink and he was flirting outrageously with the waitress and ordering rounds of cocktails on the Channel 7 expense account. The bar was very swish – double-height ceilings, huge modern chandeliers, wood-panelled walls, black and chrome leather sofas. Celeste was squeezed in between me and Dion on one of the large sofas; the chemistry between them was Bunsen-burner hot. Every now and then she'd touch his arm and tell him how funny he was. And a few minutes ago he'd leant in towards her and whispered something in her ear which had made her blush and giggle. And it took a lot to get Celeste hot and bothered.

Bertram waved over at Lulabelle. 'Over here!'

Lulabelle smiled at him and strutted towards our table as if she was on a catwalk, each leg arching in the air.

'What is she doing?' Celeste muttered. 'She looks like a show pony.'

'Turning heads,' I said. It was true – everyone was staring at her legs, me included. I couldn't tear my eyes away. She looked powerful, almost regal, as if she owned the room.

Lulabelle stood behind Leo and rested one of her hands on his shoulder.

'To what do we owe this great honour?' Giselle asked her cattily.

'I thought I'd join my team.' Lulabelle tossed her mane and stared Giselle down. 'Got a problem with that?'

'We're delighted you decided to join us,' Bertram said. 'Aren't we, Giselle?'

Giselle said nothing and concentrated on her cocktail.

Bertram jumped up. 'What can I get you to drink, Lulabelle?'

'Vodka on the rocks. Organic vodka. I only put the very best into my body.'

She slid in beside Dion and crossed her legs; her dress slid up her brown thighs.

'Don't let me stop your conversation. What were you talking about?'

'Girl-on-girl action,' Dion admitted.

She swatted his leg playfully. 'Naughty boy. Is that one of your fantasies? Sorry, I seem to have forgotten your name.'

'Dion.'

'Dion. How could I forget?' She smiled at him, then licked her top lip with the tip of her tongue.

Celeste stiffened.

'So how was dinner?' Lulabelle continued, oblivious. 'Did you *stuff* yourself, Elizabeth? You rather look like you did.'

'I did, thank you, Lulabelle,' I said. 'And did you enjoy your carrot shavings?'

She laughed but her eyes were flinty. 'There were two olives in my vodka martini – that was plenty for me. But you are sweet for asking.'

Celeste opened her mouth to say something, but Leo got there first. 'Celeste and Libby were telling me they've been friends for over twenty years, Lulabelle. Isn't that something?'

Lulabelle laughed. 'Gosh, you are old, girls. I was a baby twenty years ago.'

'Hardly,' Leo said. She threw him a look.

'What age are you exactly, Lulabelle?' Celeste asked, leaning forward. 'The papers put you anywhere between twenty-three and thirty.'

Lulabelle smiled icily. 'Don't you know it's rude to ask a lady her age?'

'That's why I'm asking *you*.'

Lulabelle gasped. 'Leo, did you hear what she just said to me?'

'Hello, Lulabelle, I'm right here beside you,' Celeste said, waving in her face. 'If you need your minder to protect you from the odd joke, I suggest you leave right now. The night is young and I'm only just getting going.'

'Girls!' Leo said. 'Let's not—'

'I'm twenty-five,' Lulabelle snapped. 'OK?'

Celeste snorted.

Bertram appeared with a loaded tray in his hands. 'Organic vodka.' He balanced the tray on the edge of the table and handed her a frosted glass. 'More cocktails, anyone?' He nodded at the tray. 'Don't ask me what they are. I told the barman to do his worst.'

'I can see the night has already disintegrated.' Alex appeared and tried to squeeze in beside me.

'Alex, there isn't enough room, pull over a stool.'

He dragged one over. When he sat down, our thighs touched. I wiggled towards Celeste. Alex stank of whisky.

'Where have you been?' I asked him.

'Working in my room. Toni's pissed with me. And she's demanding more tube and DART ads. I had to talk to the marketing department. Plus she hates the cover. She should have said something before the book came out – it's a bit bloody late now.' He rubbed his eyes with a knuckle. 'I should never have signed her up.' He lowered his voice. 'I really need to get back to London to sort all this out. Toni's not the only one complaining. But Lulabelle would have a fit.'

'You go and I'm going too,' I said. 'Don't you dare abandon me again, Alex Sharpe. Crime writers aren't the only ones who can devise horrible ways to maim people.'

He laughed. 'You can be one feisty lady when you want to be, Libby. And you're looking hot tonight. Like the dress.'

'Thanks.' I'd made an effort this evening, worn a dress. Celeste had insisted. I tapped my glass against his. 'You're not looking too bad yourself.'

'And how's my book coming along?'

'*Your* book?'

He grinned. 'You know what I mean.'

'It's not like you to be interested in the actual writing process, Alex. What's going on?'

'I'm always interested, Libby. How many words have you belted out in total?'

I laughed. 'That's more like the old Alex. Almost thirty thousand. And counting.'

He wrinkled his nose.

'What?' I asked. 'That's good.'

'I hope you're making it nice and juicy. I'll be expecting lots of sex scenes.'

'Alex!'

'What? You're good at sex. Always have been.'

I giggled and looked around. 'I hope no one's listening.'

'In your books, I mean. Although the way you look tonight, I'd love to find out if you're as hot between real sheets.'

I laughed, this time uneasily. 'Stop teasing me.'

'I'm not. I think I'm in love with you, Libby.'

I hooted with laughter. 'Don't be so ridiculous.'

And then I noticed his face. He seemed genuinely hurt.

'Alex, you can't be serious. It's very sweet of you, but I'm really not your type.'

He grabbed my hand. His palm was slightly sticky. 'That's just it. Maybe I've been chasing the wrong kind of skirt all this time. You're pretty and funny. And very loyal. I could do worse.'

I pulled my hand away. 'Alex, you're making me sound like a rescue dog. And I'm sorry, but it wouldn't work.'

'Why not? We could at least give it a try.' He put his hand on my leg. I swatted it away.

'I don't think so. But it's a nice offer, all the same. And how much have you had to drink, exactly?'

'Just a couple of whiskies in my room. Needed it after Toni.' He stopped. 'Are you laughing at me?'

'No, of course not.' I was desperately trying not to.

'And please don't say anything to Celeste. Not that she'd be interested. She's all over that Channel 7 guy. It's disgusting. He's too young for her.'

I looked over. Sure enough, Celeste's arm was draped over Dion's shoulder and she was laughing enthusiastically at something he'd just said. Lulabelle was looking on, her mouth set rigid.

As I watched, Lulabelle stood up, wobbled on her heels and then fell straight into Dion's lap, her skirt flipping up and revealing a tiny white lace thong. Dion jumped to his feet and helped her up. Lulabelle turned on the most remarkable Bambi gaze I'd ever seen, eyes wide and fluttering. Dion practically melted into a puddle.

'I think I've done something to my ankle,' she mewed. 'Dion, would you be an absolute angel and bring me to my room?'

'I'd be honoured, Lulabelle.'

She hobbled out on his arm. At the doorway she turned back, looked directly at Celeste, and smiled smugly, nestling her head on Dion's shoulder.

'Bitch,' Celeste muttered, knocking back her cocktail. She shuffled along the sofa towards me and Alex.

'Round one to Lulabelle,' Alex said, licking his finger and drawing it down in the air. 'She snaffled him from right under your nose. That's gotta hurt.'

'Shut up, Alex,' Celeste snapped. 'At least I'm not fawning over one of my clients.'

'Keep me out of this,' I said, standing up. I suddenly felt utterly exhausted. To my surprise, Leo stood up too.

'Libby, may I escort you to your room?' he said, ultra politely.

'Um, yeah, sure,' I stammered, instantly wishing I hadn't had that last cocktail. Just keep your mouth shut, I told myself.

We walked into the lobby. I also wished I hadn't worn Celeste's silver peep-toes. They were a whole size too big and I was having trouble keeping them on my feet. I lurched and grabbed Leo's arm.

'Seems to be a night for falling off your heels,' Leo said.

'Although something tells me Lulabelle's fall was no accident. Celeste looks livid. What's Dion got that I don't have?' He gave a fake pout.

I laughed and then stumbled again. It was no use, the heels would have to go. I bent down and pulled them off.

'Sorry,' I said. 'Don't want to break my neck.'

'Why don't we sit down for a second?' He pointed at a sofa tucked into an alcove. It looked inviting. 'I'm in no rush to get back to the suite. Who knows what Lulabelle and Dion are up to? I'd love some company.'

'Why did you leave the bar, then?'

'Honestly?'

I nodded.

'I wanted to talk to you. Alone.'

Talk to me? I felt a surge of disappointment. I was obviously in trouble with Lulabelle – again.

He smiled. 'Don't look so worried. I'm not a great fan of noisy bars. Despite my origins. I'm from Dublin. Didn't Alex tell you?'

'No.'

He shrugged. 'I first met him at a Joseph O'Connor reading in the Soho Club. We got talking and discovered we'd both left Ireland in our late teens. I guess that's why we hit it off. And he's a bloody good literary agent. Got a great deal for Lulabelle.'

I smiled. 'He has his moments.'

Leo stopped a passing waiter. 'What do you fancy, Libby? Anything your little heart desires.'

'A hot chocolate. I know it's summer, but I just fancy something sweet.'

He smiled. 'Can you do that?' he asked the waiter.

'Of course. Marshmallows and whipped cream?'

Leo nodded. 'Sounds perfect. Two please.'

I collapsed on to the sofa and Leo sat down beside me, pulling my feet on to his lap.

'What are you doing?' I asked, taken aback.

He started to massage my feet, holding one of my ankles with one hand and rubbing his firm thumb over the ball of one foot and then the other. It was heavenly.

'Lulabelle has you well trained,' I said. 'How long have you known her?'

'We were childhood friends. I moved to Boston when I was seventeen and we lost touch for a while.'

'Why Boston?'

'One of my friend's older brothers was already working over there. He put me up for a while. I didn't exactly see eye to eye with the old man. He wanted me to go to medical college. I didn't know what I wanted to do, but I sure as hell didn't want to be a surgeon like him. I guess I ran away. After a few years I followed a girl to London.'

'She still around?'

'No. She wanted to move back to the States, I wanted to stay there.' He shrugged. 'Wasn't meant to be.'

'I have to ask, how do you find working with Lulabelle?'

He gave a laugh.

'What?' I asked, paranoid I'd said something wrong yet again. I'd tried to phrase it carefully.

'You said "with". Most people say "for", as if I'm Lulabelle's little lapdog. It gets to me sometimes.'

'I can imagine. But I know how much work goes on behind the scenes. Believe me, if Alex is anything to go by, being a manager or an agent is a tough job.'

'Yep. Anyway, you asked me about working with Lulabelle.' He whistled. 'Let's just say it's interesting.'

I rolled my eyes. 'I bet.'

'She grows on you, I promise.'

'So you keep saying. But from her behaviour this evening, I'm not sure I believe you. The way she targeted Dion like that. She must have known Celeste liked him.'

He looked bemused. 'Why do you think she did it?'

'That's pathetic.'

He smiled. 'I know. But can we stop talking about Lulabelle? I spend all day talking about the bloody woman. I need a break.'

I laughed and he smiled at me, a lovely warm, genuine smile.

'Here comes our order,' he said.

I was in chocolate heaven for several minutes, giving my full attention to the smooth, creamy drink and stealing several of Leo's marshmallows with my spoon. He didn't seem to mind.

'Alex seemed keen this evening,' he said, eyes down as he stirred the last of his drink. 'Are you interested?'

'No! Euew.' I wrinkled my nose. 'So not my type. He's such a big kid.'

'In that case, would you like to have dinner with me? In Paris?'

'*Oui.*' I smiled. '*Je suis* delighted to.' The very idea sent tingles up and down my spine.

'Your mastery of the French language is impressive.'

'*Merci, monsieur.*'

'More, more.'

'Stop!' I laughed, then swatted him. He grabbed my wrist and used it to pull me towards him. The next thing I knew we were kissing, his firm lips pressed against mine, the sweet tang of chocolate on his lips. After a few seconds I pushed him away.

'What's wrong, Libby?'

'I'm sorry, it's just that I haven't been with anyone apart from my fiancé for years. It's all a bit overwhelming.'

He smiled. 'I'll go slowly, I promise.' He moved towards me again. 'We have a lot to talk about,' he murmured, 'but right now I'd like to kiss you.'

My heart melted. Cute and sensitive – a deadly combination.

'Come here,' he murmured, his voice as rich and creamy as the hot chocolate. This time I didn't push him away.

Chapter 20

Lulabelle

Once outside the hotel bar, Lulabelle shook off Dion's arm and sashayed towards the lifts. She'd thundered down Irish catwalks in heels twice this height.

Dion stared after her. Her ankle seemed to have miraculously healed.

She called a lift and one of the six doors pinged open instantly, revealing the lush purple-velvet interior. She walked in and held the door open with her leg – her long, tanned leg. He couldn't take his eyes off it.

'Coming in?' She looked directly at him, a smile lingering on her lips, her eyes lazy and hooded.

He nodded and jumped in beside her, standing so close he could smell her musky perfume. He was too nervous to do anything, although he wanted to. He quivered at the mere thought of sweeping her up in his arms, covering her lips with kisses, moving down her neck, towards her magnificent breasts . . .

'Well?' Lulabelle was staring at him, hands on hips, expecting an answer. She'd obviously just asked him a question.

Luckily, at that moment the lift doors swished open and he followed her wordlessly into the penthouse lobby.

'What's your name again, honey?' she asked as she punched a code into the key pad.

'Dion. Dion Sunny.' He followed her into the penthouse. As

soon as Lulabelle kicked the door shut, she dimmed the lights in the hallway and stepped away from him, towards the mirrored wall.

'Do you want me?' she asked him, rubbing one leg against the other, sticking her bum out and thrusting her chest forward.

Dion tried not to laugh. Lulabelle's pose reminded him of a porn movie he'd watched when he was a teenager. But he didn't want to insult her.

'Of course,' he said politely and truthfully. She had no idea.

She ran her tongue over her lips.

'How many vodkas have you had, exactly?' He smiled and cocked an eyebrow.

'Enough. I've been a bad, bad girl. Wanna spank me?' She lifted the back of her dress, exposing her curvaceous bum cheeks, dissected by a wisp of lace.

Dion's hormones went into overdrive. Blood surged towards his crotch. His breath quickened.

Lulabelle looped a finger under one strap of her dress and the silky material slid down her upper arm and rested in the crook of her elbow. 'Oops, my dress seems to be falling off.' Then she did the same with the other strap, holding the front of the dress against her breasts with one arm.

'Tell me how much you want me,' she purred.

Dion looked into her eyes – he could see her burning need to be adored. He'd been with models before – he knew exactly what to say, the right buttons to press, but with Lulabelle it was different.

'You are the most beautiful woman in the world,' he said genuinely. 'I've wanted you since I first set eyes on you.

He walked towards her slowly, his eyes never leaving hers.

Lulabelle shivered and then gasped as he knelt down on the carpet in front of her, took her hand in his and kissed it. Then he began to suck her fingers, and for the first time in years she felt a flicker of real desire in her lower stomach. After a few more seconds her knees started to feel weak and she staggered and put both arms on the mirrored wall; her dress fell to the floor in a silken puddle.

'You are a goddess,' he said, drinking in her incredible figure – and those breasts! Golden and firm, nipples reaching for the sky.

'Lulabelle,' he groaned. 'What are you doing to me?' He wanted to bury his face in her cleavage and wallow, like a hippo in mud, but he stopped himself.

Lulabelle smiled. This was the reaction she lived for – true admiration and awe.

'That's right, worship Lulabelle,' she whispered under her breath, pulling him to his feet.

She turned around to face the mirror. Then she backed into him, grabbed his hands and placed them firmly on her breasts.

'Touch me,' she said. She caught his eye in the mirror. 'Watch,' she whispered. She snaked one hand down her stomach and wiggled it inside her lacy knickers. Then she closed her eyes and threw her head back against Dion's chest.

'Touch Lulabelle,' she whispered again, and then gave a low moan.

Dion did as he was told.

'Lulabelle?' She was curled up on a sofa in the enormous sitting room, a white cashmere rug thrown over her almost naked body. Dion had lifted her there after her rather dramatic climax several minutes ago.

He was now sitting on the floor, watching her. He hadn't expected the tears, or the slap. His cheek still stung.

'Are you asleep?' he asked gently.

'Get out,' she said without opening her eyes. 'You got what you came for, didn't you? Now you can leave.'

'Is that what you think of me?'

She made a little snorting noise.

'Lulabelle, I'm not like that.'

She snapped open her eyes. 'Don't kid yourself. All men are like that. You're a photographer, for God's sake. You fuck models every day.'

'Cameraman, not photographer. And I resent that.'

She sat up a little. 'You've never slept with a model?'

He gave a smile. 'OK, you win. But you're different.'

'Yeah, right.'

'I mean it. There's something about you. Yes, you're beautiful, but you're also smart.'

Lulabelle's face visibly softened for a second. Then she narrowed her eyes. 'Stop with the sweet-talk. Club Lulabelle is closed for the night, get it?'

Dion continued, unperturbed.

'You have so many different projects on the go – your novel, your website, the reality show, the modelling gigs. Most models find it hard enough to get up in the morning and throw a few poses for a magazine shoot.'

'Elizabeth's writing the book. I'm just helping her.'

'But you're the driving force behind it. You remind me of my mum.'

'Jesus, Dion!'

His face was a picture. 'No! God no, not like that. I just mean the way you juggle all the different projects. She's a designer. Fashion mainly, some household stuff.'

'Is she famous? Name?'

'Stitch Sunny.'

Lulabelle gasped. Stitch Sunny was one of the most innovative designers in the business. 'Wow! I have one of her bags. I can't believe she's your mum.'

His stomach rumbled and he grinned at her. 'Sorry, I'm starving. I was editing earlier, missed dinner. The footage looks great, by the way. Do you mind if I order a burger and a beer? I'll pay for it, of course. Are you hungry? Would you like something?'

She stared at him and shook her head. Then a chorus line of French fries danced in front of her eyes. Skinny, crispy, just the way she liked them.

'I might manage some chips,' she faltered. 'Just one or two.'

'Excellent.' Dion rubbed his hands together and grabbed the room service menu from the coffee table. 'Another drink?'

She smiled. 'Why not? A vodka tonic. Organic vodka and slimline tonic.'

He laughed.

'What?'

'That's my mum's drink.'

As he picked up the phone and ordered, Lulabelle frowned. This man seemed to have a serious mother-fixation. It wasn't healthy. However . . .

'I do love her bags,' she purred. 'If you ever want to give me a little present . . .'

'Done. Now, let's stop talking about Mum and concentrate on Lulabelle.'

'Absolutely.' Lulabelle rolled on to her back. 'Where were we?'

'Whoa there. Until the food comes, we're going to talk. Where are you from, Lulabelle?'

Lulabelle folded her arms across her chest huffily. 'I'm not much of a talker. Can't we think of something else to do?' She inched the rug slowly down her chest.

'Put those lethal weapons away. Tell me about this book you're writing with Libby. What's it called, for starters?'

'You really want to know?' She was surprised. George hadn't given a toss about her novel. His eyes had glazed over whenever she'd mentioned it.

Dion nodded. 'Yes. Can I read it?'

'It's not finished yet.'

'When it's finished?'

'Certainly not!'

'What? The whole world's going to be reading it in a few

months, Lulabelle. The details are already up on Amazon. In fact, I've pre-ordered it.'

'You have? Why?'

He blushed a little. 'I keep telling you, Lulabelle – I'm mad about you. I've been following your career for years.'

'But you're English. I haven't had any profile in England until this year.'

'Gran's Irish. I used to spend my school holidays in Dublin 'cause Mum was always travelling. You're pretty famous in Ireland.' He grinned.

'What?'

He shook his head. 'Nothing. I'm not telling you.'

'Please? You're freaking me out here. What do you know?' Her eyes flashed. 'Is it something about my family? Was someone in Ireland gossiping about me? It's all lies, you know. Don't listen—'

'Take it easy.' He reached over and stroked her forehead gently. 'I kept a scrapbook, that's all.'

'A scrapbook?'

He stared down at the carpet. 'The year you entered Miss Ireland, I was so obsessed with you I kept a Lulabelle scrapbook.'

She started to giggle. 'Really?'

He blushed. 'I shouldn't have said anything. It's so stupid—'

'No, it's sweet. I don't mind, honestly. But I have to ask you something – what age are you, Dion?'

'Twenty-four. And you?'

'Don't you know it's rude to ask a lady her age? But if you must know, I'm twenty-four too.'

A smile played on his lips.

'OK, OK, I'm twenty-five.'

Dion gave a laugh. 'I have the scrapbook, remember? You were seventeen when you entered Miss Ireland, and that was—'

Her eyes darkened. 'Jesus, Dion, if you ever, ever tell anyone, I'll kill you, understand?'

'I've dated models, remember? I know the score. Once you hit thirty—'

'I AM NOT HITTING THIRTY!' she roared. 'Not now, not ever. Got it?'

He just laughed. 'You'll be the only person on earth who doesn't age, in that case. You look incredible, Lulabelle – what are you afraid of?'

Just then the doorbell rang, and Dion got to his feet. 'I'll go. You're not exactly dressed for it.'

Lulabelle rolled over and stared at Dion. He was breathing heavily, his breath catching a little in the back of his throat. If he told the press her real age, her whole career would be down the toilet. She had to keep him on side until she figured out what to do. At least he seemed to like her. And he was easy on the eye, so it wasn't exactly a trial. If only he wasn't so damn nice. Lulabelle didn't do nice, and she didn't do nobodies – not in public, anyway. In private – well, that was a different matter.

Chapter 21

Libby

'You idiot,' Celeste said the following morning when I told her about my clinch with Leo. 'Why didn't you shag him senseless? I could have found somewhere else to sleep.'

I wrinkled my nose. 'Celeste! It wasn't like that. It was a nice, romantic smooch in the lobby, that's all. We're taking things slowly. Starting with dinner in Paris.'

Celeste gave an excited squeal and beamed at me. 'I'm so happy for you.'

'Calm down, it's just a date.' But I couldn't help grinning back. In fact, I'd been smiling all morning. Leo's handsome face kept swimming in front of my eyes.

My mobile rang on the coffee table and I whipped it up.

'Every man's fantasy. Can I help you?'

'What are you on about, Elizabeth?'

I sank down into a chair feeling instantly deflated. 'Hi, Mum.'

'Why have you been ignoring my phone calls?'

'Two phone calls, Mum. And I was going to get back to you today.'

'I know you're busy, but this is urgent. Which dry-cleaners do you use?'

'What's so urgent about that?'

'Don't use that tone of voice with me, young lady. Not when

I'm in the middle of a crisis. One that you should be dealing with, I hasten to add. He's not my fiancé.'

'Mum, what are you talking about? Is there something wrong with Jeremy?'

'Yes! He has to go to the Sporting Hero Awards tonight and he can't find his tuxedo. He says it might be at the dry-cleaners. That you're always forgetting to collect things. But he can't remember which one you use.'

For a second I was speechless. 'Tell him to go and buy another bloody tuxedo, or rent one.'

'Elizabeth! I most certainly will not. The poor man's in enough distress as it is. Isn't jilting him enough?'

'Jilting him?' I gave a laugh. 'Is that what he's telling everyone? You know exactly what happened, Mum. Or should I say *who* happened.' I paused. 'They stayed at our house last weekend. Bet he didn't tell you that. Shagging in our bed.'

'Don't use that language with me, young lady. And maybe if you'd paid more attention to his ... his needs, the indiscretion would never have happened.'

'Plural.'

'What?'

'Indiscretions. There was more than one affair.'

'Stop inventing things, Elizabeth. Jeremy told me everything. And you know as well as I do that he only took up with Ruth-Ann because he felt neglected. Your house is always a mess and you spend far too much time cooped up in that study of yours. I have no idea what went on in the bedroom, but, quite frankly, if it's anything like your cookery skills—'

'Stop right there! There was nothing wrong with our sex life. And this isn't the fifties, Mum. Jeremy's got arms – he could tidy the house too, he just chooses not to. You're enjoying all this, aren't you? You never wanted me to marry him in the first place. And now you get to say "I told you so".'

'You're wrong. And I admit I may have had my reservations at first, but I do want you to marry Jeremy. And as you seem to have conveniently forgotten, it's all arranged. Right down to the embroidered napkins and the guests' treats. I've put months of work into it already. And you, young lady, are going to stop all this nonsense, come home and honour your commitment.'

'Honour my commitment? You've got to be joking. I wouldn't marry Jeremy Small if he was the last man on earth. I hate him. He's ruined my life.' My voice caught. 'He's a pig.'

'If you hate him, then why does all this upset you so much, Elizabeth? Think about it. And for God's sake tell me which dry-cleaners you use.'

'Jeeves,' I said, too upset to argue with her any more. 'In Sandycove. And now just leave me alone.' I clicked off my phone and threw it on to the coffee table with a clatter.

Celeste clapped. 'Bravo! That's telling her.'

I put my hands on my face, feeling overwhelmed. Tears started to prick my eyes and within seconds they were running down my cheeks.

'Why does she always have to make me feel so small?' I wailed.

Celeste gave me a hug. 'Never, ever listen to a word that woman says, understand me? You're an amazing person, Libs. That's why I love you. And at least your dad's a pet.'

I nodded and attempted a smile.

'That's better. Now go and take a shower,' Celeste said. 'It'll make you feel better. We're due in the lobby in fifteen minutes and I'm not going anywhere without breakfast. I'll meet you in the restaurant.' She smiled gently at me. 'Go on, get. You look a state. We can't let Leo see you like that.'

As I stood in the shower, the powerful jets of water pummelling my shoulders, I thought about Leo. What was I doing? I couldn't go out with Leo; if I was still crying over Jeremy, I clearly wasn't ready. I'd have to cancel our dinner. I'd only end up getting my heart mashed again. What was I thinking? Failed writers didn't get happy endings. I should have learnt that by now.

'You'd better read this before Lulabelle does.' Celeste slid an A4 sheet along the breakfast table.

'What is it?'

'My column. And before you ask, yes, I've just filed it. Serves her right. And I don't understand why they can't have breakfast in her suite. Her greasy cleavage is putting me off my food.'

At a nearby table Lulabelle was feeding Dion strawberries. Her décolletage was slick and glittery, and he couldn't keep his eyes off it. Lulabelle caught my eye and, distracted, dropped a strawberry down her tight white vest. She stood up and started to wiggle, pulling her vest away from her tummy. Out popped the strawberry and a passing waiter picked it up off the floor and strode on wordlessly, as if it happened all the time.

Celeste stood up abruptly. 'Little hussy. I've had enough. Coming, babes?'

Chapter 22

Lulabelle

'How could she?' Lulabelle wailed, waving the sheet in Dion's face. 'Am I really a bad role model?'

Dion wished Lulabelle had never found Celeste's article. He'd read it three times now and he knew from experience – having had to deal with his mother after one of her collections had been slated in *The Sunday Times* Style magazine – that telling Lulabelle she was overreacting wasn't going to help matters. It was still scorching, and after almost a whole day filming, Lulabelle had every right to be a bit tetchy.

'Of course not. Come here.' He put his arm around her shoulder and pulled her towards him. Her silk-clad bottom glided along the leather of the limo's seat as if it had been sprayed with WD-40 and her ribs collided with his hip bone.

'Ow!' she yelled and began to rub her side.

Dion swallowed down a sigh. Now she really was overreacting. Although it seemed to have stopped her crocodile tears, which was something.

He pulled a packet of tissues from his rucksack and handed one over. 'We're nearly at the hotel. Don't let Celeste see you're upset. Be the bigger person, Lu. Rise above it.'

She glared at him. 'No one calls me Lu, understand?'

Dion didn't like her tone.

'Let's get this straight,' he said in a low voice. He wanted to make himself clear, but he had no intention of embarrassing her in front of the driver. 'I like you, Lulabelle. A lot. Last night really meant something to me, even if we didn't, you know . . .'

'I'm sorry, I was just so sleepy after all those chips and cocktails.'

She'd eaten a total of seven chips (she'd counted them out), but he let it slide.

'Yes, I think you're the most beautiful woman in the world,' he continued, 'but I want to—' he broke off. 'I mean, I think I—' He stopped abruptly.

'What?' Lulabelle was intrigued. Of course she loved the flattery – who wouldn't? But Dion seemed genuinely smitten. Which served her purpose – for the moment. She only hoped he didn't get too attached. She'd have to make sure he didn't.

'I like you too, Dion, and while we're filming let's spend some more time together. In private. The press don't have to know. It'll be our little secret.'

She ran her hand up his leg and rested it at the top of his thigh. She felt his muscles contract under her touch.

'Nothing complicated, understand? Let's keep it very . . .' She moved her hand over a little.

'Very . . .' She moved it up again until it rested lightly on his crotch. 'Simple.'

She took her hand away.

'But—' he began, his breath coming hot and heavy.

She put a finger on his lips. 'No buts.' She winked at him. 'Unless you get very lucky.'

'OK. But I warn you, Lulabelle, I plan to make you fall in love with me.'

She gave a short laugh. She knew it was cruel, but she just couldn't help it. 'You do that, baby boy.' She patted him on the knee.

'I'll give you baby boy.'

He pushed her hand away, threw a leg over her lap, pressed his body against hers and kissed her passionately.

In the background Lulabelle could hear the limo driver's partition buzz into place.

'Dion!' she gasped as he plunged both hands inside her dress.

Chapter 23

Libby

Celeste and I were approaching the hotel after a spot of retail therapy in Union Square when a black limousine pulled up beside us and Lulabelle jumped out, followed by a sheepish-looking Dion. Her cheeks were flushed and she was clutching a sheet of paper in her hand. I tried to hide my Macy's bag behind my legs.

She ignored me and thrust the paper in Celeste's face. 'What the hell is this?'

Celeste snatched it out of Lulabelle's grasp and studied it.

'That would be my latest *Irish Express* column,' she said calmly. 'I take it from your face that you're not a fan of my writing.'

'It's all about me, bitch,' Lulabelle barked, her eyes sparking angrily.

'And why do you think that?' Celeste asked. She scanned the sheet. 'I don't see your name mentioned.'

'Don't be so smart. Of course you didn't name me. Then I could have sued your sorry ass. But as I'm the only Irish model currently filming a documentary on plastic surgery, it wouldn't take a genius to work it out, now, would it?'

'What's going on here, ladies?' Bertram had just arrived in a yellow cab.

'Celeste slandered me in one of her stupid columns,' Lulabelle said.

'What does it say, exactly?' Bertram asked with interest.

'That I'm glorifying the whole aesthetic surgery industry and pressurizing teenagers into having plastic surgery,' Lulabelle said. 'Which is rubbish. I've never said teenagers should have plastic surgery.'

'But you've never said they shouldn't,' Celeste pointed out. 'Let's face it, you're the poster girl for plastic surgery, Lulabelle. Young girls look at you and want what you have – money, fame, Galaxy models . . .'

Lulabelle glared at her. 'I never tell people what they should or shouldn't do. I leave that to sanctimonious columnists who think they have a God-given right to judge others when they don't have a clue what they're talking about. You're just pissed Dion chose me. Admit it.'

'Ouch,' I murmured.

Dion mouthed a sorry at Celeste. Then he put his hand on Lulabelle's arm. 'I don't think—'

She shook it off and narrowed her eyes. 'Go on, Celeste, be woman enough to admit it.'

Celeste gave a laugh. 'Chose? Lulabelle, you shoved your Grand Canyon cleavage in the poor man's face. Some choice.'

Lulabelle gasped and opened her mouth to say something, but Bertram cut her off, putting his hands in the air and saying, 'Ladies, please. I think you should discuss this in private.'

'No!' Lulabelle said. 'I want her sacked, Bertram. Immediately. If she thinks she's still working on my website after all this, she's sorely mistaken.'

'Calm down, Lulabelle,' Dion said. 'I think—'

'Shut up, Dion,' she snapped. 'I'm not interested in what you think.'

'Fine,' he muttered. 'I'll be in the lobby if you need me.'

'Bertram?' Lulabelle demanded, ignoring Dion's departure.

'I'm afraid I have no authority to sack Celeste,' Bertram said. 'That would be Leo's call. And I believe he's at the bank this afternoon. He said something to me about clearing funds.'

Lulabelle keyed a number into her mobile.

'No, I am most certainly not all right, Leo. That hag of a journalist slandered me in her stupid *Irish Express* column.'

'It's not slander if it's true,' Celeste said loudly.

Bertram shushed her.

'What?' Lulabelle asked Leo. 'Why? . . . If you must . . . But her skanky ear's not going near my phone – I don't want to catch anything. I'll put you on loudspeaker.'

She clicked a button and we all heard Leo say, 'If you must, Lu. Celeste, are you there?'

'Yes,' Celeste said. 'And Lulabelle's being completely unreasonable. OK, my column was about plastic surgery, but I didn't mention Lulabelle's name once.'

'What *did* you say then?'

'I'll read you an extract.' Celeste smoothed out the sheet which was still in her hand.

Botox is now seen as so 'normal' that soon you'll be able to buy DIY kits in Boots. Have any of your friends or family succumbed yet? Be warned. It's only a matter of time.

An Irish 'model' is currently making a reality documentary on her plastic surgery exploits, ramming home the message yet again that surgery is normal. As many of her fans are teenage girls, how many of them will follow her down the surgery route, ashamed of their own flaws and imperfections? Women should be supporting other women, not making them feel inadequate about their bodies. Shame on you!

Celeste looked up. 'I presume that's the bit Lulabelle finds objectionable.'

Deathly silence.

Finally Leo said, 'Have you filed the column, Celeste?'

'Yes. It's running today. Look, I didn't slander Lulabelle – it's all true.'

'True but hurtful,' Leo said.

'And what she did last night wasn't hurtful? She knew I liked Dion. I had my bloody arm around the man – she's not stupid. Friends don't do that kind of thing to each other.'

Lulabelle was staring at Celeste. I couldn't read the expression on her face.

Then she grabbed the phone from Celeste and said, 'Thank you, Leo, I'll take it from here.'

She looked at Celeste. 'I have decided to be the bigger person and forgive you.'

For a second the two women's eyes locked furiously.

'But be warned,' Lulabelle added. 'I'll be studying the website content carefully before it goes live, understand? Anything snide or disrespectful and you're history. Get it?'

'I'm not sure if I want to work on it now,' Celeste said.

'Celeste!' I hissed. 'Sunglasses fund.' I'd seen her credit-card bill and it wasn't pretty. Plus she'd just bought Chanel sunglasses and two pairs of Seven jeans on the back of it.

'Fine,' Celeste said. 'I'll do it.'

Then Bertram stepped in. 'I'm glad all that's sorted. You go and rest, Lulabelle. And Celeste, I'd like a word with you, please.'

He pulled her to one side and they had a heated conversation. Bertram was in full swing when Celeste glared at him, turned and stalked into the hotel, without a word to me or Lulabelle, her face like thunder.

Lulabelle looked at me smugly. 'My team are very loyal. Now, back to work, Elizabeth. Don't think I haven't spotted the Macy's bag.'

When I opened the door to our hotel room, I fully expected Celeste to be angrily pacing the floor. Instead she was sitting on the sofa, giggling away to herself.

'What's going on?' I asked.

'Bertram's delighted with my article.'

'I don't understand.'

'That was all for show. Bertram wants to keep Lulabelle sweet. He's no fool – wants to whip up lots of controversy before the show airs. He's chasing ratings, Libs. Doesn't give a hoot about Lulabelle.'

'He's not going to make her look stupid, is he?'

'Honestly, you're far too nice for your own good. He'll just show her in all her glory, warts and all.'

I didn't like the sound of that, but I kept quiet. Now wasn't the time to take Lulabelle's side.

Chapter 24

Libby

The following evening, we were sitting in a booth at a local diner when Celeste said, 'What do you think of Bertram?'

She ran her finger down her chilled beer bottle, making a wavy line in the frosting, then started picking at the curling label. We'd both been working hard all day and had collapsed into the diner for a burger and beer, or, in Celeste's case, several beers.

'Bertram? What do you mean? As a director?'

'No, as a guy. He's pretty cute when he's pretending to be angry.'

'He's wearing a wedding ring,' I pointed out.

'Tell me about it.' She put her head on my shoulder. 'All the best ones are married or going out with someone. But they can't all be happy. Half the married men I've met seem bloody miserable. Some of them will boomerang back on the market eventually. It's just a matter of biding my time.'

I said nothing.

She looked at me. 'Shit, sorry, Libs – that was crass. I didn't mean—'

I could feel my eyes smart with tears, and I blinked them away. 'It's OK. Forget it.' I stood up. 'I'll be back in a minute.'

'Libs, don't be like that. Come on, I'm sorry.'

I locked myself in a toilet cubicle and had a little weep. It had been such a long day – up at six to work on the book with

Lulabelle, an afternoon spent typing up the next three scenes. My lower back was stiff from the crappy hotel chair, I missed my desk at home, missed Dad, even missed Jeremy in an I-know-I-shouldn't-but-I-can't-help-it kind of way. Here I was, in sunny San Francisco, with my best friend, and I felt miserable.

I checked the messages on my mobile.

And there it was.

Libby, your mum says you still have feelings for me? Is it true? Libs, just say the word and I'll dump Ruth-Ann. I need you, Libby. It's you I love, it's always been you. X Jeremy

I started crying again. Why now? Then I sat up a little. How dare he? Was he serious? Or was he just bored of Ruth-Ann? Thoughts raced through my head. I knew I'd be a fool to believe him, but . . .

Why was everything so hard? I sighed. Right, I'd just delete the message, pretend it had never happened. If Celeste saw it she'd probably try to ring him and give him a piece of her mind, and I'd had enough drama for one day.

When the tears had stopped, I rejoined Celeste.

'Everything all right?' she asked.

I nodded wordlessly.

'Have you spoken to Leo yet?'

'Oh, don't start, Celeste.'

'What have I said now?'

'You know damn well I haven't talked to Leo. I've been with you all day. I haven't had a chance.'

'Sorry, grumpy boots – I thought you'd snuck off to ring him.' She looked at me suspiciously. 'You were ages. And your eyes are a bit red.'

'I was in the loo. I'm constipated, OK. It's all the enormous American portions. Now stop going on at me. I've had just about enough. Lulabelle spent all morning having a go at me about wasting valuable writing time in the shops.'

'I hardly had to drag you.'

I put my hand up in the air. 'Don't interrupt, Celeste. You're always interrupting me. Then you say Jeremy clearly wasn't happy and it's no wonder he had an affair.'

'You're talking nonsense, Libby. I never said any such thing. But you have a point. If Jeremy was so fecking delirious, why did he shag Ruth-slapper-Ann, then? You have to take some responsibility for your shambles of a relationship. I've tried warning you what he's like countless times. I even told you what he did at his thirtieth, but you didn't want to know. You had a strop with me for telling you. Not Jeremy, *me!*'

'I don't want to talk about it.' I put my hands over my ears. 'Just shut up.'

She pulled my hands down. 'You never want to talk about it. But you have to face facts, Libs. He pushed me into the spare room and demanded a birthday quickie.'

'He was drunk,' I snapped. 'He didn't know what he was doing.'

'Stop defending him! I only told you because I didn't want you stuck with that little shit for the rest of your life.'

I gave a laugh. 'You told me because you were jealous. For all I know, you made the whole thing up.'

Celeste scrunched up her face. 'Are you mad? Why would I do that?'

'Because you wanted to ruin things for me. Because you've always been jealous of me and Jeremy.'

'If you want me to say I'm jealous, if it makes things easier for you, then I will. But I'm not jealous. I'm disappointed. That you can't see past Jeremy's smile, past his confidence, all that money he splashes around—'

'That's not fair. It's not his fault he's good at what he does.'

'Are you defending him again? Even now?'

'Yes. I mean, no. Oh, I don't know.' I looked down and started to rub at a mark on the table.

Celeste stared at me. 'There's something going on, isn't there? Something you're not telling me? We've been friends since we were kids – you can't hide from me.' She shut her eyes, tight, and then opened them again. 'Tell me you're not taking him back. Oh Christ, Libs, please. Not again.'

More tears pricked the backs of my eyes and I pressed my eyeballs with my knuckles, willing them away.

'Am I supposed to write off the last six years of my life? Is that it?'

'Jeremy has left your self-confidence in tatters. You used to love writing. Now it seems to be like pulling teeth.' She shook her head. 'He's pure evil, Libs, and still you're holding a torch for him. I bet if he asked, you'd go trotting back to Ireland and play the little girlie again. You'd drop all this silly novel business – he always hated you having your own career. But what happens in two year's time? When someone else catches his eye? There won't be a fine man like Leo around to hold your hand. Your career will be completely down the toilet and you'll be alone. And I won't be there to pick up the pieces. I can't stand back and watch him destroy you again. I won't do it. You go back to him, and you're on your own.'

She stood up.

'It's me or Jeremy.'

With that, she walked out.

I felt completely drained; hollow. I knew in my heart that if I took Jeremy back, he'd only humiliate me again. And I didn't want to – *couldn't* – live without Celeste. She was my rock. But without Jeremy, who was I? Who was Libby Holliday?

Chapter 25

Libby

'Another day, another airport.' Celeste sighed. 'Such is the life of a grubbing journalist.' She smiled. 'But it sure beats the office.'

I studiously ignored her, my eyes fixed on my notebook. I was reading the same sentence over and over, finding it impossible to concentrate, but there was no way I was letting Celeste draw me into a conversation.

'Come on,' she said. 'You have to talk to me at some stage. Don't be so stubborn.'

I lifted my head. 'I am talking to you, Celeste. I'm just busy. I'd appreciate some peace and quiet, otherwise I'll have to move.'

'Move, then, grumpy boots,' she snapped. She crossed her arms tightly. 'In fact, don't worry about it, I'll move. Somewhere I'm actually wanted.'

I arched an eyebrow. 'You're flying back to Dublin?'

'Ha-bloody-ha.' She stood up. 'I'll see you on the plane. Hope you get lots of work done.'

She gave a little smirk. She knew I was at a sticky point in *Stay Beautiful*. Usually I'd talk it over with her, discuss the characters' motivation and how to progress the plot, but today I was damned if I was going to involve her in my deliberations. Not after last night. She had such a nerve. It was none of her business whether I wanted to get back with Jeremy or not. I was so angry I could thump her. Instead I stuck out my foot. She tripped over it, then sat on the grey airport floor, glaring up at me.

'Libby, that's so childish.'

'It was an accident.'

She shook her head and pulled herself to her feet. 'I don't know why I bother with you sometimes.' With that she walked away.

I sighed, then looked around. Alex was staring out of the plate-glass window, jabbering into his mobile. I had no idea where Leo was – probably swanking around with Lulabelle in the VIP lounge. I slumped against the uncomfortable departure-lounge seat. Our flight had been delayed and there was nothing to do – except work. I stared down at my notebook again.

I'd broken the novel up into ten sections and I was now on section three. And stuck. I couldn't quite nail the scene where Chloe saved Fly. It was flat, unrealistic.

Think, Libby, think. I chewed the top of my pen.

I started to consider Lulabelle's real story. According to a celeb website, Marcus Valentine had dumped her and taken up with another model, Titania, a 'friend' of Lulabelle's. After Lulabelle had paid off a considerable amount of his gambling debts. Talk about a double betrayal.

I thought about how that must have made Lulabelle feel. I closed my eyes and there he was – Fly: leather trousers, ripped T-shirt, sunglasses hiding his druggy-drunk eyes, dirty black hair. I watched as he threw a handful of pills into his mouth and washed them down with tequila. Then he staggered around his dressing room before collapsing, his legs caught under his body like a broken doll.

Chloe walks into the room, screams and crouches down beside him. He coughs and vomits, his puke tinged with white foam. Chloe rings for an ambulance and never leaves his side.

I opened my eyes and started to scribble, getting everything I'd seen down. Then I added the next scene – Chloe sitting with him in the hospital, alone. Everyone else has deserted him – his family, his so-called friends. His band sends a basket of fruit. He hits it to the ground, scattering grapes all over the floor. Chloe clears them up.

He comes out of hospital a week later, saying it was bad pills, man. The doctors have warned him to stop drinking and taking drugs – his liver and kidneys are shot – but he has no intention of changing. Chloe takes him back to her house, looks after him, tries to make him eat properly.

I paused, my pen poised over the notebook, and then I smiled. There it was – the double betrayal. Chloe saves his life and now he's going to throw it all back in her face.

I started scribbling again.

Chloe comes back from work and finds him in bed with Anita, her friend. Fly says he's leaving, moving in with Anita, and they walk out together, leaving Chloe shell-shocked.

I stopped and blew out a big sigh. Yes! Now we had the low. Now we had the place Chloe had to fight back from and it was real, alive and blistering off the page. I felt energized, raring to go.

'I would like to inform passengers that the Air France zero-eight-three flight to Paris has been delayed for a further forty-five minutes due to a technical problem. We would like to apologize to passengers for any inconvenience this may cause.'

There was a collective groan from the passengers. I was trying to contain a whoop. I could stay with the story. I went on, describing the depths of Chloe's despair, the days spent locked in her apartment, not talking to a soul, lying on her sofa watching television. And then . . . Liam.

Liam banging on her door, threatening to break it down unless she opened it; Liam spooning chicken soup into her, bringing her back to life. Chloe curled up on his knee, watching that very first ad for the modelling competition on the telly. Liam stroking her hair, saying she'd win it no problem, she'd show them all – Fly, the girls at work, everyone. That first flick of ambition switching on in Chloe's head.

I tapped the pen against my teeth. *But it's not quite enough*, I thought. *What else drives her to that competition?* I sat back and closed my eyes again. This time I saw Fly and Chloe. They were in her bed. *Oh, Chloe*, I thought. *Not again. He doesn't love you, can't you see that?*

Chloe's just mentioned the competition, asking for his advice, willing him to encourage her, to say, 'Yeah, Chloe, go for it, babe,' like Liam did, but instead he throws back his head and roars with laughter. Right in her face. She slaps him, he hits her back, hard, catching her lip with a ring, making it bleed.

She gets up wordlessly, pulls on her clothes and walks out. NEVER TO RETURN, I add in heavy block capitals. My eyes are wet with tears. Poor, poor Chloe.

'Flight AF083 to Paris is now boarding. Could all passengers seated . . .'

I stared down at my notebook. It was bulging with freshly written pages. I felt a lightness in my stomach I hadn't felt for an awfully long time. I smiled to myself and blinked back my tears. Excellent. Chloe's story was making me cry. If it could do that to readers too – bingo!

'It's back,' I whispered to myself. 'The old writing magic. Thank you, God.'

'Hello, stranger.'

I looked up. Celeste smiled at me. 'I was watching you work. You seemed to be really going for it. Did you get over the hump?'

I was feeling so mellow my anger just dissolved. 'Yes. But I'm sorry, Cel, I want to stay in the story. Do you mind if I we don't talk?'

Celeste shrugged. 'No problem. You novelists are one weird breed, Libs, you know that? I'll help you type up your pages later, if that would help. I'm probably the only person in the world who can actually read your writing.'

I grinned. 'Thanks, Cel. That would be fab.'

'Pleasure, babe.' She hesitated. 'We OK?'

I nodded and smiled. 'Now, stop distracting me.'

When I woke up on the plane my pen was still in my hand. I stretched out my fingers. They throbbed as I wiggled them around.

'Your hand was twitching in your sleep. I've heard of sleep-walking, but never sleep-writing.'

I turned my head. Celeste's black eyemask was sitting on her forehead. Sooty mascara stains pooled under her eyes, and her hair was matted at the back.

I rolled my shoulders and something clicked alarmingly. 'Ow.' I rubbed the spot with my hand.

'Turn around and I'll give you a massage,' she offered.

I started to protest, but she was firm. 'You've been working for hours, hunched up over that notebook. Once you ran out of pages and realized there was nothing left to scribble on, you were out like a light. I put a blanket over you but your fingers and your pen were practically fused together, I couldn't prise them apart.'

She found my knots and kneaded them with her fingers, then her knuckles.

It was so good I moaned loudly.

'Can I have some of that?' Alex was standing in the aisle. Unlike Celeste, he looked fresh as a daisy.

'What has you so chipper?' Celeste demanded. Her eyes narrowed suspiciously. 'You disappeared a couple of hours ago. You weren't bothering an air hostess, were you?'

He laughed. 'I'm so glad you're keeping a good eye on me. Shows how much you care.'

Celeste rolled her eyes. 'As if.'

'If you must know,' he continued, 'I was in Lulabelle's rather plush first-class seat. Slept like a baby.'

'Where's Lulabelle?' I asked.

'Booked herself on to Dion's flight. They wanted to travel together.'

'How sweet,' Celeste said caustically.

Alex chuckled. 'Don't be such a sore loser, Celeste. It doesn't suit you.'

'Shut it, tranny,' she snapped.

'Temper, temper. What has you so bad-tempered?'

'You! Why didn't you give Libby that seat? She spent most of the flight writing that damn novel while you lorded it up in a comfy seat. You're unbelievable, Alex. Selfish doesn't go near describing it.'

Alex looked surprised. 'You're right, I should have thought of that. Next time, I'll give Libby the best seat, I promise.'

'Stop it, the pair of you,' I said. 'You're like children. How long is this bloody flight anyway? We must be nearly there.'

'Just over eleven hours,' Alex said. 'Another two to go.'

I groaned. 'I can't bear it. I'm stiff all over.'

'Move, Alex.' Celeste got up and wiggled into the aisle. 'You're swapping with Libby. You heard her, she's in bits.'

His face dropped. 'I meant next time.'

'You're not weaselling out of it now.' Celeste offered me her hand. 'Up you get, Libs.'

Chapter 26

Libby

Five hours later I was lying on my four-poster bed in the *très* swish Hôtel Minard, Montmartre, Paris. Even during a recession, Lulabelle was a five-star girl, and after the San Francisco hotel fiasco Alex had obviously decided it wasn't worth trying to palm me and Celeste off with a cheaper hotel. He'd even booked us into separate rooms this time. Ooh, la-la!

'Are you hungry?' Celeste asked. She was perched on the end of my bed, flicking through the hotel's room service menu. 'It's all very old school – pepper steaks, lashings of cream. But they have chips, all right. Sorry, *pommes frites.*'

'I don't know. I feel very peculiar. What time is it?'

Celeste checked her watch. 'San Fran time or Paris time?'

I laughed. 'I finally understand how pop stars confuse the city they're in. By the end of a tour their poor old body clocks must be all over the place.'

She smiled. 'It's midday San Fran time, but Paris is nine hours ahead. So it's nine in the evening. We've lost a good chunk of the day. And I'm starving. Come on, let's order some chips, then hit the bar.'

'The bar? Are you crazy? The only thing I'm hitting is my bed.'

'Come on, Libs, don't be such a party pooper.'

I was having none of it. 'I'm exhausted. And you have to watch

Lulabelle's boob surgery tomorrow, or had you conveniently forgotten?'

'And you're wondering why I need a stiff drink? I have to stare at those freak hillocks for hours and then write about it.'

I woke up at three a.m. Paris time feeling very disorientated. I lay with my eyes closed, listening to the hum and click of the old-fashioned air conditioning and the rattle of pipes from the bathroom. Hôtel Minard was built in the 1920s and was charming in an olde worlde way, but I did miss the silent plumbing of the Stanza. *Hark at you, darling,* I giggled to myself. *This five-star lifestyle is starting to go to your head.*

I stretched my arms above my head, rolled my super-stiff shoulders, then opened my eyes. Orange light bled in through a crack in the curtains, catching the mahogany desk and my notebook and laptop. I rolled over and tried to get back to sleep, but it was no use – my body was telling me it was time to get up, and Chloe's story was still sloshing around in my head. After ten minutes, I gave in, switched on the lights, threw a cardigan on, sat down at the desk and flicked on my laptop.

I stretched my fingers and then poised them over the keys. I'd take Celeste up on her offer to type up the text from my notebook, so right now I could concentrate on moving Chloe's story forwards. I started typing. Seconds later, Chloe had picked herself up (with the aid of lovely Liam, of course) and entered the competition. And that's when the fun started – bitchy contestants, a rather fine competition organizer called – um, let me see: Blake? No, too American. Dex? No, he wasn't a Dex or a Brad, he was a Rick – yes, a Rick. Rick Sneed – that was a good name for a slimeball . . .

*

There was a knock on the door. 'Anyone there?' came a muffled voice. It didn't sound like Celeste, but it could hardly be anyone else.

I looked at my watch. It was eight-thirty a.m. Paris time, which meant I'd been working for over five hours.

'Just a second.'

I saved my text and clicked on my word count. Four thousand, three hundred and fifty-seven words. Excellent: I was really sucking diesel now. And combined with the chapters I'd written on the plane, I'd have loads to send the editor at New Haven, Patty Pope-Hurley, who sounded frighteningly head-girlish from the emails and calls we'd exchanged so far. She'd loved the last chapters, thank goodness, and had set her assistant editor straight to work on the text.

As I walked towards the door, I tightened my ponytail and tucked the stray strands of hair behind my ear. The pink bits were now a strange shade of coral; I'd have to do something about it when I got a chance.

I pulled the door open. Lulabelle stared back at me, fully dressed in white jeans and a white vest top, her breasts straining against the cotton. She was also fully made-up, her lip-liner like a pink tattoo under the slick of gloss, and the front section of her hair was piled on top of her head in an elaborate back-combed quiff. No wonder she was staring at me. I must have looked like a bag lady.

I pulled my cardigan around my chest. 'I've been working. Haven't had time to get dressed yet.'

'Can I come in?'

'Oh yes, sorry.'

I stood back from the door. She wrinkled her nose a little and looked at the unmade bed and mess of clothes on the floor. I'd pulled everything out last night to find my buried pyjamas and I hadn't had the energy to hang it all up. I reefed the curtains open a little too roughly, pulling the first foot of the right-hand drape off its hooks.

'Why don't you use this?' Lulabelle put her hand on the string controls, making me feel like a right ninny.

'I'm sure you're wondering why I'm here,' she said, walking towards the desk and running her fingers over the top of my computer screen. 'How's Chloe's story going?'

'Good. I'm on section five now. Chloe's just entering the competition. I'll need to get some background – what a modelling competition is like, how supportive the other girls are—'

'Supportive?' She gave a wry laugh. 'You're joking. Pack of witches. I spent the whole time watching my back. At least I didn't have to live with them all, like in some of the reality shows. That would have been appalling.'

'I think Chloe's going to live with them,' I said nervously. 'If that's all right. I thought it would make for lots of drama.'

'No kidding.' She smiled. 'That's a great idea. If I have time, I'll tell you what my competitors got up to. Nasty stuff.'

'Great. It'll all help. How about today?'

She studied her nails. 'I'm in surgery, remember?'

'Of course, sorry.'

She looked at me, and then her eyes flicked down to her nails again.

'I'm going for bigger implants, and I don't trust the Channel 7 team.' She sounded nervous. Her eyes met mine again. 'I want to ask you something. I want you to promise me you'll be there during the surgery. That you'll stop them doing or saying any-thing inappropriate when I'm under.'

'Like what?'

She shrugged. 'Something snide about my body. I'll be totally exposed on that operating table; out cold with everyone staring at me.'

I felt for her. I wouldn't fancy it either. 'I'll do my best.'

'Promise?'

'Yes. But what about Leo? Won't he be there?'

She studied her nails again. 'No. Let's just say we've had a bit of a disagreement.'

'Why?'

'You'll have to ask him that yourself.' She stared at me, her eyes flinty. 'And if anything inappropriate is recorded, no matter how small, I will hold you personally responsible, Elizabeth. Have I made myself clear?'

I bristled. 'You don't have to threaten me. I would have looked out for you anyway.'

She seemed surprised. 'Really?'

'We're writing a book together – that's got to count for something.'

She waved her hand in the air. 'That's just work. You are my employee. Please remember that. Nothing more, nothing less.'

With that she strode out of the room and shut the door firmly behind her.

'No wonder everyone hates you, arrogant cow,' I shouted after her. I wondered if she'd actually heard me. For a few seconds I stood still, expecting her to pound on the door, demanding an apology. But – nothing.

I sat on the side of the bed, relieved but strangely hollow. I wouldn't have minded a good fight with Lulabelle – it might have woken me up a bit. I was starting to feel horribly jet-lagged and rather crotchety.

Employee indeed.

Chapter 27

Libby

'This place gives me the creeps,' Celeste whispered. We were standing to one side of a small, brightly lit operating theatre in a rather grand stone building near the Louvre, waiting for Lulabelle. The Channel 7 team were also packed into the room. Dion and Bertram were checking the equipment, and Giselle was checking her make-up in any shiny surface she could find. We were all wearing disposable green surgical scrubs, including caps and dinky covers pulled over our shoes – very *Grey's Anatomy*.

'Shush, you'll get us thrown out,' I said.

She smiled rather smugly. 'I don't think Christo will do any such thing. Did you see the way his eyes lit up when I said I was a journalist? Sure sign of a publicity junkie. And what does he look like?'

We both stared at Christophe de La Tour, or Christo, as he'd asked us to call him, in his black surgical scrubs, with his pale, almost luminous skin and his dark, slicked-back hair. He reminded me of Dracula.

Christo caught Celeste's eye. 'You want to interview Christo while we wait for the victim? I tell you about the world – get this down – *world*-famous Christo technique.'

Celeste clicked on her Dictaphone and he took it from her and held it directly under his mouth.

He began: 'The world-famous Christo Technique uses a zigzag

cut on the edge of the areola, the pigmented area round the nipple, making the scar practically invisible.' He demonstrated by swirling his finger in the air, circling one of Celeste's breasts.

She stepped away from him. 'So you feed the implant into the breast through this cut?'

'*Précisément*. In this case we will remove the old implants and replace them with new ones made of cohesive gel silicone. My nurses call it the *petit pimousse* implant, after a sweet.'

Celeste looked intrigued. 'What kind of sweet?' she asked. Celeste was a details girl.

'A jelly. Like a fruit gum. Soft yet firm.'

I shuddered at the thought of someone cutting into my nipple. Dion was obviously having similar thoughts. He gave a wan smile, his face pale. Poor man. If Lulabelle had threatened me, God knows what she'd said to him.

Celeste said, 'I interviewed one of your colleagues in the world of aesthetic surgery, Mr Tony Sisk. Do you know him?'

'Indeed. How eez dear old Anthony?'

'Excellent. He was telling me about his art collection.'

'Collection? Pah. He dabbles. Now, *I* 'ave a collection to boast about.' He hit his chest with his open palm. 'On my walls: Warhol, Lichtenstein, and the Surrealists. I have passion with the Surrealists. I own two Magrittes; he was Flemish, of course, but French was his native language. The de La Tour collection is world-famous.'

'Who do you consider beautiful?' Celeste asked.

'George Clooney. Brad Pitt. Johnny Depp.'

'Any women?' she asked.

He thought for a moment. 'Naomi Campbell. She has spirit.'

'Have you had any work done yourself?'

'*Certainement*. I use Botox. My boyfriend insists.' He laughed. 'And fillers, of course.' He touched his cheeks gently.

'But no surgery?'

'Maybe in a few years.' He shrugged. 'I 'ave not ruled it out. We will see how the face holds up.'

'What is the strangest thing you've ever been asked to do as a surgeon?' Celeste continued, obviously determined to throw as many questions as possible at the man.

'Easy. One young girl, she ask me to make her look like an alien – pointy ears, narrow cheekbones, elongated eyes. I refer her to a psychiatrist.'

The door opened and a male nurse walked in, pushing Lulabelle in a wheelchair.

'Now we finish the interview.' Christo handed the Dictaphone back to Celeste.

'Ms Ryan is a little woozy from the pre-op meds,' the nurse said.

As Christo helped Lulabelle on to the operating table, she caught my eye. I couldn't tell if she was arching her eyebrows at me, or if that was the Botox. I gave her a nod. She seemed satisfied and turned her gaze to Dion.

An anaesthetist joined us. Just after he'd put Lulabelle under, music rang out – a piano concerto.

'*Non, non,*' Christo said. 'Ms Ryan is Irish. Some U2 today, I think.'

The nurse changed the CD.

Once 'With Or Without You' was playing, he crossed himself, which was a bit disconcerting.

'Better,' he said. 'I cannot work without my music. Now, Bertram, eez the camera ready? We shall begin.' He waved his hands in the air, as if conducting his own private orchestra.

Bertram nodded. 'Ready, team?'

They all shuffled into their places – Giselle beside Christo, Bertram holding the sound boom just over her head, Dion focusing his camera on her face.

'And . . . action,' Bertram said.

Giselle beamed at the camera. 'Lulabelle is now under general anaesthetic and we are about to watch her breast augmentation. Of course, her current breasts are already enhanced, so the *world-*

famous Parisian surgeon, Christophe de la Tour, or Christo, as he is better known, will remove her old implants and give her even bigger ones, using his famed "Christo Technique". Ideal for an aging model who wants to remain in the limelight as she races towards her thirties.'

'Hang on,' Dion piped up. 'Aging? That's hardly fair. Or accurate.'

Giselle put her hands on her hips. 'Why?'

'Lulabelle's only twenty-five.'

Giselle shook her head. 'Tut-tut. Is that what she told you? Poor deluded boy.'

'Shut it, Giselle,' Dion snarled at her.

'People!' Bertram snapped. 'We'll edit out the last line, Dion, OK? And no more catty comments, please, Giselle.'

'May I proceed?' Christo asked. 'Please put on your masks before I make the first incision.'

Giselle stared at him. 'How can I talk if I'm wearing a mask?'

'Voice-over,' Christo said firmly.

'He certainly knows his stuff,' Celeste murmured.

Giselle made a huffy noise. 'Bertram?' she whined.

'Voice-over it is. Just get on with it.'

Christo pulled back Lulabelle's surgical gown, revealing her chest. We all gasped. There they were, Lulabelle's extraordinary breasts, pointing directly upwards like cruise missiles. If you looked closely you could see faint light pink and silver scars in the crease under each one. She looked so vulnerable lying on the operating table, so fragile, it made me want to cry. I pulled my eyes away.

'The implants.'

Christo picked up a clear oval bag from the stainless steel kidney dish and passed it from hand to hand, as if he was juggling a water balloon. 'And now I will make the first incision, using my world-famous Christo zigzag.'

The nurse handed him a scalpel and he started to cut into the skin just under Lulabelle's nipple. Blood flowed on to the operating table.

THUNK. Dion fainted dead, and the camera clattered to the floor.

'Man down,' Christo said evenly, bloody scalpel poised in the air. 'Someone pick 'im up, please.'

Five minutes later, Dion had been helped outside, Bertram was behind the camera and I was holding the sound boom over Christo's head. It was a lot heavier than it looked.

'How long does the average operation take?' Celeste asked Christo, looking over at me anxiously.

'Thirty minutes, maybe an hour if there are complications.'

After ten minutes, I had to pass the boom to Celeste. It wasn't the weight, it was the surgery. My stomach was churning and I felt light-headed. I was aware I'd promised to keep an eye on Lulabelle, but I had to pass that mantle on to Celeste.

I told her what she had to do. She wasn't impressed.

'What do you mean, inappropriate?' she murmured. 'Like drawing a moustache on her upper lip?'

I smiled. 'Exactly. Pretend it's me on that operating table, Celeste, OK? Please? Do it for me? I gave her my word. Show a bit of female solidarity.'

'Oh, all right. But I'm not happy about this.'

'Stop chattering, you two,' Bertram snapped. 'Libby, are you staying or going?'

'Going.'

I scrubbed my hands in the sluice room and pulled off the scrubs, but the medical, bleachy smell still clung to my hair and clothes. Dion was sitting in the reception area, flicking through a plastic surgery magazine and wincing. He looked up as I walked in.

'Not you too.'

'I didn't pass out,' I said. 'Not quite. It just made me sick to watch. I don't know what I expected, but it wasn't that. It took two of them to pull the old implants out of Lulabelle, and they were covered in—'

'Stop!' Dion put a hand to his mouth. Then he took it down and sighed. 'Poor Lulabelle. She was really worried about this one. I tried to talk her out of it – there's nothing wrong with the size of her breasts – but she insisted. Said the viewers wouldn't be satisfied until they saw her blood running on to an operating table.'

'Who told her that?'

He shrugged. 'Bertram said blood was good for ratings, but it was Lulabelle's idea. Leo had a fit.'

'Is that why he isn't here today?'

'Yep. Said he'd have nothing to do with it.' He put down the magazine. 'You didn't hear this from me, OK? Lulabelle would kill me.'

'Do you think there's anything going on between Leo and Lulabelle?'

He stared at me. 'Why? Do you?' His voice was sharp.

'I don't know. But managers don't usually get so involved with their clients.'

He tilted his head. 'You don't get it, do you?'

'What?'

'Why everyone loves Lulabelle so much.'

'Why you and Leo like her – is that what you mean?'

'No, the public. She's hugely popular. All kinds of people adore her; even my mum thinks she's great. Not that I've said anything to her about me and Lu, of course. It's early days yet.'

Then I remembered – Mum. Bizarrely, Mum was a huge Lulabelle fan. I think she was actually rather impressed with my new job, apart from the fact that it meant 'abandoning' Jeremy, not that she'd said anything of the sort. 'Writing a book for someone else, Elizabeth?' she'd said with a sniff. 'Surely proper writers don't do things like that? I've never heard of John Banville or Anne Enright *ghostwriting.'*

'Maybe I am missing something,' I admitted to Dion. 'But she can be a bit difficult.'

He smiled. 'No kidding. But once you get to know her, she's like a big kid.'

I must have looked sceptical because he said, 'Honestly. She's had to develop this tough-as-nails exterior to protect herself. Have you any idea what it's like being followed every single day, paparazzi trying to get shots of her with her skirt tucked into her knickers? One guy even poked a camera under a loo door in a nightclub the other week. Can you imagine? You're trying to do your business, and *click.'*

'Horrible,' I agreed.

'She has no idea who to trust, so she trusts nobody. Apart from Leo. It's sad, really.'

'She's obviously trusts you, Dion,' I said gently. 'She's lucky to have someone decent to talk to.'

'Shit, Libby, you won't go talking to anyone about all this, will you? Especially Celeste. Lulabelle would kill me if any of it got into the papers.'

'I keep telling everyone, Celeste isn't a gutter journalist.'

'But you have to admit that last column she wrote was a bit low.'

'That was different. She was annoyed with Lulabelle for—' I paused. 'Anyway, that doesn't matter now.'

From the smile on Dion's face, he knew what I was about to say.

Then he went a bit sheepish.

'Look, I'm sorry about all that. Celeste's great. But shit, man, Lulabelle Ryan. Would you turn down Lulabelle Ryan? If you were a man, I mean?'

'Yes! And Celeste's my best friend, remember?' I studied his face. 'What age are you anyway? Twenty-two?'

'Twenty-four.'

I sucked my teeth. 'Just be careful. Don't get hurt.'

'Don't worry, me and Lulabelle are meant to be,' he said simply. 'It's fate.' Then he smiled dreamily.

Dear Lord, the man was dangerously delusional. They deserved each other.

Chapter 28

Libby

The morning after the whole Christo experience, Celeste holed herself up in her room to write her column – there was yet another bank scandal back in Ireland and she had to talk to her contacts in the economics world. I'd been banned from distracting her. It made a change.

'Evil stuff, banking,' she'd said over a rushed breakfast. 'But crises keep my column topical and my bosses happy. I always get hundreds of letters of support after giving out about financial institutions or the waiting time in A&E. When in doubt, give out, that's what I always say. Should have it tattooed across my writing hand.'

Last night had been a bit of a non-event in the end. I think everyone was still shell-shocked after watching Lulabelle's surgery. We'd had a quick dinner with Bertram and Giselle in a local bistro. Celeste had 'forgotten' to tell Alex where we were eating, even though she'd promised him she would. Dion hadn't joined us. Apparently Lulabelle wouldn't let him see her and he was distraught.

I had been a bit jumpy all evening, expecting Leo to walk in at any moment. He'd told Bertram he might join us, but he never appeared. It was probably just as well. I still couldn't shake Jeremy's text from my head.

After breakfast I sat in the lobby and people-watched for a while before deciding I couldn't legitimately avoid work any longer. I sat down at the desk in my hotel bedroom and chewed the top of my pen for a while, trying to imagine what living in a house full of models would be like for Chloe. As I didn't know any models (apart from Lulabelle), this was proving tricky. The phone rang. Celeste must have finished her column. I whipped it up, delighted with the interruption.

'Yello? You 'ave reached ze room of ze very special Parisian ghostwriter. 'Ow can I help?'

'Libby, it's Leo,' I could hear the smile in his voice. 'Is this a bad time? Are you writing?'

I blushed and put my hands on my cheeks, even though I knew he couldn't see me.

'Yes, hard at work for your slave-driver of a client. But it's fine – fire away.'

'Sorry to bother you, but I need your help.' His voice sounded flat and lifeless.

'Are you all right, Leo? You sound exhausted.'

'Didn't get much sleep, to be honest. I was up most of the night with Lulabelle. She was in terrible pain. She'd sent the nurse away and I couldn't leave her on her own.'

'How is she now?'

'Putting a brave face on it. At least the pain has eased off a bit. In fact, she wants to see you – says it's urgent.'

'Is something wrong?'

He gave a laugh. 'Poor Libby. She does make you nervous, doesn't she? No, I think she just wants to work. Take her mind off things.'

'She's just had a serious operation. Surely she needs to rest?'

'Try telling her that. Oh, and by the way, speaking of rest, I hope we're still on for dinner. I'm sorry I haven't had a chance to talk to you properly since we arrived, everything's been a bit manic – all the travel and the surgery and—'

'Elizabeth!' a familiar voice cut in. 'What happened during the surgery? Were they respectful?'

'Hello? Lulabelle, I believe I was talking to Leo.'

'Well?' Lulabelle continued, oblivious. 'I'm waiting, Elizabeth.'

Clearly, interrupting phone calls was perfectly normal on cloud Lulabelle.

'I wasn't there for the whole thing,' I admitted. 'I'm not very good with blood and it was all a bit gory.'

I heard Leo make a disgusted 'Ugh' noise.

'But Celeste stayed to keep an eye on your interests, Lulabelle,' I added quickly. 'And yes, I believe you were treated with due respect and, um, decorum.'

'What?' Lulabelle's voice thundered down the line. I held the phone away from my ear. 'I specifically told you to stay for the whole operation. You're as bad as Dion. What is it with you people? Have you never seen a bit of blood before?'

'Not during a surgery, no.' I stopped, remembering that Leo was still on the line. I knew he didn't approve of her procedures.

Hang on, I thought, how did I get dragged into this conversation in the first place? I was supposed to be talking to Leo.

'Lulabelle, can you please put the phone down,' I said firmly. 'I'd like to speak to Leo in private. And I can't believe you were listening in to our conversation. There are privacy laws about that kind of thing.'

'Privacy laws?' She harrumphed. 'Ha! Don't be so ridiculous. Leo works for me. And so do you, for that matter. I asked him to ring you for me, but then I decided to pick up the phone and do it myself. He's so bloody slow sometimes.'

'Lu,' Leo warned. 'Libby, I'm sorry our phone call was so rudely interrupted. Lulabelle's clearly not well, and I apologize for her abrupt manner.'

'I'm perfectly able to apologize for myself when it's called for, Leo,' Lulabelle said. 'Kindly allow me to make an arrangement with Elizabeth. We have a lot of work to do.'

'Lulabelle!' Leo sounded furious.

Things were getting out of hand.

'It's OK, Leo,' I said quickly. 'We can continue our conversation later. And it would be helpful to get Lulabelle's input today. I need to find out how models treat each other.'

'Thank you, Libby, for being so professional.'

'Oh, just get off the phone, Leo,' Lulabelle said wearily. 'I'll take it from here.'

'Lulabelle,' Leo growled. 'I'm warning you.'

'OK, OK, I'm sorry,' she said. 'I appreciate all you do for me, Leo, truly. But right now Elizabeth and I have a book to finish. I'd be most grateful if you'd leave us to it.'

'I'll talk to you later, Libby,' he said. 'And Lulabelle – play nice.'

As soon as the phone clicked and Leo was off the line, Lulabelle's tone changed.

'I want words with you, Elizabeth. In private. Get over here right this minute. And I'll thank you not to bring that Klingon Celeste anywhere near me.'

I felt an itch of irritation run up and down my spine.

'You can shove your private words where the sun doesn't shine,' I said. 'And for your information, Dion made Bertram cut out one of Giselle's lines about being an aging model, and when your gown rode up your legs, Celeste pulled it down and made sure it stayed there. I made her promise to look after you, and she did.'

'You're lying. Celeste hates me.'

'But she loves *me*. I asked her to pretend it was me on that operating table. She promised she would, and Celeste never breaks her word.'

For a few seconds there was silence on the line, then she said, 'So are you coming to my room or do I have to stagger over to you and rip my stitches open? I want to tell you about the kinds of dirty tricks the models could play on Chloe.'

Darn it, she'd got me there.

'I'll come over if you apologize for speaking to me like some sort of servant. I just want to be treated with a bit of respect, Lulabelle.'

Silence again. 'OK,' she said eventually. 'I'm sorry if you took offence at my not at all disrespectful tone.'

I gave a breathy laugh. 'Ha! That's hardly an apology.'

'It's all you're getting. I feel like I'm going to throw up, and I'm sweating all over.'

'Is that normal?'

'No. The nurse says I've got some sort of infection. Happens sometimes. Stupid woman was annoying me again – I sent her away. But for God's sake don't tell Leo any of this. He'll have me back in London on the next plane and *Plastic Fantastic* will completely fall through.'

'See?' I said.

'See what?'

'You *can* have a normal conversation, Lulabelle. You just have to be honest.'

'Oh, stop going all Oprah on me and get over here. There's something I want you to do.'

Chapter 29

Libby

Ten minutes later, after a speedy shower and a rummage in my suitcase for clean underwear, I knocked on Lulabelle's door – the Presidential Suite – and Leo opened it. Before I had a chance to say a word, he walked out of the door and shut it behind him, almost making our noses collide.

'Sorry,' he said, stepping sideways. 'I don't want Lulabelle to hear me.'

I just stood there, drinking him in. He really was rather lovely.

'And I'm also sorry that Lulabelle interrupted our phone call like that. Her manners are appalling sometimes. Like a spoilt child's.' He put his hand around my wrist and pulled me towards him. He lowered his voice. 'I have to talk to you. It's important.'

Our eyes locked and I could tell there was something eating away at him. He opened his mouth to continue, but then the door swung open and there she was – Lulabelle – her breasts swaddled with bandages. She looked like a pantomime dame, her chest swollen out of all proportion. She was using her portable drip like a walking stick, leaving on it heavily. Her eyes were bloodshot and there were beads of sweat on her forehead, sitting on top of her heavy make-up. There was an angry rash on her neck and upper chest. From the red and white tracks on her skin, she'd obviously just been having a good scratch.

Leo dropped my hand. 'Get back into bed, Lu.' He put his arm around her.

'I thought I heard the door,' she said. 'I shouted for you—'

'But I'd already gone to answer it. Come on. Back to your room.'

I followed them inside.

'Excuse me just one second.' Leo guided Lulabelle along the hallway by the elbow, opened a door and stood back politely to allow her to enter. 'Libby will join you in a minute, Lu. Give us a moment, please. We have publishing business to discuss. Nothing important.'

He closed the door firmly behind her. Then he walked back towards me, smiling.

'Before dinner tomorrow night – if you're free, of course . . .' He gazed at me, his brown eyes melting my heart yet again, all thoughts of Jeremy flown out the window.

'I'm looking forward to it,' I said.

'Good. Before dinner, I'm going to tell Lulabelle about us.'

Us? That sounded promising. I beamed at him.

'But first there's something I want to tell you. Lulabelle doesn't like people to know, says it sounds unprofessional, but I'm actually—'

'Did you hear that?' I asked. 'It sounded like a bell. Is it the fire alarm?'

'Ignore it. It's not the fire alarm. Please, Libby, just listen to me for a second.'

But there it was again, even louder. And it seemed to be coming from Lulabelle's room.

'What is it, then?' I asked.

Leo sighed. 'It's Lulabelle. The concierge found a hand bell for her. God knows where he got it – the thing looks ancient. She wants something. Probably wondering where you've got to.'

A hand bell? I tried not to laugh but it was no use. I started to giggle rather hysterically.

He rolled his eyes. 'I know. What's she like?'

'Elizabeth!' Lulabelle bellowed through the door. 'I'm waiting.' Then, 'Ow, ow!'

'I'd better see what she wants before she does herself an injury,' I said. 'We can talk later.'

I smiled at him and he smiled back, his eyes crinkling at the edges. He really was quite delicious.

The bell was now ringing continuously.

'*Coming, mistress,*' I shouted through the door. 'I'll see you later, Leo.'

I walked inside. Lulabelle's bedroom was impressive – three floor-to-ceiling windows with blue and cream fleur-de-lis drapes, a four-poster bed swathed in the same material, a mahogany desk, a three-piece suite, a crystal chandelier . . .

She was almost lost in the bed, like a tiny broken Barbie against the snowdrift of pillows propping her up.

'Elizabeth, stop dawdling and get over here.'

I stood my ground.

'What are you waiting for?' she demanded.

'I didn't hear you say please.'

'Oh, for fuck's sake, I don't have time for any of this. I'm in pain and I need you to take my mind off it. You want to talk bitchy models, let's talk bitchy models. Grab your notebook and shift your behind.'

I smiled. She reminded me of Jeremy when he was sick. The very worst kind of patient – tetchy and frustrated. I sat down on the side of the bed and pulled my notebook and pen out of my bag. While she took a sip of her bottle of Evian, I had another quick peek at her chest. There were two thin plastic tubes poking out from the sides of the bandages, and as I watched, yellow liquid tinged with what looked like blood spurted downwards. I followed the tube, wondering where it went.

'Stop staring at my drains,' she snapped. 'Don't know why the bloody man didn't take them out yesterday. And yes, that's blood in the tubes. Blood, blood, blood. But for Christ's sake, don't faint. Dion came over all queasy this morning. I had to send him away.'

'Did he give you those?' I nodded at the pale pink tea roses on her bedside table. 'They're beautiful.'

'That's none of your business.'

'Lulabelle,' I warned. 'I'm a human being, remember? It wouldn't kill you to be pleasant.'

'It's the drugs. And before we get started, there's something I want you to do. Go and scrub your hands and nails.'

'Excuse me?'

'You heard me.'

I winced. 'Let's just get this straight. I'm not going near those tubes.'

'It's nothing to do with the drains, woman.' She made a peculiar noise at the back of her throat, like a cat bringing up a fur ball. 'I want you to move some filler, OK? It's slipped a little.' She pointed at her right cheek. 'I can't be filmed this way and Bertram wants to take some post-op shots later.'

I moved closer and studied her face. There was a lumpy patch just underneath her cheekbone, like a ring of tiny bee stings.

'Is it new filler? Didn't you just have your cheeks done in San Fran?'

'Again, that's none of your business. But if you must know, it's a cutting-edge filler called FreshPearl. Christo's nurse gave me the name of someone who does it. It's not on the market in the UK yet. But the bloody stuff seems to have shifted.'

'It's hardly noticeable,' I said.

'The camera will pick it up. I need to look perfect.'

'Even when you're sick?'

'I'm not sick, I'm just post-op.'

I had another look at her face with its scarily high, angular cheekbones. 'Are your cheekbones real, Lulabelle?' I'd always wanted to know and it seemed the perfect time to ask.

She didn't answer for a moment. 'They're enhanced,' she said, her eyes challenging me. 'With filler. Filler that has just slipped. Haven't you been listening at all, Elizabeth? As it's pretty fresh, you may be able to massage it back up. I rang the doctor and threatened to sue his sorry ass. He admitted that it sometimes happens if the filler is too close to the skin and told me what to do. Dion tried, but he kept fainting, useless man. I'd do it myself, but I don't have the energy to stand for long enough. I'm asking you nicely.'

'I'm really not comfortable—'

'I'll pay you.'

'It's not about that.'

'Please.' She looked at me, her eyes glistening, turning on her full Bambi power. 'I don't have anyone else. Please.'

The thing was, ever since the first day I'd met her I'd really, really wanted to touch Lulabelle's skin. It was so unreal, like a ripe peach, and I wanted to see if it felt as good as it looked.

'I'll give it a go,' I said, gulping back my nerves.

I washed my hands carefully in the en suite and sat back down on the bed. Lulabelle leaned back and rested her head on the pillows.

'Listen to me carefully,' she said. 'Put your thumb in my mouth and your finger outside on my skin and squeeze upwards, like squeezing toothpaste out of a tube. Got it?'

I stared at her in fright. 'Are you serious? You really want me to put my thumb in your mouth?'

'Elizabeth, I've just had my chest cut open and I have plastic tubes sticking out of holes in my skin. Having someone's thumb in my mouth is child's play.'

I pulled a face. 'I don't think I can.'

'Jesus, Elizabeth, stop being such a baby. Pretend it's your husband's manhood and squeeze the bejaysus out of it, OK?'

'Can I just say that this is the weirdest thing anyone has ever asked me to do.'

'Really?' She looked at me in surprise. 'You've lived a very sheltered life.' Then she smiled at me.

I started to laugh.

She laughed too, then clutched her chest. 'Oh, don't, that hurts. Say something sad.'

'I'm way behind with the book,' I said.

The smiled dropped off her face. 'Are you?'

'No. I was trying to stop you laughing.'

She narrowed her eyes. She clearly didn't believe me.

'Let's get on with this, then, so we can get back to work. I don't want Leo to catch us. He doesn't know about the new filler.'

'But shouldn't you tell him? He is your manager.'

She put a hand up. 'Just stop. I don't have the energy. And frankly, my relationship with my manager is, once again, none of your business. Now, you need to use slow, firm pressure. You're aiming to move the filler upwards and towards my hairline, get it?'

'Here, you mean?' I touched my own face on the apple of my cheekbone.

'Yes, but my cheekbones are high, so more like here.' She touched her own face, further towards her eye. 'And for God's sake, stop being so nervous. Last thing I need is a shaky hand.'

She opened her mouth wide. Even her back teeth were perfect, not a filling in sight. Why was I not surprised? They were probably all fake.

I moved my hand towards her face and my thumb hovered in front of her mouth.

'Huggy up, Gagivegeth,' she said, her mouth still gaping.

I stuck my thumb in her mouth and moved it along her warm, wet gums. Then I put a finger on her cheek.

'Ight,' she said. 'I geed ug u.'

'What?' I took my hand out.

'What are you doing?' she demanded. 'Just get on with it.'

'But I couldn't understand what you were saying.'

She shook her head. 'This would actually be quite comical if it wasn't so annoying.'

I smiled. 'Just tell me what you want to do before I put my hand in your mouth. OK?'

'Fine. After you've put your fingers back in, feel around for the lump and push it up. If you need to hold my gum with your other hand to get traction, go right ahead.'

I followed her instructions, putting my thumb and finger back in place. I felt the lump, like a little piece of plasticine just under her skin, and pressed it upwards. It didn't seem to want to budge, so I held the gum with my other hand, like Lulabelle had suggested, and kept pressing upwards. This time it started to move a little. I kept working away at the lump until I thought it was in the right place and then removed my fingers.

'Finished?'

I nodded, trying not to think about what I'd just had to do.

She whipped up her hand mirror and had a look, turning her head to the left. 'Not bad. Thank you.'

'See, was that so hard?'

'What?'

'Saying thank you.'

'I always say thank you.'

I just stared at her. 'You're joking?'

She ignored me, wiggled the skin on her face around a little and then said, 'Right, let's get to work.'

'Are you sure you're up to it?'

'Elizabeth, I'm going to tell you a few true stories about my modelling days. It's hardly work.'

'OK. Just for a few minutes. I don't need much. And I have to take a call from Patty Pope-Hurley at twelve o'clock sharp.'

'Is there a problem with the book?'

'Nah. We're just talking about the publishing schedule, I think.'

'In that case, let's work for forty minutes, until ten to twelve.'

'Done.'

As I picked up my notebook and pen, it crossed my mind that maybe Lulabelle was thawing. She was starting to compromise.

She told me some of the dirty tricks the other girls played on each other during her own reality modelling show:

1. Resetting wristwatches and alarm clocks to make other models late
2. Giving a huge box of handmade chocolates to the girl with the sweetest tooth (in the hope that she'd break out in spots)
3. Planting vodka in the handbag of a girl with a drink problem
4. Ordering a wagon-wheel pizza to be delivered to a model's house, a girl who couldn't afford to put on a single pound.

As she talked, I chuckled away and scribbled down notes. I felt we were finally starting to communicate. I even considered asking her to ring Mum and say hi. Not that my darling mother deserved it.

'So how do you know about all the dirty tricks?' I asked when she'd finished. 'Were you the one behind them?'

'No! The pizza was delivered to *my* house.' She shrugged. 'And the make-up girls liked to talk.'

At five to twelve I jumped to my feet.

'I have to run. Thanks for all the help, Lulabelle – there's some great stuff there. It's just what I needed.'

She patted her cheek. 'Tell anyone about this and you're fish food, understand?' But then she smiled a genuine, sunny smile that lit up the whole room. 'And thank you. It wasn't exactly in your contract.'

I smiled back. 'It's between us girls. And you're welcome.'

I skipped back to my room. Maybe Dion was right. When it came to Lulabelle, maybe I *had* missed something.

Chapter 30

Libby

By Thursday morning I was finding *Stay Beautiful* tough going. I'd spent most of the last hour formulating a writing timetable, one of my time-honoured procrastination devices. I'd worked out that if we could bang out five thousand words every day for the next eight days, I'd almost be on target. If I kept up the pace, I'd even be able to claw back some editing time at the end. I knew Patty kept telling me there was no time for rewriting, but I had my standards. I wasn't letting *Stay Beautiful* out of my hands until I was completely happy with it.

My niggling thoughts were interrupted by a knock on the door.

'What's up with you?' Celeste asked, bounding into the room. 'You look like you've swallowed someone's hamster.'

'Just stressing about the book.'

'Well, don't. If the chapters I typed up for you are anything to go by, it's your best yet. You probably just need a break. Meet me in the lobby in ten minutes. I just need to grab something from the minibar.'

I looked at her sideways. 'Celeste, isn't it a bit early for that?'

But she was already out of the door.

One taxi ride later we were wandering around the Père-Lachaise cemetery, stepping over gnarled tree roots and avoiding the mangy wild cats that ran across our path. Celeste was on a mission. She'd had a huge teenage crush on Jim Morrison and wanted to pour whisky on his grave. She was all ready for action with a miniature bottle in her bag.

'It's around here somewhere,' Celeste said, her nose in my Paris guidebook. 'Hang on, do you hear music?'

'Yep. Over there.' I pointed to the left. A woman's voice howled 'Jeeem, I lurve you,' in heavily accented English.

'Bingo! Follow that noise.'

A large crowd was gathered around a low, black granite grave.

'Do you think they're Irish?' Celeste whispered, nodding at a group of teenagers. The smaller ones were jumping and standing on their toes, trying to see over the taller ones' heads.

'Definitely. Looks like some sort of school trip.' I watched as a fair-haired boy pulled a girl towards him and whispered something in her ear. She nodded and they snuck away from the group, holding hands. Sweet.

As the crowd parted a little to let them through, there was Bertram standing to the left of the gravestone.

'What's he doing here?' Celeste asked.

'Still fancy him?'

Celeste frowned. 'I'm sorry about all that. I was out of order. And absolutely not. What was I thinking? He irons his jeans.'

I laughed. We inched our way through the crowd and spotted Lulabelle swaying gently to the music, the slight breeze lifting her hair, which hung softly around her face. In her white cotton dress, a denim jacket and flat Roman sandals, she looked fantastic, like a young Elle Macpherson. Until you saw her face – heavy brown foundation, boxy sweeps of blusher, Barbie-pink lips.

'She's just had surgery,' Celeste hissed. 'Shouldn't she be in bed?'

As we watched, Lulabelle picked a single red rose off the ground, kissed it and threw it on top of the grave.

'Thanks for the music, Jim,' she said to the camera; Dion was behind it. 'You'll always rock in my heart.'

Celeste shrugged. 'Corny but cute.'

Once Dion had stopped filming and the crowds began to disperse, we walked towards him.

'Hi, Dion,' Celeste said. 'You guys finished now? Can we bum a lift back to the hotel?'

He looked up from his camera case, shielded his eyes from the sun and smiled.

'Sure. What have you two been up to?'

'Working, mainly,' I said. 'Your girlfriend's a slave-driver.'

He looked over at Lulabelle, who was chatting to Bertram.

'I wouldn't know anything about that,' he said a little bitterly. 'I haven't really talked to her since the operation. She won't answer my calls or let me near her.'

'She's probably feeling a bit vulnerable right now,' Celeste said. 'Give her some time.' Celeste rummaged in her bag. 'Excuse me for just one second. Have to give Jim his tipple.'

Celeste walked towards the grave, stopping to say a few words to Bertram and nod at Lulabelle. As she poured the whisky over the gravel, the smell wafted towards us.

'Libby, Lulabelle seems to like you,' Dion said. 'Would you have a word with her, see what's going on? I don't know where I stand, and it's killing me.'

'I'm not sure I'm the right person to—'

'Please?' He unleashed his puppy-dog eyes and I melted. Jesus, Dion and Lulabelle were perfectly matched.

'OK, I'll do my best, Dion, I promise.'

Back at the hotel, I rang Lulabelle.

'Ms Ryan's suite.' It was Leo.

'Leo, it's me, Libby. Can I speak to Lulabelle?'

'She's not really up to it. Maybe later. She's—'

'Of course I'm up to it,' I heard Lulabelle snap. 'Who is it?'

'Libby.'

There was a scuffle and then Lulabelle said, 'Give me that. Come right over, Elizabeth. I'm sure it's important or you wouldn't be bothering me.'

'Actually—'

But the phone had already gone dead.

'Hi, Libby.' Leo swung open the door. He looked a bit annoyed.

'Be as quick as you can,' he said. 'She's exhausted. She should have been in bed this morning, not out walking with Dion.'

Walking? For a second I was torn. But I wanted to keep Lulabelle on side.

'It's just about the book, and it won't take long. Nothing urgent. I can come back later.'

'A few minutes won't make any difference.' He lowered his voice. 'Are you still OK for dinner later? I've booked the Jules Verne restaurant up the Eiffel Tower. Best view in town. Meet you in the lobby at seven?'

'Perfect.' Our eyes locked and we smiled at each other. I could feel my cheeks blush and my heart felt light and fluttery. His gaze was so intense I couldn't bear it any longer; I bit my lip and looked away.

'Stop dawdling, Elizabeth.' Lulabelle was standing in the doorway to her bedroom. 'Do you want to talk to me or not?'

'I'll leave you to it, girls. You have ten minutes, Lulabelle. Then you're back to bed.'

Leo walked towards the sitting room and closed the door behind him.

I followed Lulabelle into her bedroom. She sat down on the sofa and I perched on the edge of the chair opposite her.

'How can I help you?' she said. Her make-up had slipped down her face and there were mascara marks under both eyes. She'd taken off the denim jacket and I could see swathes of stretchy bandages under the dress. She winced and then readjusted her position on the sofa.

'Are you OK? I can come back later.'

'No, no, it's fine. Just a little uncomfortable. It's been a long day. Eiffel Tower, the glass pyramid outside the Louvre, and then Jim Morrison's grave.'

I lifted my eyebrows. 'You told Leo you were walking with Dion.'

She cocked her head, her eyes flinty. 'What's it to you? Going to tell teacher on me?'

'No, but Leo's right to be concerned. You should be taking it easy. And he's not the only one. Dion's worried about you too.'

She narrowed her eyes. 'And how do you know that?'

'I was talking to him in the graveyard. He said you won't talk to him.'

'Did he now? Kindly keep your nose out of my affairs, Elizabeth.'

'I'm only trying to help. He's upset. Why won't you see him?'

Lulabelle stood up, staggered a little and put her hand on the arm of the sofa to steady herself.

'Are you sure you're all right?' I asked.

'I'm fine,' she snapped. 'Just get out.'

'You can't speak to me like that.'

'I can and I will. Get out.' Her eyes met mine, frosty and unrepentant. 'Now!'

I took a deep breath. 'No, I'm staying right here. Dion is a good man, Lulabelle, and he's devoted to you, God help him. If you can't see that, you're completely blind.'

She crossed her arms and stared down at me. 'Have you quite finished?'

'Are you going to talk to Dion?'

Silence.

'I'm not leaving until you agree to talk to him,' I said.

'Leo!' she bellowed at the closed door. Then she walked towards her bedside table, grabbed her bell and rang it frantically.

Leo ran in. 'What's wrong, Lu? Is it your chest?'

'No, it's not my bloody chest, it's this – ' she waved her hand at me – 'this thing. Get her out of here.'

I sat firm. 'I'm not leaving until she agrees to talk to Dion. She's being really cruel and he doesn't deserve it. It's about time someone spoke frankly to Lulabelle.'

'Hello!' Lulabelle waved a hand in front of my face. 'I'm right in front of you, thunder-thighs.'

I felt a crinkle of anger. 'OK, that's it. Lulabelle, you're one of the rudest, most unpleasant people I've ever met. Don't you get it? I'm trying to help you. Dion's a keeper – he's worth hundreds of George Foxes or Marcus Valentines. And if you can't see that, you don't deserve him.'

Lulabelle stared at Leo. 'See what I mean? She's impossible. Tell her she's fired.'

'If you fire me, *Stay Beautiful* will never see the light of day,' I said.

'I don't care!' she shrieked. 'It would be worth it never to have to see you again. You're a wagon and I hate you.'

'That's a big strong, Lu.' Leo put his hand under her elbow. 'Libby's right, we need her. Now sit down. You're looking terrible.'

'I'm not moving till you get her out of my face. Carry her out if you have to. Just get rid of the fat cow. Do you hear me? This minute!'

'No,' he said firmly. 'Libby's right. And I want you to apologize for calling her fat. That was uncalled for and completely untrue. Libby's beautiful.'

Lulabelle snorted. 'Yeah, right. She's a heifer with no dress sense and the worst haircut I've ever seen. No wonder her fiancé had an affair.'

I gasped. 'How dare you, you trumped-up bitch. At least I'm

real. Real boobs, real teeth; and get this – real friends. I can't believe I put my hand in your mouth and shifted that disgusting pollyfilla stuff around.'

'Have you been at your face again, Lu?' Leo demanded. 'You promised you'd leave it alone.'

'Oh, just shut up, the both of you,' she said. 'And for the last time, get rid of her, Leo. Or you're fired too.'

'And who would look after you then?' He gave a dry laugh. 'There isn't another soul on earth who would put up with all your shit.'

'Alex,' she said smugly. 'He's already offered.'

'The snake!' I spluttered. 'What a nerve.'

He's welcome to you.' Leo held out his hand to me. 'Libby, I know it's only lunchtime but I could do with a drink. Will you join me? Get us in the mood for our date this evening.'

'I'd love to.' I gave him my hand and he kissed it. I lowered my head and gave him my best coy smile.

'Stop that flirting immediately!' Lulabelle bellowed. 'You're not going anywhere, Leo, especially not with her. She has pink hair for God's sake. You deserve someone better.'

Leo shook his head sadly. 'Give it a rest, Lu. Libby's amazing. Much more than I deserve. Shall we, Libby?' He put his arm around my shoulders.

I looked at Lulabelle. I expected to see daggers in her eyes, but instead she looked crushed.

'But you can't,' she whispered. 'You can't . . .' She collapsed on to the sofa and put her head in her hands.

'She'll be fine,' Leo whispered in my ear. 'Let's go.'

'Are you sure?'

He nodded. 'Shouting at us didn't work so she's just trying amateur dramatics.'

We walked into the hall and he shut the door behind us. He held my face in his hands. 'Thank you,' he said.

'For what?'

'For being honest, telling Lu what she needed to hear. I think you're right – Dion's the best thing that's happened to her in a long time. I just hope she has the sense to see it.'

'But what about the book?' I asked. 'Didn't she just fire me?'

'She'll come round. But let's not worry about that now.' He kissed the top of my nose and I started to tingle all over. Then he kissed my left cheek, then the right, and finally his lips landed on mine and within seconds everything was forgotten.

Suddenly there was a scream directly behind us and I broke away from his arms. Lulabelle was standing in the open doorway.

'I'm bleeding.' She pointed at her chest. Blood was seeping through the left-hand side of her elastic bandage. She staggered, threw a hand out to the door frame to steady herself, but missed and fell to the floor.

'Lu!' Leo knelt on the floor and put his hand under her head. 'Lu, can you hear me? Libby, ring reception. We need a doctor. Urgently.'

Chapter 31

Libby

'How dramatic,' Celeste said, clapping her hands together as she perched on the mahogany coffee table in my hotel room. 'So what happened after you rang for a doctor?'

'Leo lifted Lulabelle into bed and I sat and waited with him. We didn't talk much. She was awake, but not really with it. But I still couldn't make out if it was all for real or if she was putting it on.'

'What did the doctor say?'

'That some of her stitches had ripped, plus she has some sort of infection in the wound. He put her on a drip, strong antibiotics, I think, told her not to move from the bed and rang for a nurse to monitor her. He wanted to stitch her back up but Leo wouldn't let him. Said he wanted the damn butcher who had cut her open in the first place to do it.'

'And what did Leo say when Christo got there?' Celeste said a little too gleefully for my liking. 'Did he punch him?'

'Celeste!' I said. 'This isn't some sort of soap opera on the telly. I think Lulabelle's really sick.'

I picked at the skin around my thumb.

'Anyway, to answer your question, I don't know what happened next. I left before Christo got there. It was all a bit uncomfortable. I've rung Leo a few times but he's not answering his mobile and the room phone is permanently engaged.'

'Permanently?' Celeste looked at me carefully. 'How many times have you rung, exactly?'

I tried to look calm and collected. 'A few.'

'Go on,' she cajoled. 'How many?'

I shrugged. 'I've lost count.'

'Ah, Jesus, Libs, you haven't been phone-bombing him, have you?' Celeste gave a deep sigh.

I could feel my neck and ears start to redden. 'I know, but I really like him. We kissed again.'

'When?'

My whole face started to burn. 'Just before Lulabelle opened the door and found us at it. And then collapsed.'

'Ah.' Celeste smiled at me gently. 'Tricky.'

'She fired me too, just when the book's finally starting to come together.'

Celeste winced. 'Ouch. But I'm sure she'll change her mind. Look, Libs, I'll call up to his room later. Say I'm checking everything's OK. What number is it?'

'He's in the Presidential Suite.'

'With Lulabelle?' Celeste asked.

'It's a big suite,' I said. 'Plenty of space for both of them. They shared a suite at the Stanza, too. It's no big deal.'

Celeste had a funny look on her face.

'What?' I asked.

'I'm just wondering about their relationship, that's all. They seem to share a lot of hotel rooms.'

'Suites. And Leo wouldn't kiss me outside Lulabelle's door if there really was something going on, would he? And what about Dion?'

'I don't know, Libs. Maybe he hates seeing her with Dion. Maybe he was trying to make her jealous.'

'That's a lot of maybes. It was all so awkward when I left. He wouldn't even look me in the eye. He just stared down at the carpet and mumbled goodbye to his shoes. He is her manager and I'm sure he's worried about her. But thinking about it, what if you're right?' I sighed. 'I really need to know either way. It's killing me. If you're right, if he has feelings for her . . .'

'I'll go and talk to him right now.' Celeste stood up. 'Put you out of your misery.'

'Please don't say anything about me,' I begged her.

She put her hand on my shoulder and squeezed. 'It'll all work out for the best, Libs.'

Seventeen minutes later (but who was counting?), Celeste bounced into my room.

'I have good news. Leo says the book's back on.'

I slumped against the back of the sofa. 'Thank God for that. Did he say anything else?'

'Yes. He's been talking to your editor, Patty. He told her about Lulabelle's condition. She's given you an extra two weeks to finish the book.'

Celeste looked a bit shifty. There was something she wasn't telling me.

'And?' I said.

She avoided my gaze. 'Just that he'd see us all in Antigua. Lulabelle's flying back to London first thing tomorrow, to rest. Leo's travelling with her.'

I jumped to my feet. 'I have to talk to him before he goes.'

Celeste winced. 'Before you go anywhere, there's something else. He said to tell you goodbye.'

'That's it? Goodbye? Nothing else?'

She nodded silently.

I put my hand over my mouth and started to cry. Humiliation at the hands of a man – yet again. I didn't know if my system could take much more of it. Then I stood up, tears streaming down my cheeks, and walked towards the door.

'I'm so sorry, Libby,' I heard Celeste call after me. I ran along the corridor and then down the fire-exit stairs. I couldn't bear to be caught sobbing in the lift by a stranger.

Later, as I walked back towards my hotel room, eyes still swimming with tears, I saw a man in a dark suit standing with his back to me at the far end of the dimly lit corridor, his shoulder against the wall. My heart leapt. Leo! Celeste must have got it wrong.

I pressed my eyes with my fingertips and willed the waterworks to stop. I walked faster, wanting to run but holding myself back. I did have some pride.

As I got closer, he swung round and I stopped dead, my face frozen.

Chapter 32

Libby

'Alex!'

'What's wrong, Libby? You look like you've seen a ghost.'

I stared at him, my body wracked with disappointment. Tears began to stream down my face again, hot and fast. I didn't bother to hide them or even wipe them away.

'Just leave me alone, Alex.'

'I have to tell you something.'

'What?'

'I'm pregnant.'

'That's not funny. Get out of my way.'

'Stop, I'm kidding, I really do have news – about the book. Patty rang.'

'I know all about the two weeks' grace. Celeste told me.'

'Then why are you upset?' He looked at me crookedly. 'It's Leo, isn't it?'

'I'll kill Celeste.'

'Wasn't Celeste. The lobby of the Stanza isn't exactly the most private place to have a snog. Be careful, Libby. The whole situation with Leo and Lulabelle.' He stopped for a second. 'It's complicated.'

So it was true – there was something between them. I was just a pawn in their sick little game.

'Don't look at me like that, Alex. I know what you're thinking.

Stupid Libby. How can she be taken in again? I won't have you feeling sorry for me. Stop it!'

I pulled out my key card and jabbed it into the door. For once I'd put it in the right way up. I opened the door and then swung round, still holding the door handle.

'I'll finish the book and that's it. You'll get your money, I'll get mine and I never have to set eyes on Leo or Lulabelle again; everyone's happy.'

'Actually, that's the other reason I'm here. The sell-in has been brilliant; New Haven want you to do two more books. One for the spring, then another for Christmas next year.'

'Do they, now? Well, the answer is no.' I tried to close the door, but he put his foot in the crack.

'You're being a fool,' he said. 'I've already said you'd do it. In fact I signed the contract for you. I thought you'd be happy.'

'You can't do that. It's illegal.'

'So's entering a competition under false pretences, Nuala Lightbody.'

My stomach lurched.

'Leave me alone, Alex.' I kicked his foot away with a whack from my toe and slammed the door in his face.

He knocked on the wood. 'Come on, Libby,' came his muffled voice. 'We need to talk about this new contract. It's an amazing opportunity. Look, I shouldn't have mentioned that stupid New Writers' competition, I'm sorry, OK? It just popped out. You could be one of the best ghostwriters in the business, Libby. You have a real gift for collaboration.'

'Go away or I'll call security.'

'Go ahead. I'm not going anywhere. I'm staying put until you agree to write more books with Lulabelle. Patty wants to talk to you first thing tomorrow about the new publishing schedule. I don't want to threaten you, Libby, but if I have to, I will. Do the books or I'll tell Celeste about the competition. I'm not going to stand by and watch you throw your career down the fucking toilet again.'

Panicking, I ran towards my bedside phone and keyed in Celeste's room number.

'Libby?' She answered immediately. 'I was really worried about you. Are you in your room? Will I come down?'

'Yes,' I hissed into the receiver. 'Alex is outside my door and he won't go away. I just want to sleep, Celeste, I'm so tired. I think I'm coming down with something. Will you get rid of him? I told him I'd ring security but I don't want him to get locked up or anything.'

'It's not Morocco, Libs. Anyway, a bit of *gendarme* action might put some manners on him. Ha!'

I said nothing. I was terrified. About Alex and what he might do if I refused to write more damn books. I didn't want to think about it; I didn't want to talk to him; I just wanted it all to go away.

'Libby, are you still there?'

'Sorry, Celeste, I'm not in the mood for jokes. Can you come right now? He's banging the door down.' I held the receiver towards the door, which he was slapping with his palm.

'I'll be right over, babes,' she said. 'I'll get rid of him for you. Hang tight.'

A few minutes later I heard a noise outside. I walked towards the door and pressed my ear to it, but I could only hear muffled words. I opened the door a crack and peered out.

Alex was talking to Celeste in a low voice.

'I'll find you in the bar,' she told Alex. 'Now, you heard the lady – get.' She hitched her thumb down the corridor and Alex sloped off without a word.

'He's got a bloody nerve,' I muttered, opening the door to let Celeste in.

She looked at me, concern all over her face. 'Are you all right, Libby? Alex said you're in a bit of a state.'

'I just need to lie down. I feel horrible. I just want to be alone.'

'Are you sure? I don't mind sitting with you while you sleep.'

'No, honestly, I'm fine.'

'Ring me the minute you need anything, OK? Or if you want company. Even if it's the middle of the night. Promise?'

I nodded. I could feel tears pricking my eyes and I didn't want the waterworks to start again.

Celeste gave me a hug. 'Have a good sleep. It'll all seem brighter in the morning.'

Chapter 33

Libby

I woke up at eight o'clock with a mouldy mouth and a slight throb in my right temple. I rolled my tongue around my mouth and licked my dry lips, catching a tiny piece of chocolate on the tip of my tongue. Ah, yes, the wine and chocolate from the minibar. No wonder I felt a bit grotty. But it had certainly helped me sleep, even if I did have bad dreams. One involved Crocodile Dundee who was mud-wrestling with Ruth-Ann and Lulabelle, each in tiny leopard-skin bikinis (the girls, that is, not Croc himself). I'd watched the film last night after Celeste had left – the only thing I could find in English apart from Sky News.

The other involved Alex telling Celeste I was a fraud and a cheat. Which was even more terrifying. I'd woken up in a sweat, remembering he had indeed threatened to expose me – that wasn't a nightmare, that was real.

Even at the time I knew I'd be eternally ashamed of what I'd done, but, in my defence, I was at a very low ebb – it was just after I'd been dumped by both Alex and my publishers and I guess I was looking for some reassurance that I could actually write.

So I entered this writing competition – the Charing Cross New Writers' Award for unpublished writers. And I used a fake name – Nuala Lightbody (don't ask me how I came up with it, I honestly can't remember). The prize was ten thousand pounds, the chance to have your book published by a new popular fiction imprint called Calling Town Press, and representation by a top London agent.

Unfortunately, the agent who was supposed to be on the judging panel had been taken ill and Alex had stepped into her shoes at the last minute. I should have known – Alex had always been a publicity hound.

I'd almost forgotten I'd even entered the bloody thing when I got a phone call one evening.

'Hi, there.' I recognized the voice instantly. 'Could I speak to Nuala Lightbody, please? It's Alex Sharpe from the Charing Cross New Writers' Award.'

Shit, I thought. Shit-shit-shit-shit-shit.

'Jaysus, mister, I'm sorry,' I said. 'She's, urm, away. On her holliers. Won't be back for weeks.'

He laughed. 'Libby, that's the worst Dublin accent I've ever heard.'

I squeaked. 'Wha'? Who's this Libby person? Never 'eard of 'er.'

'Funny that, because you share the same phone number. Besides, I'd recognize your writing style anywhere. And wasn't *His Girl Friday* the book you pitched to Harriet that she turned down? I have to admit, you did a good job of the rewrites. Still not that pushed on the premise though.'

I sighed. Alex always knew how to make me feel even worse about myself than I already felt.

'What do you want, Alex? Are you going to tell the judges I'm a cheat, is that it?'

'Nope. None of my business. I'm keeping well out of it. Besides, all the judging was pretty much done before I came on board. I'm ringing because you've only gone and won the bloody thing, and the chair of the judging panel will be ringing you later to tell you the news. Just wanted to warn you. In case—'

'In case *what*?' I demanded. I was angry, mostly with myself.

'Nothing. You just take the award if it means that much to you.'

'You don't approve, do you? You think I shouldn't have entered.'

'As I said, none of my business.'

'Come off it, Alex. You're disappointed in me, aren't you? Admit it.'

There was silence for a moment.

'OK, you want the truth? I think you're a fucking idiot. There's a bloody awards ceremony. In London. It'll be full of publishing heads and agents. You know what they're like when there's free wine on offer. Harriet will be there. Accept that award and your career is toast, for good.' He paused. 'Is that honest enough for you?'

'Yes,' I whispered. 'God, I've been so stupid. What was I thinking?'

'It's understandable. You've had a run of bad luck lately and I guess you just self-combusted. And actually it makes you a lot more likeable. No more Little Miss Perfect with the hot-shot boyfriend and the charmed life. This whole thing might give your writing a bit more edge. In my experience, comfortable, happy people produce crap books.'

'Thanks a lot.'

'Look, when they ring, tell them you can't take the award. That you had a book accepted for publication just after you entered, and it wouldn't be right to accept.'

'Won't they check up on it?'

'They might. Which is why I've pulled in a favour at Griffin Books. If anyone rings, my mate Hayley, the fiction editor there, will tell them that yes, they're publishing a book by Nuala Lightbody, but there's no confirmed pub date as yet.'

Tears sprung to my eyes. 'You did that for me?'

'Yes.'

'Is Hayley your new girlfriend?'

He laughed. 'I'd be so lucky. Hell no, happily married. But she'll be publishing Toni Blade from next year on. So everyone wins. *His Girl Friday* will be on their publishing schedule for two year's time but will be mysteriously dropped once the competition's long forgotten.'

I felt calm and in control for the first time in ages. Alex had saved me from myself and probably rescued my writing career to boot – what was left of it.

'I don't know what to say, Alex. Thank you.'

'No problem. Oh, and by the way, you actually deserved to win. Most of the entries were utter toss. And don't worry, it's our little secret.'

There was no sign of Celeste in the hotel dining room, so I sat down for breakfast alone. I had just ordered coffee when Celeste wrapped her arms around my neck from behind and kissed me firmly on the cheek.

Hi, babes.' She swung herself in beside me. 'Great morning, isn't it? How about we hit the shops today? We deserve a little treat. Spotted some great little boutiques in Montmartre.'

I studied her carefully. Her cheeks were flushed and her eyes sparkled. She caught my eye and then looked away.

'Where's the waiter?' she said. 'I'm starving. Do you think they do a full Irish?'

Celeste rarely had more than a croissant and coffee for breakfast. Something was up.

'Where were you last night?' I asked her.

'Out with Alex. We were in the hotel bar, then hit a nightclub.' A smile played on her lips. 'He can be quite fun when you get him going.'

I gasped. 'You slept with him, didn't you?'

She gave a Cheshire cat grin. 'Jeez, I can't keep anything from you, can I? Surprise, surprise, you were right, Libs. Once Alex had a few drinks in him, he admitted he'd always fancied me rotten and I thought what the hell. Anyway, it was a mistake, it's not going to happen again.' She cocked her head. 'Why have you gone so quiet, Libby?'

'Did he say anything about me?'

'Not really. But he understands how much pressure you're under. Oh, and he's really keen for you to do more books with Lulabelle.'

'Is he now?' My mobile beeped in my pocket and I pulled it out.

Libby, we need to talk. Face to face. Get things like the house sorted out. When are you back in Dublin? J

I was utterly confused. In his last text (which I'd never answered) he was proclaiming his undying love. What had happened in the meantime?

'Libby? You OK?'

I handed Celeste my mobile and she read Jeremy's message.

'It's for the best, Libs,' she said gently, handing it back to me.

I nodded silently, staring down at the screen again and rubbing a smudge off it with my thumb, trying to hold back my tears.

If she was right, why did it hurt so much?

Chapter 34

Lulabelle

'Flowers for Miss Ryan.'

'First floor,' Lulabelle said into the intercom. 'Apartment three.'

She pressed the button to let the delivery man into the building, an old Georgian house converted into apartments, her new London base, then shuffled slowly towards the door. She was still feeling weak and even walking made her chest ache. She'd been on mega-doses of antibiotics and painkillers for a week now, and they were making her feel groggy and irritable. The lack of appetite didn't help. She hadn't eaten in days and she was now down to just over seven stone. She hadn't been this light since she was a teenager, but even that didn't make her happy.

She stood at the door, waiting. She hadn't seen a soul for two days, since she'd had yet another blow-out argument with Leo. He wanted her to stop filming *Plastic Fantastic*, abandon the project, and she wasn't having it.

'I can't,' she'd told him. 'It would be unprofessional. And it's a vital part of the brand Lulabelle plan, Leo, you know that.'

'Fuck brand Lulabelle. If you don't stop you're going to kill yourself. You heard what the doctors said – proper bed rest for at least two weeks.'

'In an ideal world I'd love to rest, but we have bills to pay, Leo. You know that as well as I do. If *Plastic Fantastic* doesn't get aired, we're in big trouble. We've invested everything in that bloody show, and I for one am not prepared to see it all flushed down the toilet. If it doesn't air, the plastic surgeons will demand to be paid, the publicity for the novel will be compromised, and everything we've done to build my TV profile over the last few months will be for nothing.'

'I'm not prepared to gamble with your health, Lu. Both doctors said putting your body through any more surgery – at least for another few months – would be dangerous – weren't you listening? Antigua is out.'

'I'm going to Antigua, and I'm having the surgery. And there's nothing you can do about it. Either accept that or get out.'

Leo had stared at her, eyes blazing. 'In that case you'll be travelling alone. And find another manager. I quit.'

'Again?' Lulabelle said dryly. 'I'll see you later. Don't forget to pick up some white bread. It's the only thing I can keep down these days. And some magazines. Oh, and if you're passing the video store—'

'Get some other sucker to do your donkey work. You can starve, for all I care.'

'Don't be like that. I'm not well, remember?' She grabbed his arm, but he shook it off.

'No! This ends here, Lu. I'll see myself out.'

'But Leo—'

He'd slammed the door behind him, leaving her staring in his wake. She was too cross to cry but kicked the sofa instead, making her chest hurt.

'Bloody men,' she'd muttered before collapsing on to the sofa cushions and picking up the remote control.

'Flowers for Miss Ryan,' the voice came again, this time from behind the apartment door. She swung it open and was greeted by a huge bouquet of pale pink tea roses, her favourite. Tears sprung to her eyes. Leo had obviously come round.

'Put them on the table, please,' she said.

The delivery man lowered the bouquet and she squealed.

'Dion! What the hell are you doing here? How did you get my address? Was it Leo? I'll kill him.'

'I work for Channel 7, remember? We have files.' Dion closed the door behind him, strode towards the table in the bay window and put the flowers down carefully in the centre. They stood proudly in their florist's box, making the whole room look warmer and brighter.

'Confidential files,' Lulabelle pointed out. She felt a sudden wave of exhaustion and rested her bum against the arm of the sofa.

'Are you all right?' he asked. 'You look pale.'

Of course she looked pale – she had no make-up on. She probably looked a right state. Her hair was tied back off her face with an elastic band and she was wearing an old T-shirt of Leo's and a pair of tracksuit bottoms.

'I have nothing to say to you,' she said. 'As you can see, I'm not well and you'll have to leave.' She flopped down on the sofa.

He looked around the room. He'd been surprised when the taxi had pulled up outside a house and not a glitzy apartment block. Inside it had been divided into flats – the hall table was overflowing with junk mail, and a bike with no front wheel rested against the grubby wall. The green carpet on the stairs looked newish, but nothing else did.

Lulabelle's living room was large and rectangular with a high ceiling. A circular glass table sat in front of the bay window, surrounded by four expensive-looking chairs; a small kitchenette was tucked into the far end of the room, with a breakfast bar cutting across the space. A white linen sofa heaped with dark pink and red cushions rested against the left-hand wall, facing bookshelves packed with books. Over the fireplace, a huge black and white photograph of Lulabelle pouted down.

The floor in front of the sofa was littered with used tissues, glossy magazines, DVD box-sets of *Entourage*, *Nip/Tuck* and 'Favourite Musicals'.

He picked up a box, smiling.

'*The Sound of Music*?'

Lulabelle leaned forward, grabbed the box out of his hands and threw it on to the sofa beside her.

'I need to rest before Antigua,' she snapped. 'Please leave.'

'You're sick, Lulabelle. Can't Bertram delay the next surgery until you're better?'

'It's just a minor infection, nothing serious.' She looked up at Dion. She'd forgotten how tall he was, the way he automatically pushed back his hair with his hand when it flopped over his big brown eyes.

'What do you care anyway? You can't fancy me now. Not looking like this. And it's hardly the Ritz, is it?' She waved a hand around the room. 'But it's only temporary. Sold my apartment to fund *Plastic Fantastic*. Now please, just go.' She hung her head and stared at the carpet.

'Good for you.' Dion dropped to his knees and held Lulabelle's hands. 'That's why I admire you. You're not afraid to take risks. And Lulabelle, I don't care where you live or what you're wearing, you always look beautiful to me. But it's more than that. I care about you, I want to make you happy.' He paused. 'I love you.'

She sighed. 'You don't love me. Don't you understand? I'm not the loving kind. Love only brings pain.'

'I do love you, Lulabelle. I love the way you scrunch your nose up when you're tired, I love the way you curl your body around my back in your sleep, like a cat. I even love the sadness behind those eyes.' He stroked her cheek. 'I don't want to love you, believe me. There are far less complicated girls out there. But I can't help it. It's you I want. Don't you feel anything for me?'

She shook her head slowly. 'No. It was a bit of fun, Dion, nothing more.'

He nodded silently. Then after a few seconds he said, 'In that case, I'll leave you alone. But if you change your mind . . .'

'I won't. But thank you for the flowers.'

'Can I get you anything? Food? You need to eat if you're going to get better. I'll stay if you like. Mum always asks me to eat with her when she's lost her appetite – says watching me wolf down my food helps. She's tiny, like you. A sparrow.'

Lulabelle's eyes tingled. It was such a kind offer. 'I can't ask you to do that,' she murmured.

He just smiled. 'I'll go shopping and then make you dinner. I do a mean lamb couscous.'

She had to admit that sounded wonderful. It had been a long time since a man had offered to cook for her. Leo didn't count.

'OK. But you have to leave straight afterwards, understand?'

He stood up. 'Understood. Don't go anywhere.'

Half an hour later, he rang the buzzer, arms laden down with shopping bags. Oranges to juice, lamb, couscous, peppers, spices . . .

No answer. He tried again. Nothing.

He stood back from the door and shouted up at the bay window.

'Lulabelle, can you hear me? Open the door.'

Still nothing. After more shouting he finally gave up. He scribbled a note on the back of the supermarket receipt, posted it through the letterbox, and, after one last fruitless ring of the buzzer, walked away.

Lulabelle sat on the sofa, her arms wrapped around her knees, rocking backwards and forwards. She knew if she let him in that would be it. Better to hurt a little now than a lot later. Because he'd leave her eventually. They all did.

'I need a date for the Harry Potter premiere tonight,' Lulabelle barked into her mobile the following day, standing in front of her bathroom mirror and layering her top lashes with even more mascara. 'Get on to it. Someone who looks good in a tux.'

There had been murmurings about an 'unexplained illness' in the press and she was determined to prove to everyone that she was just fine.

'Like who?' Alex asked nervously. He took his feet off his desk and grabbed a pen.

'A hot young actor or director,' she said. 'Single, obviously, and straight. Strictly no footballers. Last one wouldn't take his hands off me, ruined my silk dress. And no models.'

Alex didn't have any hot young actors on his books. He tapped his pen on his desk. But he did have . . .

'What about a writer?' he said.

'Alex, you're not listening to me. I said hot. Nerds with glasses hardly fit the job description.'

'Barn Weldon is a crime writer, very hot. Next big thing.'

'What kind of name is Barn?'

'His professional name, like Lulabelle. Short for Barnaby.'

Lulabelle didn't like Alex's tone. 'It's a stupid name.'

Alex winced. He'd come up with the name himself. Brian Weedon didn't have quite the right ring.

'He's going to be huge. Film rights sold and in development.'

'With who?'

'Excuse me?'

'Film rights. Who are they in development with?'

Alex thought for a second. It was a small Irish film company called Cappa Quinn.

'Warner Brothers. And he's ex-SAS. Tall, built like a tank.'

'Can he string two sentences together?'

'He's a writer, Lulabelle. Words are not a problem.'

'A writer like me who drives the project, or a real writer like Elizabeth?'

Alex smiled to himself. 'A real writer.'

'No, not interested. No one cares about writers. Find me an actor.' She clicked off the phone.

Alex put his head in his hands. Where the hell was he going to find someone at such short notice? He punched a name into his BlackBerry.

'Yes? What do you want?'

'That's no way to talk to your boyfriend.'

'Hello? You're not my boyfriend, Alex.'

'We're sleeping together, Celeste. In my book, that's boyfriend territory.'

'It happened once, Alex, and it's not going to happen again, believe me. Look, I have a whole heap of gory medical textbooks to get through. I shouldn't be on my mobile in the library. What do you want?'

'Maybe I'm just ringing for a chat.'

'*Alex!*' she hissed.

'OK, OK. Where do I find a hot young actor in London? Lulabelle needs a date for the Harry Potter premiere.'

'Use your nut – who gets a hot young writer a publishing deal?'

'Me. His shit-hot agent.'

'Exactly. For a smart man, you're incredibly thick sometimes.'

'Brilliant, Celeste. I owe you one. Hey, I have a meeting with Toni in Dublin on Friday afternoon. Can I buy you dinner Friday night? I could stay over.'

'Absolutely not! Fork out for a hotel, you mean bastard.'

Alex spent all afternoon ringing talent agencies, with very little success. Some of the agents' assistants were downright hostile.

'Lulabelle? I don't think so. Not the image our client wants to project.'

But at least he had one name for her – Tyler Jackson, ex-Doctor Who. He'd checked the actor's headshot out on the agency's website. He was aging a bit, grey at the temples, but he still looked presentable. He took a deep breath, then rang Lulabelle and read her Tyler Jackson's CV.

'I've never heard of him, Alex. And I'm not going to a red carpet do with an ex-anyone.' There was a pause down the line. 'Do you own a tuxedo?'

'Yes, why?'

'You'll have to accompany me.'

'Me?' Alex was flabbergasted. 'What about Leo?'

'I'll meet you in the bar at the Ritz. Seven o'clock. Don't keep me waiting.'

'But—'

The line went dead.

Alex stared at his BlackBerry. A Harry Potter premiere with Lulabelle. He knew he should be thrilled – what an opportunity. The place would be swarming with celebrities to sign up. These days you weren't a proper celebrity unless you had a tell-all biography and a ghosted novel behind you.

But he was considering flying to Ireland a day early to surprise Celeste. He weighed up his options – Lulabelle or Celeste? But it wasn't that simple. Celeste didn't want to see him, even after that amazing night they'd spent together in Paris. What was wrong with the woman? He needed Libby's help – she'd know how to crack Celeste's shell. But Libby was barely speaking to him.

He sat back in his chair. He should never have threatened her, but he'd been boxed into a corner by Patty and her demands and he'd taken it out on Libby. Bringing up all that stuff about the writing competition – God, he'd been a right shit. There must be some way he could make amends. He ran his hands through his hair. *Think!* he told himself. *Think!*

Chapter 35

Libby

'Libby, it's me. Alex is on the telly,' Celeste said into my answering machine. '*Xposé*, TV3. Some sort of movie premiere. Quick, or you'll miss him. And ring me back.'

I grabbed the remote and flicked on to TV3. Celeste was right – Alex was walking down a red carpet with Lulabelle on his arm. She was wearing a rather demure top – black lace with a high neck – and a black silk skirt with gold butterflies decorating the two over-sized pockets. One hand was in a pocket, the other clutched Alex's arm. Her hair was piled on top of her head and topped with a thick gold headband, matching her gold peep-toe heels. She looked stunning. I hated to say it, but Alex looked her equal, in an immaculately cut tuxedo in darkest navy. I squinted. And he was definitely wearing make-up.

The phone rang again and I snatched it up, praying it was Celeste and not Jeremy, who'd been plaguing me with calls.

It was. 'Hi, Cel. Hate to say it, but Alex looks amazing.'

'I know. And is he wearing guy-liner?'

I peered at the screen. 'Yep.'

One of the *Xposé* girls stopped Lulabelle by thrusting a large furry microphone in her face.

'So who's the new beau, Lulabelle?' she asked.

'My mystery man.' Lulabelle winked at the camera. 'He's the strong, silent type.'

I chuckled to myself. Lulabelle had obviously told him to keep his trap shut.

'Is that right?' the girl asked Alex, batting her eyelashes at him. 'Are you an actor? You look familiar.'

Celeste gave a squeal. 'That reporter is flirting with Alex! The cheek of her!'

The reporter put her hand on his arm. 'And I do love your suit. Matches your eyes.'

'Yuck!' I said. 'Did you hear that? And what's he doing now? Did he just—'

'Oh yes, I think Alex just passed that woman his business card. On national telly. Little fecker asked me out for dinner on Friday and everything. I'll kill him.'

'He's probably just touting for business. You know what he's like.' I stopped. 'I thought you said you'd made a mistake. That it was just a one-night fling.'

'I know, I know. I've been trying not to think about him, but talking to him earlier made my stomach squirm. It's not rational. It's my damn hormones – always get me into trouble.'

I sighed. 'Oh, Cel. How long have you felt like this?'

'Honestly? Since I first met him. He's always had a terrible effect on me.'

'But why didn't you tell me?'

'He was your agent, plus he showed less than no interest in me. And then he dumped you and he fell off the radar, back to his snake den of celebrity authors in London. But he's been ringing me, pestering me to go out with him. I don't know what to do.'

I tried to imagine Celeste and Alex together, as a couple. It made me feel uncomfortable. Celeste was my best friend; Alex was my agent. Both knew far too much about me.

'To be honest, I think you deserve better,' I said firmly.

There was silence down the line.

'Cel, are you still there?' I could tell she wasn't happy. 'Oh, sleep with him if you must, but don't come crying to me when it all goes horribly wrong.'

'Have you just given me your blessing?'

'Absolutely not. But a sober dinner date with the man might just bring you to your senses. My mobile's ringing – it's probably Jeremy. I've been avoiding him all week, so I'd better take it. Enjoy your date. I'll see you at the airport on Monday. And make sure you squeeze all the red-carpet details out of Alex.'

Chapter 36

Lulabelle

37 Crofton Grove,
Notting Hill,
London

Saturday

Dear Lulabelle,

As you won't answer your door or your mobile, this is the only way I can contact you. I rang Leo but apparently he hasn't heard from you in days. He says I shouldn't worry, that if you managed to make that film premiere you must be OK.

That's why I'm writing to you. I saw you on the news with Alex on your arm and I nearly punched the telly. So much for not being the loving kind.

Bullshit!

But why Alex? Am I not good enough for you, is that it? If Prada, Armani, and Gucci turn you on, just say the word, I'll wear them. They're only labels. Underneath the slick clothes, you know I have more to offer than he does.

I sat outside your house for an hour the other evening, hoping you'd see sense and open the door. The ice cream melted all over the place.

What the hell do you want? Why are you shutting me out like this?

I'm going to stop now. But know this – I LOVE YOU – despite all the games.
Yours always,
Dion

Lulabelle crumpled up the handwritten letter and threw it on the floor. She picked up her mobile and rang Leo's number, but it went straight to his voicemail.

'Leo? I want Dion off the Channel 7 team. Immediately. I refuse to work with him. He's unprofessional. And return my calls, for God's sake. We have to talk about Antigua.'

She threw her mobile on to the sofa beside her and stared into space. There must be some work she could do to take her mind off Dion's letter. She didn't want to deal with the ever-increasing pile of bills on her coffee table – too depressing. She looked around the room, and her eyes came to rest on the sample *Stay Beautiful* cover New Haven Books had sent her, propped against her Anne Tyler and Roddy Doyle hardbacks.

Chloe. She'd think about Chloe's story. Leo and Alex were determined to keep that damned Elizabeth woman on board, but Lulabelle wasn't so sure. Maybe she'd try writing the second book herself. How hard could it be? And fiction was much easier to control than real life. She grabbed a pen and started to scribble some plot notes on the back of the cover.

Chapter 37

Libby

When I walked in the door of my house for my pre-arranged 'serious talk' with Jeremy (I was staying at Mum and Dad's – it all seemed cleaner and less difficult that way), there was a black scowl on Jeremy's face.

'Your fancy-man has outdone himself.'

He pointed at the bouquet which was sitting in the hallway, practically blocking my entrance.

'It arrived just before you did,' he said. He looked like he was about to give it a good kick, so I stood between him and the flowers. They must have cost a fortune: roses, lilies, freesias and orchids, hand-tied and complete with a crystal vase.

I giggled, delighted, and hugged my arms against my chest. 'Wow!'

'Wow indeed. Who's it from?'

I pulled the gift card out of the small brown envelope and read it.

'I'm sorry, Libby. You remain my favourite romance writer. Much love and respect x x x'

That was it. No name. How deliciously mysterious.

I grinned. 'I have no idea.' But I knew who I hoped it was from.

He looked at me, his eyebrows raised. He clearly didn't believe me.

'You'd better move it or someone will trip over the bloody thing and hurt themselves,' he muttered.

I took the vase with me into the living room and rested it on the floor in front of the window. I sat down on the sofa and studied the card again, turning it over in my hands.

Jeremy snapped, 'Stop smiling like an idiot. Tea?'

I nodded. 'Please.'

As soon as he'd left the room, I studied the handwriting. It was large and curling – probably the girl in the flower shop's, certainly not a man's. No clue there. I hardly dared believe that Leo had sent it, but who else . . . ?

'Here.' Jeremy thrust a mug into my hands. 'Ruth-Ann had the kettle on.'

'She's here?'

'Waiting for me in the kitchen. This won't take long, will it?'

I was disgusted. 'I'm not discussing the death throes of our relationship while *she's* in the house.'

'Where's she supposed to go?'

'Don't be so obtuse, Jeremy. To her own apartment.'

'Stop throwing big words at me. I'm not in one of your writing classes, thank God.'

I refused to let him get to me. 'Obtuse is hardly a big word. Look, we have a lot to talk about – let's not start getting at each other already. I did ask you to make sure Ruth-Ann was elsewhere.'

'I forgot.'

I sighed. 'We're wasting time. Just deal with it, Jeremy.'

He stalked out of the room. I heard voices in the kitchen and then Ruth-Ann stuck her head around the door and said, 'Thanks a lot, Libby,' in a snide voice, then left the house, slamming the front door behind her and storming down the path.

We both watched her for a moment, and when she'd disappeared down the road, I sat down on the sofa and he sat down beside me, even though there were two perfectly good armchairs in the room. It made me feel uncomfortable, but I thought it churlish to ask him to move.

'Satisfied?' he asked me, a smug look on his face.

'What was all that about? That thanks a lot business? Actually, forget it, I don't want to know.' I put my mug down on the coffee table. The water was tepid.

Jeremy blew the air out of his mouth. 'So are you going to come clean about your mystery man? No one spends that amount of dosh on flowers unless they're getting their leg over.'

I wrinkled my nose up. 'Please! Not all men are such Neanderthals. It's not like that.'

'Really?'

'Jeremy, forget about the flowers – we need to talk about the house. I'll be back home soon and we have to sort out what's going to happen.'

'Why don't you just move in with your new man? Another writer, is it? Someone you met in Paris? French, is he?'

'Jeremy, stop. I don't know what you're imagining, but I was working in Paris, not smoking Gitanes in literary salons. Yes, there is someone interested, I think, but nothing's happened yet, I promise. I'm not sure why he sent the flowers or how he got my address, but I can assure you I won't be moving in with anyone, especially not him. He doesn't even live in Ireland.'

'So he is foreign?'

I picked up my mug, pretended to take a long sip, and then cupped my other hand around it, hoping he'd get off the subject.

No such luck.

'Oh, I know how these things go,' he said. 'One minute it's all amazing sex in hotels, massage oil, fancy underwear, the works; the next minute you're trapped in yet another stifling relationship with someone who wears T-shirts to bed.' He was starting to get very agitated. 'I won't have it!'

'You won't have what?'

'Him. Another man in my bed.'

'Jeremy Small, would you listen to yourself? And this isn't solving anything. I'm here to talk about selling the house.'

'Selling? Are you mad, woman? The property market is all over the place.'

'Jeremy, can we just discuss this rationally, please? I'd prefer not to get a lawyer, but if—'

'Lawyer? Libby, you don't get it, do you?' He jumped off his chair and knelt on the carpet in front of me and grabbed my hand. He startled me and I sloshed tea all over his sky-blue shirt.

'Libby!' He got up and brushed down his chest with his hand. 'I'm soaked.'

'Sorry, sorry.' I got to my feet. 'Take it off and throw it in the washing machine. If you catch it while it's still wet, it'll be fine.'

'Trying to get me naked, are you?' He gave me a half-smile.

'Don't be ridiculous. I'm just trying to save your shirt. I know it's one of your favourites.'

'No, Libby, it's *your* favourite – you bought it for me. That's why I wore it today. You always say the colour matches my eyes.'

He looked at me and, as he held my gaze, started to undo the buttons. I couldn't help but notice his chest – it was firm and muscular. He'd obviously been putting hours in at the gym. And he'd let his hair grow longer – blond curls were touching his nape, the way I liked it best.

'You're staring, Libby,' he said softly. 'Like what you see?'

I flicked my eyes upwards, mortified. I felt my cheeks redden and I stumbled over my words. 'Yes. I mean no.'

He reached forward, grabbed my hand and pressed it against his crotch. 'You still turn me on, Libby. See.'

'Jeremy!' I tried to pull my hand away, but he gripped it tightly and used his leg to trip me up, making me fall against the sofa cushions. It was a bit of an in-joke between us, his ability to trip me up and then catch me.

'I know you still want me, Libby.' He grinned down at me, his naked chest heaving.

'Get off me, you big teenager,' I said. 'It's not funny.' But then I started to smile. That was the problem with Jeremy – he could always make me laugh.

'Just one kiss, for old time's sake.' He kissed my cheek gently, his warm lips practically melting into my skin.

'No.' I turned my head away quickly, pinching a nerve. 'Ow!'

'Your writer's neck?'

He knew my neck was a weak spot, caused from slumping over my computer for long hours without a break. My physio had recommended setting a mechanical egg timer to ring every fifteen minutes so I could get up and stretch. She clearly didn't understand how writers work. Coming out of the story every fifteen minutes to do some exercises that made me look like a turtle just wasn't an option. I'd never get a book finished that way.

'Sorry.' He let go of my hand and sat up. 'I just got carried away. You look amazing, Libs. Never better. That old spark's back in your eyes and have you lost weight? You look thinner. Am I forgiven?'

To be honest, I was flattered. I had lost a couple of pounds, despite the hotel food. Must have been the stress of running around after Lulabelle. And it was the first time ever I'd had two men fighting over me. OK, maybe 'fighting' was pushing it a bit, but I hadn't felt wanted for such a long time, and all this male attention was rather refreshing.

'It never happened,' I said, straightening my new *I Love Paris* T-shirt and brushing back my hair.

'Ow.' I put my hand up to the base of my neck. It really hurt.

'Turn round and I'll rub it for you.'

Jeremy was rather good at massage. It wasn't just all the practice he got with Ruth-Ann and the other women; he'd actually done a proper physio course so that he could relax his sports clients during meetings. Jeremy was no fool – he probably got them into a happy, relaxed state so they'd agree to all kinds of things.

I was in considerable pain, so I said, 'OK, but go easy.'

I turned my back to him. He lifted the hair off the base of my neck and started to blow on the bare skin.

'Jeremy! Stop that.'

He gave a laugh and then started to knead the top knuckles of my spine with his fingers, pressing firmly yet gently against them. I relaxed back into his fingers.

'Take your top off,' he said.

I laughed. 'I'm not stupid.'

'Libby, do you want me to fix your neck or not? I have to move further down the vertebrae.'

'No funny business.'

He laughed. 'Understood.'

He helped me pull my T-shirt over my head.

'Lie down,' he said.

'Jeremy, I'm warning you.'

'I need to work on your spine. I'm not going to try anything, I promise. Do you not trust me?'

I laughed. 'You're joking, right?'

He looked miffed. 'I've changed.'

'What, overnight?' I was having none of it. 'Forget the massage, it's a bad idea. I'll manage.' I winced again – my neck was still throbbing.

'Stop being so stubborn,' he said. 'I know you're in pain. If you want to write again this week you'll have to let me help.'

I knew he was right, so, against my better judgement, I gave in. He helped me lie down on my stomach. My face was pressed into the carpet and it smelt a little musky, like old Indian take-away mixed with strong, sweet perfume.

'I'll be back in a second,' he said.

'Where are you going?' I asked, but he didn't hear me.

I heard him walk back into the room and, wordlessly, he knelt down and started to work on my neck and spine, moving his fingers up and down my back. His hands were slick with massage oil.

'It's not sore down there,' I squealed as his fingers teased my skin just above the waistband of my jeans.

'You need to relax, Libby,' he said in a smooth, calm voice. 'Close your eyes.'

As his hands worked on my neck, it felt even more painful for several minutes, and then the pain melted away and I moaned in contentment.

'That's so much better. Thanks, Jeremy.'

'Keep still,' he said. 'I've nearly finished.'

He unfastened my bra.

'Hey!' I said.

'Relax – I'm just centring your back.' His hands moved in smooth circles over my skin.

'You're on a desert island,' he said softly. 'Lying on golden sand, waves lapping the shore. Can you hear the waves?'

'Yes,' I murmured.

'The sun is kissing your skin, there's a gentle breeze and you're completely happy, utterly content.'

'Yes,' I murmured again.

The next thing I knew, he flipped me over and began to kiss me, pressing his lips against mine, gently yet firmly. My heart started to pound in my chest and suddenly I felt that familiar rush of warm, fuzzy sex hormones soaring through my veins. Before I knew what was happening, I kissed him back.

'What the hell are you doing, Jeremy?'

Jeremy jumped off me and I looked up. Ruth-Ann was staring at us. She looked upset, disgusted and shocked.

'I can explain,' he said.

I sat up. Unfortunately my bra decided to slip sideways, baring my breasts. She gave a horrified gasp and ran out the door.

I grabbed my T-shirt and threw it on, wincing as I tweaked my neck again.

'Jeremy, I'm sorry, but I can't be around you any more – you're dangerous. I'll always love you, but it's not enough. Maybe you should go after Ruth-Ann. See if you can salvage things.'

He stood in front of me. 'You love me?' he asked, ignoring all mention of Ruth-Ann.

'Of course I do, you idiot. Why do you think I've put up with your behaviour all these years? But I don't trust you. And I don't like you. Loving you isn't enough.'

He grabbed my arm. 'I was a fool to let you go, Libby. Give me one more chance, please?'

I shook his hand off. 'You didn't let me go – I threw you out, remember? And right now I'm leaving. For good.'

His face twisted up. 'You just want to be with your new boyfriend. I'm begging you, Libby, forget about him, stay with me. He'll never love you the way I do.'

I shook my head. 'You have to let me go.' I pleaded with him, my eyes swimming. 'I can't do this any more. Please, Jeremy?'

He nodded and stared at the floor again. 'You can go for now. But it's not over,' he whispered. He looked up, his eyes steely. 'You'll change your mind. You always do.'

Chapter 38

Libby

That afternoon there was a knock on Mum and Dad's front door. Dad was at the library and Mum was in the back garden, deadheading the roses. I was keeping well away from her. She refused to accept that Jeremy and I were over, and kept suggesting ways to 'mend' our relationship, as if it was an old sock that could be darned back to use.

I peered out of the living-room window, worried I'd find Jeremy standing there, invited over by Mum herself. But it was Alex, and I was in no mood for him. I gritted my teeth, then opened the window and stuck my head out.

'What the hell are you doing here?'

He swung round and gave me a wide, crocodile grin which only made me even more cross with him.

'Hi, Libby? How's tricks? Celeste gave me your parents' address. I have to talk to you.'

I made a mental note to kill Celeste later.

'No,' I said simply.

'What do you mean, no?'

'No to everything you have to say. Got it?'

I closed the window a little too vigorously, making the glass shake in the frame.

As I watched, he walked across Mum's lawn, stepped into her flowerbed and rapped on the window with a knuckle.

'Libby, I know you're in there.'

I walked into the hall.

Next thing I knew the letterbox flap lifted.

'Lulabelle told me something about her past,' he shouted in. 'About herself and Leo. I think you'll want to hear it.'

I grabbed my mum's silver letter-opener off the console table, ran towards the letterbox and poked at his fingers with its tip.

'Ow!' He pulled his hand back. 'Jesus, Libby,' he shouted. 'What's got into you? That hurt. Open the door.'

'No!' I bellowed at him. 'I'm in a very bad mood and I can't be responsible for what I might do to you.'

He gave a laugh. 'I'm prepared to risk it. Come on, Libs, I know you're dying to hear about Leo and Lulabelle.'

I ignored him, pulled my mobile out of my pocket instead and punched in Celeste's name. I walked into the kitchen so I was out of sight and earshot.

'Celeste?'

'Oh, hi, babes. Listen, Alex told me he'd sent flowers to your house and I told him you're staying with your parents. So he said he'd send more there. He seemed pretty insistent. I think he feels guilty about upsetting you in Paris. But you might want to nip over to your place—'

My heart sank. Of course the flowers weren't from Leo. I was being stupid, yet again. Leo had no interest in me. Why was it taking me so long to accept that?

'Too late.' I explained what had happened this morning.

Celeste laughed. 'So Jeremy thinks you have a new man? Good! Pity the truth's a bit less romantic.'

'Celeste, what does Alex know about Leo and Lulabelle? Please, put me out of my misery.'

'Are you OK, sweets? You sound a bit hassled.'

'Hassled?' I gave a manic laugh. 'I just kissed Jeremy, Ruth-Ann caught us at it, and Alex is standing outside my front door, yelling through my letterbox, saying he knows something about Leo and Lulabelle. What do you think? I'm cracking up. What does Alex know?'

'Jeez, Libs, you nearly took my eardrum out. Look, he was at some film thing with Lulabelle last night and she had a couple of glasses of pink champers too many and told him something about their past. But the bastard refused to tell me, said he wanted to talk to you first.'

'Think, Celeste. He must have given you some clue. Were they lovers, is that it?'

'I have no idea, honestly. You're going to have to talk to Alex. But it all sounds intriguing.'

There was a knock on the kitchen door and I saw a tall, dark shape through the security glass.

'The bloody man is at the back door now. Must have gone through the side gate. I have a good mind to ring the guards.'

Then Mum's face appeared at the window.

'Coo-ee,' she shouted through the glass. Her face looked very flushed. 'You have a visitor. A man.' She wiggled her eyebrows at me. 'Should keep Jeremy on his toes.'

'I'm on the phone, Mother,' I yelled back, pointing at my mobile.

Mum waved her fingers at me. 'Not to worry, dear. I'll keep him company. I'm sure we'll have a lovely little chat.'

'I have to go, Cel. Mum's outside with Alex. Heaven knows what she'll tell him. Or vice versa.'

Celeste sucked in her breath. 'Yikes. Ring me as soon as you find out the Lulabelle gossip. Promise?'

'Promise.'

I clicked off my mobile, and when I turned round there he was – Alex, standing in the kitchen, looking the freshly painted cream cabinets up and down.

'Nice,' he said. 'Your mum said to come on in. Lovely woman.

Said if things didn't work out with Jeremy, I might be in with a chance.' He leaned against the central island, his hands folded loosely across his chest. 'I'd love a coffee, if you're offering.'

'I'm not.' I shook my head. 'And you are not to go saying anything to my mother, understand? Just spit it out, the Leo and Lulabelle stuff, and then kindly scoot. I don't have time for all this.'

He gave a smile. 'You're not being very sociable, Libby.'

'I'm warning you, Alex – I've had a lousy day and I'm this close . . .' I put a balled fist under his chin.

He pushed my fist away. 'First you stab me with a knife—'

'Letter-opener.'

'Is that what it was? Then you threaten to punch my lights out. I'm hurt, Libby.' He paused for a second. 'Tell me how to get Celeste to fall for me and I'll tell you every delicious word.'

'I don't want you anywhere near Celeste. You're not good enough for her.'

He winced. 'You think I don't know that?' He held out his hand and started to count on his fingers. 'I've treated clients badly, I've misrepresented them, I've gone out with girls 'cause they look good on my arm. And I upset you, opening the whole writing competition can of worms when I swore I'd never mention it again. Which I won't – not to Celeste, not to anyone. You have my word.

'I admit it, I'm a shit – but that's not who I want to be any more. But I can't do it on my own.' He put his hand on his heart. 'Celeste gets me, here. She makes me want to be a better person, work harder for my clients, put down some real roots. If I don't have her, I'll turn into an even bigger prick. She's the only one strong enough to save me.'

I scoffed. 'Turn into one?'

'I'm trying to apologize here, Libby. Give me a break? Please?'

I thought for a few seconds, then said, 'OK, Mr Honest – first of all, how many times did you practise that little speech? And secondly, what happened to the German translation rights of *Different for Girls*? One minute the Germans were all over the book, next thing they said *"nein"*. Why? I want the truth, Alex.'

He bit the inside of his lip. 'It was their loss. Don't worry about it.'

'If you want my help with Celeste, answer the question.'

He blew out his breath. 'They gave me a provisional yes based on your earlier books. Then the editor read the manuscript.' He shrugged. 'There was nothing I could do.'

Realization dawned. 'She hated it?'

'No. She just didn't love it enough.'

Always the diplomat. 'And what was wrong with *His Girl Friday*?'

'Libby, this isn't very constructive—'

'Answer me.'

He sighed. 'If you insist, I'll tell you. It was baggy and meandering; and the main character was up her own ass.' He stopped for a second. 'Mary. Was that her name? Mary Smith? Even the name's tedious.'

I nodded, amazed that he'd remembered.

'There was far too much backstory and not enough action. In fact, feck all happened. It was, in short, brutal. But I did like the sister. Mina.'

'The nymphomaniac?'

He grinned. 'Yes. Now, she was fun.'

'Why didn't you tell me all this at the time?'

'I didn't want to upset you.'

I raised my eyebrows.

'OK, OK,' he said. 'The truth. I didn't want to deal with all the emotional fall-out. You were very attached to that book. Refused to take my earlier plot suggestions on board, remember? Got quite huffy about it, in fact. Thought you knew better.'

'So you sent it out to Polly. Who rejected it for you.'

'It was a cowardly thing to do, and I'm sorry. But your work with Lulabelle is back on track. The best thing you've ever done, in fact. Fantastic plot. Races along.'

'Lots of sex, you mean?' I raised an eyebrow. 'I know you, Alex. When in doubt, whip it out.'

He laughed. 'Libby, your readers' lives are generally pretty ordinary. Most people are too knackered to have much of a sex life, too broke to travel the world, stuck at home minding snotty kids or elderly parents who don't remember who they are half the time. That's why your books are so important to them. Think of all those letters and emails you get.'

'Used to get,' I said. 'They've tailed off recently.'

'And you'll get them again. In their thousands. Once you get your writing back on track. Here's the thing – your stories and your characters have to be bigger, funnier, more exciting than reality. Life can be pretty crap sometimes, and if your novels can give people a bit of time out, a bit of escapism, great.'

Something went ping in my head. 'That review,' I murmured. 'In the *Irish Standard*. "*Different for Girls* is just like watching paint dry, only less interesting."' My face dropped. 'Are all my books boring, Alex?'

He shook his head. '*Wedding Belles* and *Baby, It's You* were brilliant, but then you seemed to run out of steam. Lulabelle's book has made you try another direction. You'd never have written about the modelling world without it.'

Tears started to spill down my cheeks. 'I can't believe my books had started to send people to sleep. And I'm sorry, Alex. I know you tried to warn me, but I didn't want to hear it.'

'That's why I dumped you. To shock you out of your stupor. I always hoped you'd bounce back.'

I brushed away my tears with my knuckles. 'I hated you at the time, but I'm beginning to understand. And from now on, every page will sizzle. I'm not writing any more scenes set in kitchens. No more women moaning about the lack of single men. I'm sending my characters on exotic holidays, giving them inspirational jobs and sensational sex.'

Alex clapped. 'That's the spirit.'

'And I'll help you with Celeste,' I added. 'But you still haven't told me about Leo and Lulabelle.'

He smiled. 'I was getting to it. Leo is Lulabelle's brother. Changed his name by deed poll when he was eighteen. He's Leo Ryan.'

I felt instantly dizzy. Alex pulled out a kitchen chair and I sat down.

'Brother?' I shook my head, then gave a laugh. 'No wonder they're so close. But why didn't they just tell people? I don't understand.'

'Lulabelle thinks it's unprofessional to be represented by your brother. She said it would make her look like she couldn't afford anyone else. And you know Lulabelle – she's all about appearances.'

I grinned. 'No kidding.'

'And in the early interviews, when Leo was in Boston, she told people she was an only child. Said she didn't want anyone asking questions about Leo and why he'd left Ireland. Apparently their dad was a real bully, but even so, Leo was always trying to please him. Did a year of med school 'cause the man wanted him to, but his heart wasn't in it and he failed the exams. The old man had a fit, told Leo he was a useless bugger and if he failed the repeats he'd be out on his ear. Leo told him to fuck the repeats, he was leaving anyway. Used the money he'd got for his eighteenth to fly to Boston and hook up with his cousin. After a few years, he ended up in London.'

'Where he found Lulabelle again,' I added. 'Just like Chloe in the book. It's all starting to make sense. Thanks for telling me, Alex.'

He shrugged. 'Hey, I know you like the guy.'

'Liked. Past tense. But thanks anyway.' I nodded at the kettle. 'Fancy a coffee? There are chocolate biscuits. And then we'll talk Celeste.'

He smiled. 'Deal.'

Chapter 39

Libby

After our heart-to-heart, Alex spent three hours helping me plan a dramatic, action-filled ending to *Stay Beautiful*. By the time he left – after promising to make me the next Jilly Cooper – I was feeling rather chipper. I returned Celeste's seven increasingly impatient phone calls and broke the news about Lulabelle and Leo.

'Duh!' she said. 'Now that you say it, it's so obvious. I should have guessed. Some journalist I am.'

Now we were on our way to Antigua, leaving Ireland, Jeremy and Mum far behind us. For some bizarre reason (according to Dad she'd found the perfect mother-of-the-bride outfit and was determined to wear it, which I think had a lot to do with it), Mum seemed to think that if she nagged me enough, I'd forget all about our murky recent past, rush back into Jeremy's arms and proclaim the wedding full steam ahead. I'd tried to explain to her that it was *over*, that I'd just spent hours cancelling the cake, the dress, the cream Rolls-Royce, the hotel, the honeymoon (the Maldives) – all at great expense. Cancellation fees were no joke. But she was having none of it. The way things were going, she'd still turn up at the church on New Year's Eve, wedding or no wedding.

The clergyman, Reverend Linden, had been the most understanding of all, surprisingly.

'If you're not sure, best not to rush into anything, my dear,' he'd said. 'No matter what others might tell you. Especially family members.'

He'd given a cough. Then he'd added that Adele, my mum, had already been on to him and to pass on his regards. Lord knows what she'd said to the poor man – even saying her name made him sound twitchy.

Like the Reverend, Dad was being very understanding. 'Give your mother time,' he'd whispered over dinner while Mum's back was turned. 'She'll come round. And enjoy Antigua.' He'd winked. 'Lucky you. Where are you staying?'

'In a villa near English Harbour. Has its own pool.'

He'd smiled. 'I've always wanted to go to the Caribbean, but you know what your mother's like in the heat. Forget about all the wedding stuff and have a ball, Libby.'

Celeste peered out the aeroplane window. 'I think I see land.'

Sure enough, the clouds parted, revealing an island rising out of the turquoise ocean. I pressed the back of my skull into the headrest, scrunched my eyes shut and then opened them again.

We'd been travelling for hours – Dublin to London, London to Antigua – and I felt stiff and sweaty. Plus my neck was complaining a little. I'd scribbled in my notebook for the first two hours of the flight, spurred on by Alex's timely suggestions, which in retrospect was rather foolish. But I wanted to finish *Stay Beautiful* and start working on one of my own novels again.

Last night my mind had gone into overdrive thinking up fresh ideas. Stories about ordinary women like me who'd been plucked out of their everyday routine and thrust into an exciting new career or lifestyle. Joining and saving an ailing circus; meeting a mysterious man who turned out to be a multi-millionaire and being whisked away in his private jet; inheriting a vineyard in France and fighting with the hunky yet sullen and uncooperative wine-maker who just happened to have a dark and tragic past. Yes, some of them were a bit over the top, but at least my writer's brain had started to kick in with a vengeance. The sooner I finished *Stay Beautiful*, the better.

'Hey, girlfriend,' Celeste said in her best Caribbean reggae accent. 'We're almost there. Get ready to party.'

'Antigua, Antigua,' she started to rap, jiggling around in her seat and using her mini-champagne bottle as a microphone. 'Let's party in Antigua, with your blue, blue sea, and your hist-or-y, I really wanna see ya.'

I laughed hysterically. 'That's terrible, Cel. And people are starting to stare.'

She grinned and blew her hair out of her face. 'Who cares?'

We landed at the small airport and stepped out of the plane into the blazing sun. The warm air smelt of petrol fumes and bananas, and as we walked towards the arrivals hall I smiled to myself. The Caribbean. How exciting was that?

The hall was pretty basic, more like a giant cow shed than an airport. But nothing could dampen my good humour, even the long, noisy delay while we waited to be herded through customs and immigration, and the even longer delay to collect our luggage.

Finally we heaved our bags off the shuddering conveyor belt and walked outside. We were immediately hit by another blast of warm, fruity air.

'Lulabelle Ryan's villa?' A local man in long shorts and a black T-shirt, with dreadlocks tied back in a thick ponytail, ran up and down the edge of the crowd waving his hands. 'Hello, London flight. Anyone for Lulabelle Ryan's villa?'

Celeste nudged me. 'That's us.' She waved back at the man. 'Over here.'

After forty minutes in the car, the last part juddering and shaking over a rutted earth lane, our driver pulled up outside the gates of a large wooden chalet painted eggshell blue.

'Villa Bristo, ladies,' he said. 'Enjoy.'

'Will I open the gates for you?' Celeste asked.

He grinned. 'No, lady. The goats will escape.'

'Pet goats?' I asked, intrigued.

He laughed loudly. 'No, lady. Goats for eating.' He shrugged. 'But you probably be eating lobster. Down in English Harbour. No goat for rich ladies.'

I was about to protest that we weren't rich at all, but I stopped myself. Compared with the driver, who'd told us he lived in a shack and fished and waited tables as well as driving his uncle's cab, we probably were.

A figure waved from the outside deck of the house. I squinted and stared up. Leo. My heart skipped and I took a couple of deep breaths.

'He's here,' I murmured.

Celeste followed my gaze and then stroked my cheek with her fingers.

'I know you want to confront him about Lulabelle and everything, but not now, Libs. You're tired and you might say something you'll regret. Let's grab showers and get something to eat first.'

Leo took the wooden steps which led from the house to the stony drive two at a time and ran towards us. He was wearing plain navy board shorts, flip-flops and nothing else. My eyes were pinned to his chest – lightly tanned, toned, with a triangle of dark hair. I forced my eyes up, away from his heavenly body.

You're delusional, Libby, I told myself. *You mean nothing to him, nothing. Stop torturing yourself.*

Cel and I had talked the whole Leo/Lulabelle thing over and over, until we had covered every earthly possibility and permutation (including some unearthly alien-inspired ones), and we'd both come to the same, rational conclusion: if he hadn't told me about his relationship with Lulabelle, then he wasn't worth hanging my hat on. After my experience with Jeremy, we both agreed that when it came to men, honesty was the number-one deal-breaker.

But seeing Leo standing there, tantalizingly close, in all his manly glory, it was hard not to long for him.

Celeste nudged me with her shoulder. 'Leo asked us how our flight was.'

'Good, thanks,' I said brightly, coming out of my lust-induced stupor. 'And isn't this weather heavenly?'

Leo smiled. 'There's a swimming pool cut into the hill behind the house. One end's covered with a sun awning. Fancy a dip? I'll ask Sabrina to whip up some cocktails and we can drink while floating around on the blow-up armchairs.' He stretched his arms over his head and I got a heady whiff of fresh sweat which sent my hormones buzzing.

After tipping the driver outrageously, we walked towards the house, Leo leading the way.

'I take it from the fact that you're actually out here that you're still working for Lulabelle?' Celeste asked him.

'Alex talked me into it. Says he's happy to deal with the publishing end of things, but not her media commitments. Needs more time to concentrate on his other clients, including you, Libby. He can be quite persuasive when he wants to be.

'I hate all the plastic surgery stuff,' he continued, 'but she needs me. She pretty much begged me to come back; apologized, for a change. Properly, too. Promised that this liposuction would be the end of it.' He shrugged. 'Maybe she's finally starting to see sense.'

Celeste added, 'And of course you and Lulabelle have a special bond.'

He stared at her, but she just smiled back sweetly.

A slim black woman in jeans and a white shirt walked out of the house, drying her hands on a tea towel. She gave us a wide, toothy smile, which made her conker-brown eyes crinkle at the corners. Her hair was shaved and her head smooth and perfectly oval, like an egg. She was so beautiful I couldn't help but stare.

'Welcome to Villa Bristo,' she said. 'I'm Sabrina. You want something, you just ask, OK? Food, drinks, anything. I'll show you to your rooms. You Lulabelle's assistants, that right?'

I laughed. 'Not exactly. I'm working on a book with her, Celeste's a journalist. She's writing Lulabelle's website.'

Sabrina's brown eyes widened. 'Writers? How exciting. I love to read. You Irish, yes? You not Maeve Binchy?' she asked me. 'Or Marian Keyes?'

'No.' I laughed. 'Libby Holliday. I write as Elizabeth Adams.'

She considered this, then shook her head. 'No, sorry. Never heard of you.'

'You will,' Celeste said firmly.

After Sabrina had shown us to our room – firing us dozens of questions about Maeve and Marian as she did so – she left us to shower and change.

Celeste sat down on one of the compact single beds and ran her hand over the plain white cotton bed-cover. There was a rectangular window in the room, high up in the wall so we couldn't look out, a ceiling fan, and a small but clean en suite bathroom with a shower, complete with metal shower tray.

The beds swamped the compact space, and after hanging a few things on the hooks on the back of the door, we left the rest of our clothes in our suitcases and slid them back under the beds so we could actually close the door.

'I think we're in the servants' quarters,' Celeste said. 'But at least it's clean.'

I felt a tickle on my skin and looked down. 'Apart from the ants.' I shook my foot to get rid of the line of black dots crawling up my instep. 'Yuck.'

Celeste wrinkled her nose. 'Should we look for a hotel?'

'We'll only be here to sleep. And I for one intend to spend most of my day writing on the veranda, or floating in the swimming pool. We'll just have to find the nearest supermarket and stock up on the strongest mossie and insect sprays they have.

Alex said the island's riddled with creepy crawlies. He has a thing about them.'

'It's a pity he's not here,' Celeste said rather wistfully. 'To kill the insects, I mean,' she added quickly.

I just looked at her, a smile curling my lips.

'What?' she demanded.

'You've been talking about Alex a lot today.'

'No I haven't.' She stood up and grabbed a towel from the end of the bed. 'Can I go first in the shower?'

'Celeste! Stop avoiding the subject.'

She sat back down. 'I'm crazy about Alex, OK, but I don't want to get too involved. We both know he has quite a track record when it comes to the ladies, and I'm not prepared to be just another notch on his bed-post. It's only my hormones – it'll pass. Speaking of which, did you get a load of Leo's abs? Hubba-hubba. Not that I was looking, of course.'

I grinned. 'Of course.'

'Maybe I was a bit hasty, Libs. You could always have a bit of a holiday fling. Might do you good.'

'I thought we decided I should steer well clear of Leo Knight, or Ryan or whatever his name is? Don't go changing your mind now. I'm not strong enough to resist him on my own.' I paused. 'But what am I saying? He's not interested.'

'You're right. I think it's the sun. Turning us both into sex maniacs. Anyway, I'm off to shower in our luxury marble bathroom, darling. Toodle-ooh.'

Twenty minutes later, I slid into the pool, deliciously cool water lapping at my skin.

Leo was swimming laps in a slow, easy front crawl.

Celeste drifted towards me on a blow-up armchair, sipping a cocktail through a long straw.

'Why are you wearing a T-shirt over your swimsuit?'

'I'm just being cautious. I have very sensitive skin.' The truth was, I didn't want to expose too much bare flesh in front of Leo.

I scrambled on to a lilo and closed my eyes. 'This is bliss,' I murmured, drifting off.

A piercing voice woke me from my catnap.

'What the hell are you doing?'

I snapped open my eyes. Lulabelle was standing at the edge of the pool, hands on hips, wearing a white cotton sundress and a straw sombrero.

'You're all supposed to be working,' she continued. 'Get out of the pool.'

Leo stood up, water streaming down his face.

'No,' he said calmly. 'The girls have been travelling all day and they deserve some time off. Throw on your bikini and jump in.'

She glared at him. 'It wouldn't be good for my scars, Leo.'

'You can still sunbathe,' Celeste suggested. 'Or even just sit in the shade and have a cocktail. They're delicious.' Alex had obviously mellowed her Lulabelle-rage.

Lulabelle seemed to waver for a moment. Then she said, 'No, I have to catch up. My Facebook site is jammed with questions.'

'Lu, I'll find someone to do the web stuff for you,' Leo said. 'You shouldn't be replying to the fans yourself. You don't have time.'

'I make time,' she said. 'Like now. You guys enjoy lounging around. I'll see you later.'

'You're a workaholic, Lu,' Leo shouted at her back.

She swung around. 'One of us has to be.'

'You're pushing yourself too hard,' he added.

'Stop babying me.' She stormed off.

Celeste paddled towards me with her legs. 'Classic bossy big brother, spoilt little sister behaviour,' she whispered. 'You could confront him right now. Pretend it's just a hunch, see what he says.'

'And spoil my first day in paradise? No thanks. I'll talk to him tonight.'

But I never got the chance. Neither Lulabelle nor Leo appeared for dinner.

Celeste slid her hand over mine. 'Cheer up, babes, there's always tomorrow.'

Chapter 40

Libby

I knew I was starting to get on Lulabelle's nerves. We'd been working on the final chapters of *Stay Beautiful* for over two hours, and she still wouldn't see sense.

'I know we've been over it before, but can I just explain how I see the book ending?' I said patiently. 'Please?'

'If you must.' Lulabelle sat back in her chair and stared out of the window at the goats.

'I'm listening,' she added, after I gave a short cough.

I began. 'Chloe has entered the competition and makes it to the final, against all odds. Then all the models have a cat-fight.'

'Except Chloe.'

'Except Chloe.' I'd wanted to make her fight too – far more fun – but Lulabelle wouldn't have it.

Lulabelle pressed her fingers against her eyelids. 'Yes, yes. Continue.'

'Then we have the scene that you're not happy with. Where she meets an ordinary guy in a café. A sweet, funny guy who doesn't watch reality shows and has no idea who she is. She spills her coffee down his leg and he's very nice about it. They get talking and he asks her out.'

'And I keep telling you, Chloe doesn't need a boyfriend. She's completely self-sufficient.'

'Everyone needs someone. And our readers will expect a love interest.'

She sighed. 'Why, exactly?'

'I know it's old-fashioned, but most women want a Cinderella ending. It's escapism, not real life. Look, we're not writing literary fiction here, we need a happy ending and that's that.' I sat back and crossed my arms in front of my chest.

Lulabelle sniffed. 'I think winning the competition and having a fabulous modelling career is enough.'

'But she's still alone. Chloe needs someone to share her happiness with. She has to let someone in. Someone she's not related to.'

'Related to? What are you talking about?' She stared at me.

'Metaphorically speaking,' I said quickly. 'I mean Liam. If you won't let her end up with Liam, who is her natural soulmate if you ask me, we'll have to introduce another man instead.'

'No! I won't have it.'

I gritted my teeth and then said, 'The book's not going to work unless Chloe ends up with someone decent. Can't you see that?'

'No! The last scene will be the final of the competition. Chloe wins. She's happy. The End.'

Lulabelle was starting to sound very grumpy and I didn't want to push her too far. But I also knew from experience that our readers would not be satisfied unless there was at least a whiff of a man on the horizon for the heroine.

'I see.' I blew out my breath. 'We're obviously not going to reach a consensus today.'

'So what do we do now?' she asked.

'Work on another scene instead and talk about the ending again after your surgery.'

Lulabelle gave me a look. 'You think you can change my mind about the man thing, don't you?'

I said nothing. Instead I stared down at my notebook and read back some of my notes. Turning the page, I found a folded sheet of paper. Ah yes, I'd almost forgotten the rather strange note Lulabelle had pushed under my bedroom door during dinner last night.

I held up the note. 'We need to talk about the final flashback scene and your new suggestion.'

She nodded curtly but said nothing. So I continued.

'Originally we had Chloe's father having a heart attack,' I said. 'You suggested that we change that to a suicide – an overdose. And you also suggested that Chloe finds the body.'

'That's right. But there's no need to discuss it further. Just write it in.'

I put my notebook down and looked at her, trying to keep myself in check. 'It doesn't work like that. If you want to go with the suicide thing – and I hate to say it, because it's a lot of extra work for me, but I think it's actually very clever – I'll have to go back through the whole book and weave it in. Discovering your dead father's body would have a huge impact on anyone, especially someone sensitive like Chloe. We can't just throw it into the plot. It has to be worked in from the very beginning.'

Lulabelle bit her lower lip, then said, 'What if her dad shot himself in front of her? How would that affect her?'

I thought about it for a second. 'It's a bit CSI. We're not writing a crime novel. And it's hardly realistic.'

'It happened to an old school friend of my mum's,' Lulabelle protested.

'Just because it happened in real life doesn't mean it will ring true in a book. No, I think it's too much.' I tapped my pen against my teeth. 'But I do like the whole finding-the-body thing. It explains a lot about Chloe.'

'What do you mean?'

'Why she's so driven, yet so fragile underneath.' I paused. I knew I was taking a huge risk here, but something made me continue regardless. Maybe it was my irritation at the way she was trying to control the ending of *Stay Beautiful*. Perhaps it was sheer wilfulness. I don't know.

'Why she craves attention,' I continued, 'wants everyone to love her, even complete strangers, but won't let anyone get truly close. I think she's afraid to love and be loved.'

I think Lulabelle would have frowned if her forehead wasn't frozen. Instead her eyes went cold.

'Is that how you see Chloe?' she asked.

'From how you've described her, and what I know of her, yes. Look, all I'm saying is you can't throw random bits of other people's real lives into Chloe's story and expect it to work. It has to make sense.' I tut-tutted. 'I wish I had more time to research all this – what Chloe would feel like the moment she found the body. What dead people look like . . .'

'You've never seen a dead body?'

I shook my head. 'A dead dog, yes. A dead human, no.'

She gave a derisive laugh. 'God, you've lived such a sheltered life.'

I looked at her in surprise. 'How many dead people have you seen?'

'Two. My granny and . . . and someone else.'

'Excellent.' I grabbed my pen and turned to a fresh page in my notebook. 'What do they look like, then? Skin colour, that kind of thing?'

I caught her eye.

'Sorry, I don't mean to be insensitive, but it would be really helpful for the book.'

'I understand.' She flicked her eyes out of the window again and shifted a little in her seat. 'Small. They look small. And peaceful. But their body is just a shell – they've completely lost their essence. Their soul I suppose you'd call it if you were religious.'

'Tell me more,' I said, scribbling away. 'How did you feel when you saw the bodies?'

'In my granny's case, I felt sad but also relieved for her. She was old, in her nineties, and she'd been sick. In fact she looked younger – her skin had collapsed against her skull and her wrinkles had smoothed away.'

'Like she'd been Botoxed?'

Lulabelle stared at me. 'That's sick! Ninety-year-olds don't get Botoxed.'

'Some of them do. Celeste found all kinds of weird cases on the internet. Anyway, I digress. Tell me about the other dead person. Was that a family member too?'

Lulabelle stared at me. 'Must you be so flippant?'

'You're right, I should have more respect. I apologize. My curiosity gets the better of me at times. Do you want to stop? I have loads here to be getting on with.' I tapped my notebook with my pen. 'If you're tired—'

She shook her head. Her face was pale and she seemed agitated, but she waved me silent with her hand.

'Yes, he was family,' she said softly. 'Younger than granny – fifties, so it was more of a shock. His jaw had dropped open and he looked like something from a horror film.'

'How did you *feel*?' I asked again.

She gave a shiver. 'Terrified at first, then numb. Then angry.' Her eyes glazed over a little and she turned her head to stare out of the window again.

'Angry?' I asked, fascinated.

'At what he'd done.' Her voice was strangely distant. 'He must have known I'd find him. It was a Saturday. Mum was out, some sort of bridge tournament in Wexford, asked me to fix him something to eat. Brady's ham, potato salad, coleslaw – funny the things you remember. Anyway, I knew he was going to complain bitterly about having to eat a cold lunch, but I was supposed to be studying for my summer exams, so any distraction was good.

'I knocked on his study door at one on the dot to tell him his food was on the table – he was fussy that way – but there was no answer, so I walked in. And there he was, slumped over his desk. I tried to rouse him, but I couldn't. There was all this white foam coming out of his mouth, and his eyes—' She stopped abruptly.

I realized I'd been practically holding my breath, so I took a gulp of air. I looked at Lulabelle, but she was still staring out of the window. I stayed quiet, too shocked and mesmerized to say anything.

'I can't remember much after that,' she continued in the same trance-like voice. 'I could have been there for minutes or hours. I have no idea. At some stage Mum came in and screamed. I remember that. She must have called an ambulance – medics certainly arrived. And then the Guards. Someone took Daddy away. I never saw him again. Closed coffin, you see. Mum couldn't bear to look at him. Hated him for what he'd done to her.' She sniffed. 'To *her*. She wasn't the one who'd found him.'

I stared at her. I remembered what Leo had said – that Lulabelle was only fifteen when her father died. Poor Lulabelle. How did you get over something like that? I began to understand why Leo was so protective of her, and why he put up with so much of her demanding behaviour. If my timing was right, he'd been in Boston when this had happened to his little sister. Poor man must be riddled with guilt.

'I'm so sorry,' I whispered. I reached over the desk for her hand, but she ignored my gesture, got up and stood facing the window.

'I do like those goats,' she murmured, holding the side of the window frame. 'They seem very content, just eating and dozing in the sun.' She paused, rubbing a smear on the glass with the tip of a finger. 'I'm sure you have plenty of gory detail for the book now, Elizabeth. Please see yourself out.'

I was flabbergasted. 'But Lulabelle—'

'You heard me – get out!'

'No. I'm not leaving you like this. You're upset and it's all my fault.' I walked towards her. 'I'm so sorry for talking about dead bodies like that—'

She swung round and screamed 'Shut up!' at me. Her eyes were wide and fixed. She put her hands over her ears.

'Shut up, shut up, shut up!'

She started slapping my chest and shouting, 'I hate you, I hate you, I hate you,' over and over again.

The door swung open.

'Lu!' Leo rushed in and pulled her off me. 'What's going on?'

'No! I can't, I won't . . .' Lulabelle collapsed into Leo's arms, her eyes flooding with tears.

Leo looked at me, horror in his eyes. 'Libby, what happened?'

'I'm so sorry,' I murmured, and ran out of the door.

Chapter 41

Lulabelle

Leo grabbed his sister's wrists. 'You can't, Lu. Your system is still in shock. And you promised me – no more general anaesthetics, just the liposuction.'

'Sculpture.' She pulled her arms away, walked over to her bedside table, picked up her Valentino sunglasses case and checked inside. Nothing. She rummaged around in her handbag without success, then muttered, 'Where are the fucking things?'

'On your head,' Leo said.

She patted her crown, gave a nod, 'Thanks,' then sat down on the side of the bed.

'We both know I have to do this,' she said calmly. 'And then no more for a while, I promise.'

'For a while? You're perfect, Lu. You were perfect before all the surgery. You tricked me into coming over here – admit it.'

She sighed. 'And you call *me* a drama queen? Look, are you coming with me today or not? I could do with the support.'

'No. I don't want any part of it. I should have put a stop to this madness a long time ago. I'm flying back to London on the first plane I can get, flashbacks or no flashbacks. Where's Libby?'

'Why? Finally plucked up the courage to tell your little girl-friend about us, is that it?'

'You can be such a bitch, Lu. I should have told her ages ago, but to be honest I wanted to give you both time to get to know each other better. Thought you might warm to each other.' He laughed. 'What a joke. I'm not surprised she sees right through you. And yes, I'm going to try and salvage something. Convince her we're not having some sort of sordid affair.'

Lulabelle threw her head back and hooted with laughter. 'Affair? That's hilarious.'

'I'm glad you think so. Goodbye, Lu. Take care of yourself.'

'Don't be such a baby, Leo. Look, I'm sorry for teasing you about Elizabeth, but you don't honestly like her that much, do you? With that ridiculous hair and . . . and . . . all that cellulite?'

He stormed out. She followed him into his bedroom, where he was stuffing his clothes into his travel bag.

'Leo, come on. I'm sorry.'

He looked her in the eye. 'Will you cancel the operations, stick to the liposuction?'

'I can't. *Plastic Fantastic* depends on it.'

He threw his bag over his shoulder and strode past her, knocking into her shoulder.

'Ow, that hurt! I'm in recovery, remember?'

He swung round. 'For the last time, where's Libby?'

'With Celeste. They went to English Harbour. Said they were doing research, but I heard Celeste say something about shopping.'

'I'll find her. Now keep away from me, Lu.'

He asked Sabrina to order him a taxi and sat on the veranda to wait. A few minutes later a car pulled up and a tall, blond man stepped out of the passenger seat.

'This Villa Bristo?' the man shouted up.

Leo looked him up and down. In a cream linen suit, he was far too well dressed to be a paparazzi or reporter, but you never could tell.

'Who are you looking for?' Leo asked.

'Libby Holliday. I'm her fiancé.'

Leo said nothing for a moment, his mind numb. Finally he managed, 'She's out.'

The man smiled. 'But she's staying here?'

Leo nodded.

The man rubbed his hands together. 'Excellent. I'll try again later. Don't say a thing – she's not expecting me and I want it to be a surprise. Need a ride? I'm going to St John's.'

Leo made a decision. 'Thanks, but the airport's the other way.'

The following morning, Lulabelle shivered. She knew it was irrational but she had a bad feeling about this surgery, and Leo's huffy departure hadn't helped. She'd presumed he was only bluffing about flying back to London, but Sabrina said he'd taken a taxi to the airport, so now she was on this bloody island pretty much alone.

She stood up again and walked towards the open window. Voices carried on the wind – women's laughter and the clink of ice against glass. She strained her ears. It sounded like Libby and Celeste. For some reason this upset and irritated her in equal measure.

She had a thought. She checked her make-up, lowered her sunglasses over her eyes, dropped a floppy brimmed sunhat on her head and went outside.

'Celeste?'

Celeste sat up, spilling her pineapple cocktail down the front of her white T-shirt. She brushed the liquid off.

'You gave me a fright, Lulabelle.'

Lulabelle peered through her dark lenses. 'I'm visiting Mr Avalon this afternoon and I'm sure you need to interview him for my website. You can come with me.'

'Actually I've already spoken to his secretary. I've arranged to talk to him tomorrow.'

'He's expecting us. Be ready in ten minutes. And you'll need to change into something smarter. And clean.' She looked down her nose at Celeste's denim shorts.

'How are you feeling today, Lulabelle?' Libby asked, her voice quivering a little.

'What do you care?' Lulabelle said. 'And you're supposed to be working.'

With that she tripped off in her highest strappy sandals, almost crippling herself when one of the heels got stuck between the wooden slats of the veranda's floor. Luckily she was out of sight of Libby and Celeste.

'Libby's worried about you, Lulabelle,' Celeste said as soon as their taxi pulled out. 'She said you freaked out yesterday.'

'I did nothing of the sort, and that was bloody indiscreet of her,' Lulabelle snapped. 'And if there's so much as a sniff of anything in the press, I'll sue you, understand?'

Celeste bristled. 'Whatever it was, she's still pretty shaken. She refused to tell me what happened – she's annoyingly loyal to you for some ungodly reason – but she's worried about you. She explained that sometimes writing can trigger things from your past, painful things. And I don't work for the gutter press, Lulabelle. I'm a columnist. A columnist who happens to be writing some damn fine website content about all your crazed plastic surgery.'

'What do you mean crazed?'

Celeste waved a hand up and down Lulabelle's body. 'Look at you, for God's sake. You're stunning. Why the hell you keep shaving bits off your body I don't know. And as for this liposuction thing—'

'Liposculpture. And cut the lecture, Celeste. I've already had one from Alex this morning.'

'You were talking to Alex?'

'Yes. He is my agent and I wanted to complain about Libby. Her research techniques are most unprofessional.'

'Stop acting like a spoilt bitch. You don't deserve Libby's loyalty and you were extremely rude to her on the veranda. I think you should apologize.'

Lulabelle gave a snide little laugh. 'Like that's going to happen.'

'Grow up. You have poor Dion moping around the place like a kicked puppy, and your brother—' She stopped abruptly.

'*What?*' Lulabelle shrieked. '*How the hell*—? Who told you? Leo?'

'I'm not saying.'

'And you're calling me childish? Answer me!'

'No. And before you ask, no one knows apart from me and Libby.'

'Libby? Are you sure?'

'Positive. She was going to confront him about it—'

'But he's gone back to London, and once this damn book is finished she's unlikely to see him again. So keep it to yourself or you'll have my lawyers to deal with. No leaks, understand? Or I'll sue your sorry ass. And now stop talking to me. I have a blinding headache. Not another word until we get there.'

Lulabelle stared at the doctor. Mr Avalon wasn't at all what she'd expected. He was far older, for a start – at least sixty. His salt and pepper hair was cropped short and he had a matching beard and twinkling brown eyes. If it wasn't for his olive skin, he'd be a ringer for George Clooney.

'Ladies,' he said warmly, his arms outstretched. 'Welcome to my office. Make yourselves comfortable. And please call me Raul.'

Lulabelle studied the two orange plastic chairs which sat in front of the simple wooden desk and waited.

'Yes, yes,' he said, gesturing at the chairs. 'Right there.'

Celeste sat down and pulled her notebook and a pen out of her handbag. Lulabelle followed her a little reluctantly, worried that the seat of the chair might mark her white jeans. It looked clean enough, but you could never tell with plastic.

As Raul stepped outside for a moment, Celeste whispered, 'Now this looks more like the doctors' surgeries I'm used to.' She sniffed. 'Even smells properly medical – bleach and sweat.'

Lulabelle looked around the walls. 'Where's the art?' All she could see were framed certificates and photographs. 'They can't all be his children and grandchildren, surely?'

Raul walked back in the door and shut it firmly behind him. 'I see you've noticed my pictures.'

He tapped the photograph of a smiling boy with curly brown hair and a sweet button nose. He couldn't have been more than three or four.

'One of my first hare-lip patients. Little Remo. If you look very carefully, you can just make out the slight scar under his right nostril. That was taken a few months after his operation. The scar's barely noticeable these days.'

'Are they all your patients?' Celeste asked, waving at the walls.

'Every one.' He picked up a wooden picture frame from his desk. 'But this is my wife, Pilar, and our four granddaughters. Beautiful, no?'

Lulabelle studied the photograph – a woman with blue eyes and dark blonde hair smiled back at her. She was walking on a beach, three little girls surrounding her, one in her arms, all laughing. She had a lopsided smile, deep marionette lines and was a good size sixteen.

'Yes,' Celeste said.

Lulabelle kept her mouth shut.

'Now, my dear.' Raul sat down behind the desk, put his tanned arms on the table and templed his fingers. 'You are thinking of sculpting your torso, removing some of your fat, is that correct?' he asked Celeste.

Celeste gave a laugh. 'I probably should be, but no, it's Lulabelle here beside me you should be talking to. I'm Celeste O'Connor. I'm updating Lulabelle's website to tie in with the telly series. You know all about that, I presume?'

He smiled. 'Humble apologies. My mistake. And yes, I've been speaking to Bertram many times.' He gave a hearty laugh. '*Plastic Fantastic*. Great name.'

He turned to Lulabelle. 'Why liposuction?'

'Liposculpture,' she corrected him. 'I'd also like you to make my belly button more oval-shaped. It's too round.'

'I can do that,' he murmured, making some notes. He looked up. 'But back to the liposuction. And whatever you call it, it's still sucking away fat. You are a slim woman, a size what? European eight to ten?'

'Eight,' she said firmly.

'So I ask again, why liposuction?' He waved his hand down her body. 'I see no fat.'

She looked at him in surprise. She wasn't sure she liked his tone. She much preferred the word sculpture to suction – it sounded far more refined, less medical. And none of the previous doctors had asked her why she wanted a procedure. The psychologists, yes, but that was their job, to make sure you didn't have unrealistic expectations about the surgery. They always asked, 'How do you think plastic surgery will change your life?' And she always gave the same reply.

So she gave Raul her stock answer. 'I think it will make me more confident about my body, less self-conscious. It won't make me happy, I know that. Happiness comes from within.'

And when he didn't respond, she added, 'Look, I lost a lot of weight in my late teens and the skin on my stomach has always been loose and it seems to be getting worse. Exercise doesn't seem to help. So I'd also like a tummy tuck.'

Celeste cocked an eyebrow at her and Lulabelle glared back.

'I exercise,' she said defensively. 'All the time. In private.'

'Any children, Lulabelle?' Raul said, stepping in.

'No. But I would like a baby in the future.'

'I see. Abdominoplasty is a serious operation. I'll talk you through the various stages and then you can decide if it's really for you.'

Doesn't this man want my money? Lulabelle thought crossly before remembering that, according to the Channel 7 terms, he wasn't actually getting a penny.

'There really is no need. And I think Celeste has some questions.'

'Which I'll be happy to answer in a moment.'

Raul gave Celeste a smile.

'Now Lulabelle, are you nervous about the surgery, about having a general anaesthetic? About recovery after the operation? I believe you had problems recently—'

'I guess Bertram told you about the surgery in Paris, right? I had a slight infection, nothing serious. I'm perfectly fit now.'

'Are you on any medication?'

'No.'

'And you feel well?'

'Perfectly. Can we just get on with this, please?' she said curtly.

Celeste coughed.

Lulabelle glared at Celeste. The damn woman was even more annoying than Elizabeth. She didn't know why she'd bothered bringing her along in the first place. Unfortunately the doctor's receptionist had insisted. 'Mr Avalon likes all his patients to have support during the consultations and after surgery,' the woman had said. 'And it's not optional.'

Raul looked at Lulabelle. 'Let me make myself very clear, Lulabelle. A tummy tuck is a very serious operation. I will explain: once you are under general anaesthetic, I cut down from the belly button to just above the pubic bone and part the adjacent skin, like a curtain.'

Celeste shivered. Lulabelle felt like joining her. No other surgeon had been quite so graphic.

'I loosen the skin up to the ribs,' he continued. 'Then I lace up the stomach muscles with interrupted sutures – basically a chain of stitches. I pull down the skin and anchor it at the pubic hairline and put in drains.'

Raul tilted his head and looked Lulabelle in the eye. 'Now, my dear, are you sure you want to go ahead with the surgery?'

She sniffed. 'Anyone would think you're trying to put me off. But I don't scare easily.'

'I can see that. I just want to make absolutely sure you know what you're getting yourself into. Plastic surgery is a serious business.'

'Believe me, I know.'

He sat back in his chair. 'How many surgeries have you had, Lulabelle?'

'In the last year?'

'Ever.'

'Mr Avalon, Raul, I'm a model – my job is to look beautiful.'

'Define beautiful.'

'What?' Lulabelle was confused. Was this a trick question? 'I don't know. Someone who looks perfect – perfect body, perfect skin, perfect hair, perfect teeth, perfect everything.'

Raul tapped his fingertips together. 'Interesting. Karl Lagerfeld once said, "There is no beauty without strangeness." I happen to agree with him. When you look into a woman's eyes and see a good heart, to me, that's true beauty.'

'I thought you meant physical beauty,' Lulabelle said stiffly. 'Inner beauty is a different matter.'

'Do you feel beautiful inside, Lulabelle?' Raul's eyes were gentle.

'Oh, for heaven's sake, I don't have that body dismorphic thing – I know that's what you're implying. But there are things I want to improve, things that will give me the edge in the modelling world. Is that so bad?'

He smiled gently. 'No, my dear. As long as you are in control of what you are doing. And as long as your body can take it. I understand that for you, surgery is a means to an end. A way of boosting your career and your celebrity. Especially with this television show. And you have every right to do that. It's your body.'

He stopped for a moment and picked up the photo frame.

'My daughters are now in their twenties, Lulabelle. After the first was born I felt such a surge of love, pure love, I swore to myself that from that day on, if I was to continue as a plastic surgeon, I'd look after every patient like one of my children. Before that, of course, there was the fire, which made me set up the clinic in the first place, but that's not important right now.'

'I was hoping to talk to you about the Angels' Clinic later,' Celeste said. 'After you've finished with Lulabelle. Would that be OK?'

He smiled at her. 'Of course, my dear. Why do you think I'm doing the television show? It's hardly for the fame.' He laughed. 'That has no appeal. But media attention for my clinic – that interests me very much. Makes raising funds so much easier. Bertram has promised that this *Plastic Fantastic* will be shown all over the world. Is that correct?'

'I believe so,' Celeste said.

'What are you talking about?' Lulabelle interrupted. 'What clinic?'

Raul leaned forward and clasped his hands together. 'I run a clinic in São Paulo – the Angels' Clinic. We operate on children with deformities: burns, harelips, tumours. But do not bother yourself with it, my dear. Just concentrate on your surgery.'

Lulabelle got the feeling she was being slighted.

'Tell me about the clinic,' she said. 'I'm interested too.' She gave Celeste a look. Why hadn't the bloody woman told her about this clinic thing?

Raul shrugged, then smiled. 'You want the whole story, I tell you the whole story.'

He pointed at an old sepia photograph on the wall. A dark-haired woman in a plain black dress sat holding a baby on her knee, a small boy in a white shirt and shorts standing by her side.

'This is me, my mother and my little brother, José. We lived in a favela – a shanty town – near Heliopolis. There was a gas explosion, a great fire. They died. I managed to get out. I was five.'

Celeste gasped.

'How terrible,' Lulabelle murmured.

'Yes.' Raul sighed. 'But I was lucky. A friend of my mother's took me in, Helena. She was a teacher. Brought me to school with her every day. I worked hard and won a scholarship to college, studied to be a surgeon, to make her proud. Met my wife in college. Like Helena, Pilar is a teacher.'

He stopped for a moment, picked up his pen and tapped it lightly on the desk.

'There was another terrible fire in 1982, same favela. Nearly three hundred people died. Children were wandering the streets screaming, their skin burning. As soon as I saw the pictures on the news, I knew I had to do something. At that stage I was running my own plastic surgery consultancy in São Paulo.'

He gave a smile.

'It was Brazil. Beach heaven. Plenty of demand. Many of the best surgeons in my year went into aesthetics. But that day I cancelled all my surgeries and drove to the hospital, explained who I was and what I wanted to do. They thought I was insane, but they were desperate – they let me take some of the children back to my clinic. I worked for four days and four nights solid.

Those poor children – the pain.' His face collapsed and he shook his head. 'Some of them died in my arms. But many of them survived. Over there, that is my Heliopolis wall.'

He waved his hand at a collection of photographs. A couple of the children had strangely smooth, pink faces, many were badly scarred, and one girl had only one hand, but all were smiling.

'Any one of those children could have been me. I knew what I had to do. So with Pilar's blessing I set up the Angels' Clinic. I work here in Antigua, so I can help the little ones back in Brazil.'

'Why not do your plastic surgery in Brazil?' Celeste asked. 'Wouldn't that be simpler?'

'Here I can charge three times as much for the same procedures. I work the main tourist season in Antigua, then fly back and devote my time to the clinic.' He shrugged. 'Suits me and my family best.'

'You deal with very, um, different patients in both clinics,' Celeste said. 'How do you cope with that?'

Lulabelle looked at her, but Celeste was avoiding her gaze.

Raul sighed. 'All my patients are in pain in one way or another. For some it is physical pain, for others it is mental suffering or anguish. Both just want to be happy. Which brings me back to Lulabelle's surgery. We will talk more about the clinic later, yes?'

Celeste nodded.

Raul turned his gaze to Lulabelle. 'Now, my dear, I must tell you I am happy to do the belly button surgery, but you do not need either liposuction or a tummy tuck, and no reputable surgeon would go ahead with those procedures. I most certainly will not.'

'What?' Lulabelle sat back in her seat. She was completely shocked. 'I don't understand. You told Bertram you could do all three.'

'No, I told him in theory I could do all three, but in practice I wanted to have this consultation to confirm that you needed the operations. Lulabelle, you do not have enough body fat to warrant liposuction, and doing an abdominoplasty on someone so young, someone who has not yet had children, would not be medically recommended. I am sorry, but it's your belly button or nothing.'

Chapter 42

Libby

'I'm telling you, Libs, Raul Avalon was extraordinary,' Celeste gushed, collapsing in a heap on the white linen sofa in the living room at Villa Bristo. 'Like an evangelical preacher of the plastic surgery world. Get this – he only does it so he can operate on disfigured children in Brazil. And he refused to give Lulabelle liposuction or a tummy tuck. Said she didn't need them. She was disgusted.'

'Slow down there, Cel.' I was still addled from Sabrina's news: that Leo had flown back to London without so much as a goodbye. And that a strange blond man had been looking for me, but had refused to leave his name. It could only be Alex.

I sat down on the wicker armchair opposite Celeste, feeling rather despondent. The French windows were open to the veranda, and the huge, creaking Colonial fan wafted air around the room.

'And you should have seen him,' she went on. 'A real silver-haired fox. I wish you'd been there.'

I heard the roar of a car engine outside and looked out through the French windows. A familiar figure climbed out of the front seat.

'What's wrong?' Celeste asked me. 'You look like you're about to pass out.'

I was speechless. All I could do was point.

'Jesus H. Christ. What the hell is *he* doing here?' Celeste strode outside and leaned over the banister of the veranda. I followed her.

Jeremy appeared in front of us, in a cream linen suit, complete with straw Panama hat. He should have looked ridiculous, but with his toned body and light tan, he got away with it.

Jeremy beamed. 'It's so good to see you, Libby-Lu.'

'Don't you Libby-Lu her,' Celeste snapped. 'And you can wipe that grin off your face. You are *persona non grata* on these premises. On this island, in fact. Go on, get.' She hiked her thumb towards the steps.

'Nice to see you too, Celeste, but I'm here to talk to my fiancée. And to give her this.' Jeremy handed me a long turquoise box wrapped in a white satin ribbon. He knew I was a pushover for Tiffany's. 'Anniversary present. Little late, I'm afraid, but I hope it makes up for it.'

I opened the box. An old-fashioned key encrusted with diamonds nestled against the velvet, a delicate chain threaded through the top.

'It's white gold,' he said. 'Do you like it?'

I just nodded, touching the chain with my fingers. It was beautiful.

Celeste looked at me, confusion and hurt all over her face. 'What's going on here, Libby? You told me it was over, that you never wanted to see him again.'

'I know,' I murmured. I was finding it hard to talk; I think I was still in shock at Jeremy appearing out of the blue, and at the uncharacteristically lavish present.

He laughed gently. 'But you didn't mean it, Libs. Did you?' He stroked the side of my face with his hand. 'We belong together.'

'Get your paws off her.' Celeste hit his hand away. 'And if you think you're staying here, you're delusional.'

Jeremy just laughed. 'Always the little tiger, Celeste. Actually

I've booked a boutique hotel called Ocean Paradise. Honeymoon suite. Libby, go and get your things.'

I stared at him. 'What?'

'You're coming with me.'

'Jeremy, I have to work,' I protested. 'I can't just flounce off to a resort.'

'Just for one night. Please? At the very least it will give us a chance to talk – properly.'

'I need some water,' I murmured, trying to buy some time. I ran into the kitchen, pulled a bottle of water out of the fridge and stood there for several minutes, sipping, trying to collect myself.

When I went back outside, Celeste had disappeared and Jeremy was chatting to Lulabelle, who was lying on a sun-lounger on the veranda in a white crochet bikini, her breasts straining at the flimsy material.

'There you are, darling,' Jeremy said. 'Lulabelle was just filling me in on the book. Sounds fascinating. I hadn't realized she was doing so much of the work. Must be a doddle for you, just joining up the dots, so to speak.' He was sitting on the side of her lounger, looking cosy.

I looked at Lulabelle, but it was hard to read her expression behind her oversized sunglasses.

'Oh yes, she's a regular James Joyce,' I said dryly.

'And your fiancé's such a pet,' Lulabelle purred, stroking his arm.

'Ex-fiancé,' I said.

'I do hope you get over your little lover's tiff,' she said. 'He's a real catch.'

Jeremy grinned at her. He was clearly besotted, stupid man. 'Thank you, Lulabelle,' he said.

'I hear you're off to Ocean Paradise, Elizabeth.' She stood up. 'I guess I'll see you the day after tomorrow for my surgery. I'll expect you to be there, and please remind Celeste.'

She bent over to pick her magazine up off the ground, but her heel caught in the veranda's floor and she fell on top of Jeremy, her chest pressed against his face.

'So sorry,' she tittered.

'My pleasure,' he said, helping her to her feet again. 'And good luck with the surgery – not that you need it.'

'You are a darling.' Lulabelle leant over and kissed him on both cheeks, and then once again for luck. The bloody woman was pressing her breasts into his chest, I could swear it.

After Lulabelle had left, Jeremy said, 'Ever considered it, Libby?'

'Considered what?'

'Getting a bit of work done. Your boobs could do with a little help. I'd be happy to pay for it.'

I stared at him with my mouth open. 'Jeremy Small, I can't believe—'

'Phone for you.' Sabrina walked towards me, mobile house phone in her outstretched hand. 'He says it's important.'

'Hello?' I said.

'Libby, it's Alex. There have been some developments. Miramax and Warner are both showing considerable interest in the *Stay Beautiful* film rights. I need a detailed synopsis, outlines of the main characters, and as much of the book as you can send me. And I need it yesterday.'

'Alex, in case you've forgotten, the book hasn't been edited yet and I'm in Antigua.' I felt like adding, 'And Jeremy has just turned up looking like a movie star, bearing gifts and offering to pay for a boob job,' but I stopped myself.

'I know, babes. And I wouldn't ask unless it was urgent. If this film deal comes off, you and I will be Richie Rich. If I can get it to auction, there's no telling how high they'll go for film rights.'

'Does Lulabelle know about all this?'

'I'm not sure. I left several messages on Leo's phone, so I presume he's told her.'

'Leo's gone. Flew back to London.'

'Why?'

'No idea. He didn't bother telling anyone.' I tried not to sound bitter.

'Not like Leo. Anyway, probably best if you don't mention it, in that case, babes. She's a funny one. Might not like to hear it from someone unofficial.'

'Someone beneath her, you mean? Like her slave girl?'

He laughed. 'So when can you email me the stuff, babes?'

I sighed. 'I'll get cracking straight away. There's been a plot development. I have to change some of the earlier chapters so the later ones make sense.'

'But you're nearly finished, right?'

'Yes, I sincerely hope so. I'll get it to you as soon as I can. Tomorrow evening OK?'

'You're a star. I love you.'

'Yeah, yeah. Talk to you later, Alex.' I clicked off the phone.

'Bad news?' Jeremy asked.

I nodded. 'Alex is working on a film deal for the book.'

'That's fantastic. Ching-ching.' He rubbed his fingers together.

'I'll be chained to my desk till tomorrow night at the earliest.'

'You're worth waiting for.' He stepped towards me and stroked my hair. 'Have I told you how sexy you look?' He patted my bum.

'Jeremy,' I murmured, stepping away from him. 'Stop.'

'Libby, please, let's give it another chance. Dump Mr Interflora. We're made for each other. Soulmates.'

'I don't know,' I said, genuinely confused. 'And what about Ruth-Ann?'

'Ancient history.'

'How can I trust you again, after everything that's happened?'

'You can. I promise. Tomorrow night in our private hot tub, I'll prove it to you.'

My stomach lurched. He still had a terrible effect on me. 'Let me think about it.'

Chapter 43

Lulabelle

'Look at her, lying there on my table. Perfect.' Lulabelle heard Raul's voice above her. She felt groggy, as if she was under water. She tried to open her eyelids but they wouldn't budge. Maybe the anaesthetic hadn't fully kicked in yet. She tried to relax and wait for that familiar icy feeling to surge through her veins as the drugs started to take effect. But no, nothing. She could still hear everything.

'Why does she keep doing this to herself?' Raul again.

'Don't ask me,' she heard Dion say. 'She has no idea how truly beautiful she is. And I think—'

'Dion!' Bertram this time. 'Don't think, concentrate. Hold the camera steady. I want to get Raul's hands in shot as he makes the first cut.'

Cut? Hang on, if Raul was about to operate, surely she should be out cold by now? Something was wrong, very wrong. She tried to move but nothing responded – arms, legs, face, all dead.

Aaagh! She felt a dagger of pain in her stomach. She tried to lift a hand to swat it away but it was no use, her body was completely paralysed.

'Raul, her blood pressure's rising dangerously quickly.' The anaesthetist.

'Heart rate?' Raul asked quickly.

'Racing.' The nurse.

Silence for a moment. Then light flooded Lulabelle's right eye. She willed her eyeball to move, putting everything she had into that one tiny movement. There, was that enough?

'Christ!' Raul said, 'she's still awake. Put her back under – quickly, man. And everyone except my team out. Immediately.'

Lulabelle felt the world slipping away. A metallic taste hit the back of her throat, then – nothing.

Lulabelle opened her eyes. She felt terrible. Her mouth was bone dry. Her lips felt cracked and she poked her tongue out to lick them and then tried to swallow. Her head felt like it had been packed with cotton wool, and she winced as she attempted to move it.

'Try to stay still.' Dion smiled down at her and held a child's plastic cup with its own wiggly straw to her lips. It was pink with a picture of Disney's Cinderella on the side. She gave a husky laugh when she saw it.

'Like it?' He smiled again. 'I found it in a chemist's in English Harbour. I thought you should have your own princess cup. Raul said you might be in here for a few days. He wants to keep an eye on you. Told me to call him as soon as you woke up.'

There was such tenderness in Dion's eyes, in his face, in his voice that Lulabelle began to cry, huge racking sobs that hurt her tender stomach.

'The operation?' she croaked. 'My stomach?'

'Raul only made one incision, then he sewed it back up again.'

'No new belly button?'

'No. Plain old round one.'

Lulabelle's eyes welled up.

'Don't cry, my love. Your health is far more important than an oval belly button.' He stroked back her hair tenderly. For a second she considered slapping his hand away and asking him to leave, but she was suddenly frightened of being alone. Her heart started to hammer in her chest and she could feel her breath quicken. The tears kept coming, huge swollen droplets that spilled down sideways on to the pillowcase.

'Leo will be back on the first flight he can get.' Dion reached for the bell above her bed. 'I'd better call Raul.'

'Stop!'

He put his hand down. 'OK, I'll give you a few minutes. But he's worried about you, Lulabelle.' He paused. 'Do you remember anything about what happened?'

'Yes. I could hear you all talking, and then I felt a scalpel cut me open—'

He caught his breath. 'Jesus.'

'It was horrible.' She started to sob deeply, making her stomach ache again. 'I was so scared. And I'm so stupid—'

'It's hardly your fault. It's something called anaesthetic awareness. Raul said it's highly unusual but not unheard of – it sometimes happens if a patient is old or on medication. He doesn't know what caused it in your case.'

'The fucking sleeping pills,' she whispered through her tears. She'd been so frightened of this operation she'd thrown down two strong sleeping pills last night, even though Raul had warned her not to eat or drink a thing. She didn't think it would matter.

She could have killed herself, and for what? For a fucking television show?

Something inside her snapped. She'd had enough. Enough of the surgery and painful recovery. Enough of the photographers following her every move. Enough of the filming. Enough of the constant worrying – about her weight, her hair, her wrinkles, her nails, what the public thought of her. Enough of hating Libby for being a natural beauty, of envying Celeste's brains. She was exhausted.

Yet through her tears, she felt a glimmer of hope. Because right there, smiling down at her gently, without judgement, was Dion.

'I'd better call Raul,' he said. 'I promised.'

'Wait! Please don't leave me. I'm so sorry for treating you badly, and I'm—'

'Lulabelle, none of that matters now.' He held her face in both his hands. 'I'll never leave you again. I promise.'

'There's something I have to tell you.'

'What?'

She gulped back her fear. 'My real name's Lucy, Lucy Ryan. And Leo's my brother.' It was a start.

He kissed her sticky forehead. 'Hello there, Lucy Ryan. Good to finally meet you.'

Chapter 44

Libby

'The papers are going wild,' Alex grinned. 'Top Model's Near-Death Experience,' he said in his best movie-trailer voice.

Celeste smiled. 'And who exactly told them about it? It certainly wasn't me or Libby. It was hardly Leo, and Lulabelle and Dion are too busy making plans to think about publicity. It was you, wasn't it?'

'Plans? What kind of plans?' Alex looked perturbed. He didn't like being out of the loop.

Celeste just smiled knowingly and ran her finger down the side of her glass. We were sitting on the veranda in Villa Bristo, sipping fruit cocktails.

'They're getting married,' I said, putting him out of his misery. 'As soon as possible. She had a change of heart. What did she call it? Oh yes, an epiphany.'

Alex hit the table, making the jug and glasses clink. 'What? When did this happen? For feck's sake, I leave you lot alone for a few days—'

'Stop getting your knickers in a twist,' Celeste said. 'I think it's sweet. He's a lovely lad and the whole near-death thing seems to have shaken her up a bit.'

'It'll never last,' he muttered.

'What's wrong with you? Don't tell me you fancy her?' Celeste stared at him.

'Course not. I'm just worried about her. Dion is—'

'Devoted to her,' Celeste said. 'And he's no fool. He knows exactly what he's getting himself into. Is that why you flew all this way? To give Lulabelle a lecture on the folly of love?'

He laughed wryly. 'No. I wanted to check she was all right. I do care about the woman, strangely enough. And Leo said he could do with some help.'

'With the press, you mean?' I asked.

'With everything. I felt pretty useless in London. And I was finding it hard to concentrate on anything. Something on my mind. Something important.'

He gave Celeste a loaded look. 'What are you doing tonight? Are you free?'

She laughed. 'Are you asking me on a date?'

He shifted on his seat. 'Might be.'

'I'll think about it. Depends how much champagne's on offer.'

Alex grinned. 'I'll take that as a yes.'

His BlackBerry rang and he answered it.

'Yes, she's right beside me.' He looked at me. 'I'll tell her.' He put it back in his pocket. 'You've been summoned, Libby. Lady Lulabelle requests a hospital visitation. As soon as possible.'

'I can't. I have to meet Jeremy.'

Alex's eyebrows shot up. 'Jeremy?'

'It's a long story.'

'Lulabelle first, Libby,' he said. 'It sounds important. I'll order you a taxi.'

Lulabelle was sitting up in her bed. She was pale and her hair was greasy, but she put the book she'd been reading on the bedside table and smiled at me, a real smile that reached her eyes. I recognized the cover instantly. My third novel, *Never Been to Me*.

'What do you think?' I asked nervously, nodding at it.

'Not bad. But I preferred *Baby, It's You*. I think it's your best.'

'How many have you read?'

She shrugged. 'The one about weddings, the one about the divorced mum, and the one about Mary someone or other. Although I didn't finish that one. Sorry.'

'*Different for Girls*. No need to apologize. Not my finest hour.'

'You're a great writer, Libby. Your books have kept me sane over the last few days. Leo bought them for me at the airport.'

I was touched.

'I tried it, you know,' she said. 'Writing, I mean. Got bored after chapter three. How on earth do you do it every day, Libby? Is it OK to call you that?'

'Of course. And I guess I'm lucky – when it's all going well, I love writing. And don't tell anyone, but sometimes I get bored of writing too. Most writers do. When it happens I take time off, go for a walk or something, and hope it'll pass. Anyway, more importantly, how are you feeling? How's your stomach?'

'Physically, fine. It was only a nick and Bertram says it makes a wonderfully dramatic ending for the show. A brush with death and all that. Good for the ratings. Raul wants to keep me in for a few more days, just to make sure I have no more flashbacks. He's such a sweet man. He's been telling me all about the children he works with. And he asked me to be the patron of his clinic,' she added proudly. 'I'm going to give all the profits from *Stay Beautiful* towards helping to build a new burns unit. Leo's having a fit. He wants me to give them fifty per cent. But I told him one hundred per cent from this book and fifty per cent from the next two books. If *Plastic Fantastic*'s a success, I can afford it.'

She paused and looked at me. 'That's why I wanted to see you. I really want to write more books with you, Libby. And I want to put your name on the cover. *Stay Beautiful* by Lulabelle Ryan *and* Elizabeth Adams. What do you think?'

'I'm not sure. More books.' I whistled. Ideas for my own books were still coming hot and fast, but I had to admit that there was a lot more I wanted to do with Chloe. 'There are a few things I have to sort out first,' I explained. 'My fiancé's still here and—'

'I have to tell you something.' Lulabelle pushed herself up in the bed. 'I've been around and I know men like Jeremy. Hell, I've dated most of them. He's no good and he'll never change. Let him go.'

'Thank you, but I can deal with Jeremy myself,' I said tightly.

Lulabelle blew out her breath. 'Look, you'll probably hate me for this, but I have to say it. He asked for my phone number. Said he wanted to take me out when everything had settled down at home.' She put on his deep voice. ' "I think you're just the sort of girl I need. You wouldn't mind a little wifey at home, would you, Lulabelle?" And then he looked me up and down like I was a piece of meat.'

Her impression of Jeremy was spot-on, and I would have laughed if what she was saying hadn't been quite so appalling.

'Libby, he's a pig,' she added. 'Please don't go back to him. I'm begging you.'

I started to cry, shielding my eyes with my cupped hand.

I felt a hand on my shoulder. 'I'm sorry,' she murmured.

I shrugged her hand off and looked up. 'Don't touch me. You came on to him, didn't you? Tell me the truth. Admit it!' I shouted in her face.

She just shook her head, and from the look in her eyes I knew she wasn't lying. I sat on the side of the bed and stared down at the floor. The stupid thing is, in my heart I'd known all along – Jeremy was just playing with me again, the way he always did. Enough!

'It's up to you now, Libby Holliday,' I whispered to myself. 'Sink or swim.'

'I also overheard Jeremy saying you needed a boob job,' Lulabelle added. 'You wouldn't, would you? Have surgery. I mean, there's no hope for any of us if *you* have plastic surgery.

You're one of the few women I know who is actually happy with her body.'

I stared at her in surprise. 'No I'm not. I hate my thighs, and my boobs, as Jeremy so kindly pointed out, are pretty disappointing. But I guess if I was really all that unhappy, I'd do something about it. But after your experience I think that's unlikely, to be honest.'

'I envy you. You're comfortable with yourself. And Leo was right, you're naturally beautiful.' She stopped, then added, 'In your own way.'

I smiled a little. She just had to add that last bit. 'Go on, I know you want to say it. Flaws and everything.'

Lulabelle shrugged. 'We all have flaws. It's what makes us human. That's what Dion and Raul say, anyway.'

'They're right. Congratulations, by the way. On your engagement.'

'Will you come to the wedding? Celeste too.'

'Are you kidding? Any excuse for a new frock.'

'We haven't set a date yet – Dion has to talk to his mum first. I'm hoping Raul will come too. He's been very good to me.' She paused, and then asked, 'Have you ever seen a shrink, Libby?'

'No, but I probably should.'

She gave a laugh. 'Raul's found me someone back in London. He thinks I have some issues that I need help with. I'm nervous. Telling a stranger all my secrets like that.'

'Telling a *doctor* your secrets,' I pointed out. 'And it's all completely confidential. What kind of issues?' It was out before I could stop it.

'Body issues. Stuff to do with my – well, you know, my father's suicide. And the operation. I've been having nightmares. Been finding it hard to sleep.'

I had a wild thought. 'Do you think Raul did it on purpose? Not giving you enough drugs, I mean? To put you off surgery?'

She gave a hoot. 'Libby! Doctors don't do that kind of thing. You've written far too many novels.'

I laughed. 'I guess.'

'Speaking of novels, what do you think? Will you write more? With me, I mean? Alex said New Haven are offering a very lucrative deal.'

'Can we give Chloe her Cinderella ending?'

Lulabelle beamed. 'Done. Will you come and see me tomorrow? We can talk about it then; dream up some more plot lines. I've missed it.'

I smiled. 'Addictive, isn't it? I will, but there's something I have to do first.'

Chapter 45

Libby

The following morning Lulabelle's hair was tied back in a perky high ponytail and her make-up-free cheeks were rosy. She'd pass for seventeen and I'd never seen her look happier.

'You were right,' I said, walking in and sitting down on the side of her hospital bed. 'About Jeremy. He denied it at first but I could tell he was lying. Then he said he was sorry, that he still loves me.'

'Loves you?' Lulabelle looked shocked. 'Is he mad? Even *I* know that's not love. What did you say to that?'

'I told him I really didn't care any more. That love is about trust and respect, not lies and hurting people over and over again.' I sighed. I'd never forget what Jeremy had said to me at that moment.

'You've always lived on another planet, Libby. I blame those appalling books you write. Romantic nonsense. Life's not a Jane Austen novel, all devoted friends and dashing gentlemen. Wake up and join my world, Libby, the real world.'

'No,' I'd told him. 'I'd choose my world over yours any day. With good friends who love me. And a man who won't betray me. And if he doesn't exist, I'm better off alone. Goodbye, Jeremy.'

With that I'd walked away, leaving him staring after me, gobsmacked. For the very first time in my life, I knew in my heart that a man like Jeremy was not good enough for me.

I looked at Lulabelle. 'It's over,' I said simply. 'He's out of my life for good.' I blinked back tears.

'Are you OK?'

'I will be. There are only so many times your heart can be broken. The first time almost cuts you in two, after that . . .' I shrugged.

'I understand.' She smiled gently. Then she reached over and gave me a hug. She smelt like a new T-shirt. 'Thanks, Libby,' she said into my hair. 'Thanks for everything. I'm so sorry you're sad, but it won't be forever. You and Celeste have done more for me than you'll ever know. But I have a favour to ask.' She sat back and bit her lip for a second. 'I want you to give my brother a second chance.'

'Lulabelle, your sense of timing is unbelievable and he has no interest—'

'Wrong! And I'm not stupid, I know you still like him, I can see it in your eyes, even if you deny it. Think about it – you're in one of the most beautiful places in the world for four more days. Days you could be spending with a damn fine man who is mad about you.'

'Mad about me? Ha! Lulabelle, your darling brother has walked, no, sprinted away from me not once but twice, back in Paris and again here. There's only so much my poor battered heart can take. And both times he never even said goodbye which was bloody rude of him if you ask me.' I chewed the inside of my cheek to stop myself crying – it was all still so raw.

'Libby, I have to tell you something. In Paris, after I saw you kissing, I freaked out, begged Leo to stay away from you. Told him I'd kill myself if he didn't listen to me. I know it's no excuse but I was so scared of losing him, of being alone. I wasn't thinking straight.' She paused. 'Do you hate me?'

My heart pounded in my chest. How dare she? What a witch! Just as I was starting to warm to her, she goes and lands this bombshell. Well, I wasn't having it. I jumped to my feet and powered towards the door. She didn't deserve an answer.

'Libby, wait! There's more.'

I didn't turn around. My hand was on the door handle when she said, 'Leo met Jeremy, at the villa. That's why he left the island in such a hurry. He was upset and angry; he thought you'd been lying to him about Jeremy.'

Bloody Jeremy. God only knows what he'd said to Leo. I stood there in shock. What if Lulabelle was telling the truth? What if Leo did have feelings for me? I was rooted to the spot, my mind racing.

'The way he smiles at you,' Lulabelle said softly. 'The way he talks about you, defends you, there's something special there. Don't throw it all away. He's a good man and he deserves someone like you. Someone honest and clever and kind. Give him another chance. Please?'

I swung around and glared at her, angry tears flooding my eyes. There was a lump in my throat the size of an orange and I just wanted to curl up in a ball and forget about everything – Jeremy, Leo, Lulabelle. I wanted to wake up in the morning and not instantly remember how shit my life had become, how badly I'd let Jeremy treat me for so many years. I wanted safe, calm, stable, as far from the highs and lows of the last few months as I could get. I didn't want another man complicating things.

I stared at Lulabelle and for the first time I realised that she and Leo had exactly the same eyes, melty chocolate brown. Leo. His face floated in front of me and for a second I felt all warm inside and an excited shiver ran up and down my spine. Then I shook myself.

'I can't,' I said. 'What if it all goes wrong? I'm not putting myself through all that again, not for a long, long time. Right now I need to be on my own.'

Lulabelle shook her head. 'No! It can't end like this. In a few days we'll all be back in London or Dublin. You guys may never get together and it'll be all my fault. I know you probably hate me for ruining things in Paris, but I had to explain why he behaved like that. In case there was a chance. Because I love Leo so much. He's the only family I've got and I just want him to be happy. But I've wrecked everything, haven't I? I'm sorry, I'm so, so sorry . . .' She tailed off and gave a sob. Then she pressed her eyes sockets with her fingertips and took a few deep breaths.

'Libby, listen to me, please. It took a botched operation to make me realize what's important in life, and it's not money or a brilliant career or fame or anything like that, it's having someone who loves you for who you are. Who lets you be yourself. I'll be straight with you. I think Leo's in love with you. I think you guys might have a chance to be truly happy. Don't throw it all away.'

Love? OK, I wasn't expecting that. Our teary eyes locked. It was so ridiculous – Lulabelle had just told me something wonder-ful and here I was crying like a baby. I started to laugh.

'I'm sorry,' I said, shaking my head. 'I don't mean to laugh but it's all just so . . .' I tailed off.

'Messed up? I know, what are we like, Libby?' And then she smiled, and full power of her megawatt grin hitting me. She was smiling through her tears, like a rainbow through a downpour. God she was beautiful when she smiled. 'I nearly forgot,' she said. There's something I want to give you, a present. For being my ghostwriter.'

'As well as your brother?' I softened and smiled at her.

She nodded. 'Does that mean you'll talk to him?'

'I'll think about it.'

She leapt out of the bed and hugged me. 'I knew you still believed in true love. Maybe you'll be my sister-in-law one day, wouldn't that be fabulous?'

My stomach lurched. Don't get me wrong, even after her Paris confession, Lulabelle was seriously starting to grow on me, but I wasn't ready to be related to her just yet. And maybe Leo's feelings had waned; maybe she had it all wrong. But God I hoped not.

Epilogue

'Bloody London rain.' Celeste groaned, staring out the window of my hotel bedroom.

'I miss Antigua.'

'No kidding.' Images of Leo flicked in front of my eyes like a slide-show. Leo apologizing and asking could we wipe the slate clean, start all over again. Leo swimming in the azure sea while I pretended to be reading, secretly watching his every stroke behind my sunglasses. Leo feeding me crab cakes and then laughing heartily as a piece fell down the front of my sundress. Leo holding my hand as we walked along the fine white sand at sundown.

It all seemed like a distant dream.

There was a knock on the door. Celeste jumped up to open it. Alex. Two huge bouquets in his arms. White roses.

'Thought you'd like these now, Libby. Save you lugging them around the bookshop and the restaurant.' He handed me one of the bouquets and gave me a kiss on the cheek. 'Happy launch. Have a fab evening. Foxy outfit.'

'Thanks.' I smoothed down the skirt of the sleek silk dress. I was worried it looked a bit like a nightie, but Celeste (my stylist for the night) had teamed it with a black short-sleeved leather jacket and stunning red Jimmy Choo courts, my second present from Lulabelle. The first was a spa day in the Ocean Paradise Hotel in Antigua, complete with a hair cut. The hair dresser had tut-tutted over my pink bits but soon gave me the best 'do' ever, a choppy blonde bob. I wanted to look good for the launch, but more than anything I wanted to impress Leo. My new boyfriend.

I loved saying that – boyfriend. Made me feel like a teenager again. We were taking things slowly, and the fact that he lived in London and could only make it over to Dublin every second weekend suited me just fine for the moment. Every morning I woke up with a smile on my face, and, for now, that was enough. But I'd always rather fancied living in London . . .

'These are for you, sweets,' Alex said to Celeste. No kiss on the cheek for her – instead a full-on Hollywood smooch. After a moment she pushed him away.

'Watch the lipstick, buster.' She grinned and gave him a wink. They'd been getting on surprisingly well for two people who always liked to be right.

'One girl for each arm,' Alex said. 'How lucky am I? And I have news. *Sunday Times* book charts. *Stay Beautiful* went straight in at number one. Congrats, Libby.'

I instantly started to cry. I waved my hand in front of my face. 'Sorry – I always cry when I'm happy.'

Celeste rummaged in her bag and handed me a tissue. Then she changed her mind and pressed the whole packet into my palm. 'The way things are going, I think you'll be needing these.'

The Dublin Times

Ex-Miss Ireland, Lulabelle Ryan is best known for her forays into the world of reality television. Her latest in the grubby oeuvre, the horrendous-sounding *Plastic Fantastic*, chronicling her own plastic surgery experiences, will hit our screens in the spring. But before that dubious treat, she adds author to her CV, with devastating consequences for the literary world.

Stay Beautiful is as light and frothy as chocolate soufflé and has about as much substance. Set in the world of modelling (where else?), it features the usual rags-to-riches, poor-girl-done-good plot line, along with some so-so dialogue and a soupçon of wit. Banville it most certainly is not. Sadly, the great unwashed will probably adore it.

Simone Fullsome-Jeller,
author of *Sartre and his Teacups*

www.amazon.co.uk

★★★★★ (Five stars)

Oh My God! *Stay Beautiful* is the best book, ever. I looooved it. Chloe is such an amazing character and the story was brilliant. Lulabelle's such a talented writer. I can't wait for the next one. And the film. Wonder who will play Liam? My money's on Johnny Depp.

And did you catch Lulabelle's wedding in *Hello!*? Her husband is Mr Dream-Machine. I soooo want to be Lulabelle Ryan.

Heddy Smith, Tamworth